THORNE SMITH, in his brief but amazing life, established a one-man literary genre. In the seven years since his death no one has usurped his unique place as a creator of alcoholic hilarity in novel form. His faithful public will greet with joy this genuine new Thorne Smith novel, left unfinished at the time of his death and now completed by Norman Matson.

This uproarious novel recounts the remarkable consequences of the marriage of a meek and respectable man to a Grade-A witch. T. Wallace Wooly, Jr, a wealthy widower who lived a quiet and stuffy life on a diet of vitamins and vegetable juices, did not know what he was getting in for when he rescued a strange woman, entirely nude, from a burning hotel. The woman, Jennifer, became enamored of her rescuer, and Mr Wooly was a little bewildered a week later to discover that he had taken Jennifer as his wife. His bride's unconventional antics were eventually to revolutionize Mr Wooly's life. He who had never in his life drunk anything stronger than carrot juice was to find that steady alcoholic consumption was a requisite if he was to have peace of mind. There follow some of the finest binges in literature, climaxed by the memorable scene in which Mr Wooly, disguised as an old lady from Perth Amboy, appears at a Turkish bath in pursuit of his blond secretary.

The author of *Topper*, *The Bishop's Jaegers*, *The Night Life of the Gods*, etc., has never created funnier situations nor more beleaguered characters than in this new book. It's the answer to seven years of prayer by Smithomaniacs.

THE PASSIONATE WITCH

THE PASSIONATE WITCH

BY THORNE SMITH

COMPLETED BY NORMAN MATSON

WITH DRAWINGS BY HERBERT ROESE

THE SUN DIAL PRESS · GARDEN CITY, NEW YORK

1942
THE SUN DIAL PRESS

CONTENTS

THE PASSIONATE WITCH

CHAPTER I

Rendezvous in the Ladies' Room

FROM beyond the polished oaken door of the ladies' room in the offices of T. Wallace Wooly, Inc., came a slight and varied sound that lingered lonesomely in the sunny, empty rooms. It was as whispering without words, an autumn breeze sweeping dead leaves together or an intermittent leak in a steam line. Had you paused to listen to this sound for a moment, and it is to be hoped that you wouldn't, you would probably not have identified its source or its meaning; had you listened a bit longer, however, you would have infallibly recognized it as the vocalization of feminine sorrow. . . . It is just as well that we do not and cannot know how many tall blondes are at any given moment mixing their highly soluble beauty with tears, draining it off into small handkerchiefs, leaning one shoulder the while against the walls of ladies' rooms from here to Detroit, Albuquerque, and so forth, and all for love—or the absence of it. Miss Betty Jackson's case is by itself sad enough for us.

Outside sunlight and greenery filled the neat streets of Warburton, a typical Saturday afternoon, huge with pleasant promise, and tomorrow inevitably would be Sunday, further reprieve for all the little people hurrying homeward, golfward, and so on: hang-overs hovered in the misty distances, and even the horny voices of automobiles came through the open windows with a questing, yearning sound. But Miss Jackson quietly wept. All morning, ever since Mr Wooly had barked at her, she had promised herself this opportunity, this rendezvous with her grief. Now she kept it. She wept wordlessly, leaning against the wall. . . .

At long last the tears ceased to flow. She directed her eyes to the mirror, and at once it was all over.

"Look at your face," she said aloud, horrified. "Just look at it!" She began to repair as well as she could the damage she had done.

Betty was in love with her employer, T. Wallace Wooly, Jr. She wept because she was and also because of late he had been worried, preoccupied. She was concerned for him. Even if she could never have him she wanted to take care of the little man as much as she could and as he would permit. And of course her grief was not wholly bitter, for she felt it a privilege just to be near him, day after day, even if he did hardly look at her, and spoke to her, when he did, only of the business of T. Wallace Wooly, Inc., Insurance and Real Estate.

In Warburton no other man was as active in business and public affairs as Mr Wooly. He was secretary, chairman, trustee of many sorts of organizations, except, of course, convivial or frivolous organizations. He spoke often for the Chamber of Commerce, the Literary Society, the Men's Bible Study Class of the First Church. He stood, or seemed to stand, like a lighthouse, never doubting his light or his location, illuminating the dark and often confused waters of life in Warburton. In his boyhood he was called only Junior, and sometimes even now—he was thirty-nine—some old friend would call him that. He had never told anyone how much he detested it. He looked the very image of his father, the first T. Wallace Wooly, who had done so much for the family fortune. He acted like his father, too: sat at his father's desk and had even had for the first years after his father's death the same secretary, a Miss Ogilvie, who might have been part horse, but not a well-bred one, to judge by her appearance. Her appearance, indeed, was a certificate of virtue for her employer. Up to the day before she died Miss Ogilvie had been as keen, as industrious, as she had been under the reign of Junior's father. Our Mr Wooly had always loathed her, a fact he had, however, loyally concealed.

Betty Jackson, who was half a dozen of something else, a horse of quite another color, had been sent in to Mr Wooly by Simpson, the fat office manager, who chose her at once from a bevy of applicants, getting an idea about the future that had done him no good. Mr Simpson had anticipated that Mr Wooly, the kind of blind fathead who would keep such a secretary as Miss Ogilvie year after year, would be deaf and blind to Betty's loveliness. He was quite mistaken here. And, besides, from the first Betty had had no eyes for any but Mr Wooly. (In her dreaming mind she did not call him "Mister," nor Junior either, but other names, some gentler, some grander.) And as for Mr Simpson, no matter how he arranged himself in the apparent line of her vision, he might as well have been the Invisible Man himself. . . .

Since this chronicle has principally to do with Mr T. Wallace Wooly, Jr, adequate—nay, admirable—son of his

famous father, the most important fact about his character might as well be discovered to us at once. He was as
shy, underneath his strut and swagger, this suburban
tycoon, as a small brown rabbit. When Mr Wooly's
chauffeur, the domineering Swanson, drove him to a meeting he was to address, Mr Wooly would be sitting lonely
and hot on the back seat of his blue limousine, hands
tightly clenched, his stomach one yawning, tremulous
ache of apprehension—as in his first days in school and as
always since—although upon his return, ears still echoing
the applause, he would be a different man, filled with
confidence and admiration for himself. He was not, as his
father had been, all of one piece, but a mixture. He had
even once considered giving it all up and going away to
Bali in a black-hulled schooner yacht he would buy, but
somehow the routine of his days, his personal and public
responsibilities held him close.

He was, as a matter of fact, afraid of Betty, whose cool
and aloof demeanor he had completely misunderstood.
He was far from being numb to her charms. He would
look at the back of her golden head and long to know
her thoughts. (His own, he could admit to himself, were
shocking.) He was scrupulously, haughtily correct in all
his dealings with her. . . . And the reason he had barked
at her this sunny Saturday morning was simply because he
had caught himself wanting to step straight across to
where she sat and kiss her.

A sad misunderstanding altogether, one that a few
bold words could have cleared up at once.

Having done what she could for her ravaged face, Miss
Betty Jackson came out of the ladies' room. From her

neck down her rendezvous with sorrow had in nowise dimmed the beauty that was hers—her bosom was not dejected; her waist was not less trim. Her long legs were not bowed in grief, and her slender, arched feet had not gone flat with her spirit. The simple green silk, the golden belt, sheer stockings and tall-heeled sandals of green suède were as they had been. On top of her head was her golden hair, but on the front of her head, so to speak, was her now-lamentable face, the blue of her eyes falsely dimmed by the bright red glow of her eyelids, the grievous pallor of her childlike cheeks shown in too-sharp contrast with a nose red as a cherry, red as the lipstick on her sad, sweet little mouth. Blinking, with one last sniff, she walked in her firm but graceful stride to the glass door of the sanctum sanctorum, opened it, sat down at her desk there and began to work. There was work to be done. Always. He saw to that. Soon her nose, her thoughts, faded. Her beauty returned.

So did Mr Wooly.

She looked up, surprised, and smiled like an angel. He walked through this radiance, a small, neat man in a double-breasted suit. An air of restrained elegance. He looked like a field marshal in mufti, something Napoleonic, or he looked like an Episcopalian millionaire. He *was* an Episcopalian millionaire. His stride was a conqueror's, but his large brown eyes were troubled. He had returned only to ask Betty to have lunch with him. The first time. He was very nervous.

A moment of fraudulent calm at his desk, and he began to move about as if hot-nosed ants were exploring the farthest reaches of his pants. He squirmed and fidgeted—he, Mr Wooly, who had always been so calm, so deliberate; he shoved his chair and himself a foot from his desk and with one bright toe sent them whirling round, once and again and again. Miss Jackson heard the sound of this lunacy—dared not look. He stopped at last. He said loudly, angrily: "Stop that rattle-de-bang now! I've got something to say to you, Miss Jackson." Her heart sank. The can coming up! She was sure.

She turned round slowly.

He tossed his head. He laughed a laugh that was meant to be merry. It was a horrid failure. Goose-pimples, millions of them, rose all over Miss Jackson's body.

"Have you had your lunch? What's that? What are you staring at?"

She shook her head.

"Will you have it with me?" he asked her frantically, his hair fairly on end.

At last she could speak:

"I'd like to very much, Mr Wooly."

"Well don't keep me waiting!"

She was amazed, overwhelmed. They went out of the empty Saturday-afternoon office, into the main street of Warburton.

Swanson, Mr Wooly's chauffeur, a bony Swede with melancholy whiskers, moved his toe; the long blue car glided away.

It was not a hilarious event, this first lunch they had ever had together. On the way to the Barkley they were both quite silent and when they had been ushered to a corner table of this, the best of Warburton's restaurants, and were seated opposite each other, with various items of food between them instead of, as in the office, a short-hand book, insurance papers and the silver-framed photograph of the late Mrs Wooly, the situation seemed so strange that Betty had no notion of what to say and so continued to say nothing.

It was up to Mr Wooly. He filled in as best he could, betraying by not the slightest flick of expression his own great concern and uncertainty. He broke the ice with a brief statement of his attitude toward cocktails and other alcoholic beverages. "I never touch them," he said, which was news to Betty, and not very good news, as she had been thinking that this situation needed nothing so much as two or three old fashioneds, an amphibious sort of decoction or dish which she favored, claiming that while it was more edible than fruit salad, which it so much resembled, its action was nicer and quicker too.

But instead of old fashioneds they had each a glass of carrot juice, replete, Mr Wooly assured her, with vitamins. Over these Mr Wooly touched on several topics he decided might prove fraught with interest for Betty, this handsome girl he had seen nearly every day for a month and who was yet such a complete stranger to him. He discussed the education of his daughter Sara. She was fifteen years old and she attended a school in New Rochelle; there was also the matter of the Hotel Monroe policy. They had just written this, and it was a very pleasant bit of business, indeed. Apparently warmed by the carrot juice, Mr Wooly plunged into a dish of various mineral salts such as iron, calcium, magnesium, and so on. These were in the shape of celery and nuts, sliced tomatoes, cream cheese. As he crunched and crackled his way along Mr Wooly, holding her with his large brown eyes, told Betty about himself. Betty gathered that Mr Wooly in his own opinion was more like Charlemagne than, say, Charlie McCarthy, and that what he did not know about real-estate values and fire insurance was of no importance. He explained to her not only why he was such a picture of robust health but why his intellect was so keen and creative. While Mr Wooly poured his self-assertion into the limpid pools of Betty's loyal eyes the little brown rabbit that was his soul stopped running round in terrified circles; its little heart calmed down to a normal rhythm; Mr Wooly, to sum it up, had himself believing what he was saying. As for Betty, it was with her no question of being won over; she already had been won over, and what he said she believed before he said it. She was in love; she did not even resent the carrot juice but had already decided hereafter to stop eating food and drinking drinks, as had been her wont, and begin instead to take vitamins and mineral salts, for her health, which though already superb, could not, she realized, ever be superb enough for her Mr Wooly.

As they went out the headwaiter bowed, and so did some other lunchers, respectfully, cordially. "I can detect their thoughts," Mr Wooly told Betty with a droll smile. "They say to themselves: 'There he goes, the rich, the successful, Mr T. Wallace Wooly.' With more than just a touch, you know, of envy. We should never envy anyone though. And how little they understand the heavy responsibility of being a Mr Wooly. No bed of roses," said the little man. "Of course not," she breathed. Even though merely a figurative one, Betty was gratified that he should mention bed to her. She did not move away when, sinking back into the seat of the blue car, his side pressed against hers.

"It is not only," Mr Wooly said presently, "that you are a deucedly attractive woman, Miss Jackson, but you are so well spoken, if I may pay you so direct a compliment, a conversationalist, indeed; ah, they are rare these days."

"Thank you, Mr Wooly," she said in a small voice with a small, warm smile added. That she had barely said a word throughout did not trouble her, did not refute the compliment. As for Mr Wooly, his own oratory, the whole hour of it, had left only the pleasantest of echoes in his own ears, and generously he totted up some of these to Betty's credit.

Having dropped her at the door of her boardinghouse, a frame structure with a wide veranda, one of many such in a tedious street on the wrong side of Warburton, Mr Wooly sank back again, closed his eyes and thought about his secretary, quite forgetting the smile on his face, leaving it clinging there like something left over from Christmas.

Swanson's heavy voice aroused him. "Yah?"

Opening his eyes (he had been merely daydreaming, not sleeping) Mr Wooly saw his chauffeur's bony, mustached face hanging over the back of the front seat. This face was filled with disapproval. "Home, Swanson!" Mr Wooly said shortly.

Swanson shook his head slowly. He spoke: "Look before you yump, Mr Wooly."

The man was impossible. "Swanson, what do you mean
by that remark?"

He turned back to the wheel. "Ay tank you know,"
Swanson said. Though somber as ever, he was plainly
gratified. He had, at least, wiped that smile off his employer's face. Indeed, Mr Wooly's pleasure, his confidence,
was considerably diminished. Swanson, a severe and virtuous man, had been hired by Mr Wooly, Sr, a dozen years
before, and he had contrived somehow to become his
terrestrial representative. He knew and Mr Wooly knew
he knew that when Mr Wooly was smiling that sort of
eyes-closed smile after lunching with his blonde secretary
he was not thinking in a way that would have pleased
the late Mr Wooly, Sr.

Swanson drove in a silence that was packed with comment. In theory, of course, Mr Wooly could have discharged the man right then and there; he would have liked to, and he didn't because the truth was he was afraid of the man. Swanson had the psychological bulge on Mr Wooly. Even while Mr Wooly in his imagination gave him the dressing down of his life, building up to the climax: "And now you may go!" he knew perfectly well he would do no such thing.

He was suddenly depressed; he even wondered if he had been as brilliant as he had thought talking to Betty. . . .

In the distance something screamed higher than the housetops. The fire siren. Mr Wooly was a confirmed, passionate buff; that is to say, an amateur of fire, not arsonically, of course, but platonically and professionally. He was, moreover, vice-chief of the Warburton Fire Department, an honorary title bestowed upon him when he presented the town with the new fire engine.

Swanson glanced into the rear mirror. "Headquarters?" he suggested.

"Quickly, please," Mr Wooly said. If they were there in time he would be able to ride to the fire—if, indeed, it were a fire—on the new fire engine.

CHAPTER II

Out of the Frying Pan

WHILE Mr Wooly's interest in fire was intense, he did not approve of it—not when it was on the loose. It reminded him of hell, for one thing—each natural blaze seeming a signal and a warning from the supernatural conflagration that may await us. Fire, moreover, caused his companies to pay out some of the money they had taken in, which seemed to him a topsy-turvy procedure. Fire in another way fascinated Mr Wooly. Its personality, so to speak. It waved and roared and hid itself in monstrous clouds, shown on the leaning faces of the multitude. As the moth to the candle—so Mr Wooly to the fires.

The engine came howling down Brick Street. Its driver did not see Mr Wooly frantically waving from his car and of course did not stop. Very well, Mr Wooly would be driven. He told Swanson not to loiter. Swanson didn't. Evening had sifted over Warburton. In the distance there rose up a pinkish glow and a mile-high pillar of black smoke. Mr Wooly groaned. It was the Hotel Monroe, which he had insured only yesterday. They had arrived well ahead of the fire engine. The whole front seemed intact, the fire being at the other end. Mr Wooly told Swanson to wait, went in to look around.

The lobby, with its old leather chairs and its semi-circular desk, presented a scene quite calm and quite deserted. The walnut balustrade of a stairway going straight up darkly gleamed, and the polished brass wench who held a lamp above the newel post seemed uninterested. But somewhere else, in other rooms, someone muttered and spat, said *whoo* and *whoosh!* That was fire on the loose, writhing like a snake, roaring like a yellow tiger. Realizing everybody must be around in back, Mr Wooly decided to leave them there. He moved toward the street door. Suddenly the lights went and he was in darkness. It was his impulse then to run for it with all his might, and later he was to wish to heaven that he had. But he paused, hearing a woman's voice: "Help! Help me!"

He called: "Come out, come out, wherever you are!" No answer save from that invisible fire.

Mr Wooly did not want to go upstairs and be burned. He called out again, went halfway up. "Some lower-class hysteric," he muttered crossly.

A door flew open and fire leaped and billowed, crawling rapidly all around the flame, eating, snarling, was lost again in its own smoke. From the center of this dreadful display stepped a woman. She fell into Mr Wooly's arms just as he arrived. He grunted. They stood there a moment like the two sections of a stepladder. He saw there was only one thing to do with her in the circumstance, much as he disliked holding onto strange women. He hoisted her up over one shoulder. He shifted her, noting, distraught as he was, that her skin was cool to his fingers. Skin? He felt her again, here, there, wherever he could reach. He spoke at last, and for some reason he spoke in a whisper.

"Where," he demanded, "are your clothes?"

"I don't know," she said. Her voice came from behind him, well below his neck. She was lying sackwise over his shoulder, feet first.

Her answer seemed inadequate. He pressed the matter. "What do you mean, you don't know where your clothes are?"

"The hotel's on fire," she said patiently.

"I know it is. I'm the vice-chief of the fire department." This statement seemed, even in his own ears, a trifle unnecessary. "It is just an honorary title," he added. "As when the queen is made colonel of the regiment."

"What queen?" asked the woman.

"Any queen. Any regiment. Just for instance."

"You mean it's all hypothetical?" She seemed disappointed.

He quivered all over. "Don't blow against my spine," he begged. "Makes me shudder."

"I've got to breathe," she argued. "Are we going to stay here and be broiled together, like an oversize shiska-bab? Or are we going down?"

"Don't wobble," he said and descended two steps in the smoky darkness. He paused for breath. "You all right?"

She said she was. "But don't try to turn your head," she begged. "Your chin scratches. Or maybe you are kissing me?"

"I am not," he exclaimed, expressing the shock she gave him to the utmost. "What an idea!"

"Oh, I don't know," she said.

"At a time like this?" Somehow the creature involved you in argument after argument. "I assure you, all I feel about you is your weight. You're no more a person to me than a bag I might be carrying out."

She pinched him in a place most convenient to her pendant hands.

"Ow," he said and kicked backward. He was wishing that it was all over. They could not prolong their descent much longer, and when they reached bottom there would be the populace, all ears and all eyes. Even now he saw that beyond the double glass doors down there lights were moving. The fire laddies had arrived. And with them the multitude, half the town of Warburton, waiting with a fine, tolerant expectance for the old hotel to divulge whatever secrets it might have been harboring. It was an in-between sort of hotel, old and a bit shabby and not as intolerant as it had been once. It occurred to Mr Wooly that while none, so far as he knew, had seen him go in, a great many were about to see him come out. He began seriously to wonder about this, to regret the hasty impulse that sent him up the stairs to make this rescue.

Perhaps if she went out alone . . . and then he came out unobtrusively? He paused again. Behind them fire whooshed and spat at the heart of billows of black smoke. The strange woman on his shoulder had skin that was very smooth and inexplicably cool. There was an odor of roses about her, too, or had been before the smoke had thickened. Her position was not conventional, not a position usually assumed by a woman you had just met. Her legs went on before. All he could see of her was what he could see out the left corner of his left eye, a blur, a pale hill or two. He was not enjoying himself; he was quite certain of this, and yet he could not help but feel that they had already established a relationship that was somewhat intimate.

"It is getting hotter," she said.

Did she think so? He didn't mind it, he said. In fact, now that he had brought her all the way down, he was

thinking of trotting up and poking around for some other stray guests.

"I was the last," she said. "I was taking a little bath when they told me the place was on fire. So I dried myself and slipped into a negligee. When fire came in it burned the negligee right off me."

"When fire came in!" Mr Wooly objected. "You talk about fire as if it were a brush salesman."

She laughed against his spine.

It was very hot and very stifling now.

Outside the entrance doors firemen had got their floodlights focused on the hotel's façade, making everything brighter than noonday. Mr Wooly put the strange woman on her feet. "You can't go out there like that,"

he said, being careful not to look straight at her now that she was visible.

"I don't know why not."

"Well, you can go out by yourself then. And I'll stay in here for a while, till the excitement dies down."

"You'll be burned to death."

He wasn't so sure this wouldn't be better than making the appearance they were about to make before that crowd out there.

"If you insist, I could wear your pants," said the woman.

That seemed a complete solution, until he thought to ask: "And what will I wear?"

"You wear underdrawers, don't you?"

He saw the tableau clearly. Too clearly. He saw that for him to appear in his drawers while she wore his pants, just the two of them coming out the doors of the Hotel Monroe, would be making Warburton history. He wanted none of it.

"I feel much better," the woman said. "Stronger. Perhaps I could carry you out."

He considered this suggestion but rejected it also. It was no improvement. Firebrands now fell down the stair well all about them. It was really time to get out of there. What to do? The woman solved everything by the simple device of a low moan and a quick, but not too quick, faint. He caught her, raised her again over his shoulder. Firemen, who now opened the doors of the hotel, dropped back at the scene that met their eyes. The broad step beyond the columned doorway was rather like a stage. From the assembled multitude rose an appreciative sound, a murmur, a loud huzza of admiration and approval. Flash bulbs of photographers made the flare brighter than ever. For moments the good burghers, the firemen, were so impressed none came to help. At last wrenching themselves from their fascination, firemen took his burden, covered it with an oilskin coat. A cheer for the hero went up into the calamitous glow, and with it (or was he mistaken?) a laugh from somewhere. "Aha! Mr Wooly!" "Who is she?" people asked. No one knew.

Mr Wooly found his chauffeur and his car waiting just beyond the fire lines. Mr Wooly's face was begrimed, his clothes in disarray. He felt he owed some sort of explanation to Swanson.

"Rescued a lady," he reported.

"Yah?" Swanson was never one to be hoodwinked by portentous brevity. "I saw," he added and then made, as usual, the heavy comment of his Nordic silence.

Mr Wooly, pretending nonchalance, lightly brushed his lapels. "Well, it's done," he said.

"Yah? Yust begun, more likely," Swanson told him. "Out of the frying pan . . ."

"We'll go home now," Mr Wooly commanded. His tone was cold.

"Yah," said Swanson, managing to convey by that one brief syllable that while he was wholly right in his judgment of the day's adventures, Mr Wooly was as wrong as he could be.

CHAPTER III

Mr Wooly Crawls into Bed

MR WOOLY'S BED had once been the property of his great-granduncle, a gentleman who had never written his autobiography because it would have been mostly unprintable, a truth *his* son and *his* grandson had managed to conceal from our Mr Wooly. It was of Empire design with four fat posts of reddish cherry-wood, deeply carved. The initial *W* shone in gilded carving on the headboard. The bed itself was of unusual acreage. The whole Wooly establishment, the six or seven servants, including Bentley, the butler, who was quite fat, and even a horse or two, could have slept in it without feeling too crowded, though of course no such absurdity was necessary, for the Wooly residence was one of many commodious apartments. The bed's hangings were of powder-blue brocade, and the whole magnificence was roofed over with a sheet of plate-glass mirror of the finest quality. When the rose-hued reading lamp in Mr Wooly's bed was aglow he could lie there and, looking straight up into the mirror, practice facial expressions and gestures appropriate to the speech he was to deliver on the morrow at the realtors' convention or some neighborhood improvement dinner.

It was his custom to ring for Bentley, the butler, when he was ready to retire. Bentley would not undress him, but he would hang up Wooly's clothes. He would listen

with well-bred interest and approval to Mr Wooly explain how well the day had gone, how eloquently he had
spoken, how very interested all his audience had been.

Having said, "You may go, Bentley, good night," Mr
Wooly would then walk deliberately, thoughtfully, to his
bed, observe the thermostat on the wall there, wind his
watch, glance at the titles of the very serious books on
the bed table, finally with slow dignity enter his bed,
stretch out on his back and in the mirror above, meeting
his own eye, coolly, unflinchingly, murmur, "A good
speech, an excellent speech, by George!"—or some such
commendation—then switch out his light and at once go
into a dreamless sleep. He usually slept on his back,
without snoring, without flinging himself about as if he
were wrestling with trouble. Indeed, he had had no
trouble. He was so busy from the moment he awoke and
left his bed until he returned to it, and was so safe, awake
or asleep, that tomorrow merely waited—it did not
threaten, as with most of us. To tell the truth, Mr Wooly,
this upright widower of Warburton, had been, in one way
of looking at it, perfectly adjusted to life, and in another,
as good as dead, which may, on the ultimate adding machine, add up to about the same.

In any case, this night, the night after his return from
the Monroe Hotel fire, he did not call Bentley (who as a
consequence could not sleep a wink) but, having hastily
bathed, crawled into his bed. For the first time he avoided
his own eyes up there. He turned out the light at once.
He began to toss about, first on his left side and then on
his right. He sighed. He longed, for the first time, to
undo a sequence, to reject the day just finished. He was

no longer safe. He had been found. His armor had been pierced. He hardly realized the nature of these new thoughts. By the very thinking of such thoughts it becomes apparent that somewhere in him he had all along known that, though he was the busiest, most public, most important man in Warburton, he had been in hiding, withdrawn from life like a turtle.

He did not like the female he had rescued. He did not like her at all, but when he thought of her he could not sleep. The odd thing was that while his mind did not want to remember her his hand persisted in holding an echo of the sensation of her cool skin. His arms remembered. All hell was breaking loose inside him. Better, he could say to himself, *If she had burned!* Confound the woman, barging into my life! And he was not too kind, or too obtuse, to suspect her as a designing woman. Not yet forty, he had a more than adequate income and a backlog—what a backlog!—of tax-free government bonds. He was rich. Unmarried! Only the poor can be unsuspicious. Mr Wooly prayed silently. Praying, he remembered the flames. He thought of hell's fires until, gigantically growing, the whole incident at the Hotel Monroe loomed as an encounter with Himself, the Prince of Darkness. An unsavory place at best—the Hotel Monroe! He tried to think of Betty, but somehow she seemed to merge with the creature he had carried down the stairs. When he went to sleep he moved about and groaned like a soul in torment, for he began to dream at once that she was there beside him and the whole bed was afire. Alas, so was he!

CHAPTER IV

Jennifer

DR FRANK MANNIX, who had a long blue jaw and wore inch-thick spectacles, looked at Mr Wooly with eyes made small as split peas by reverse magnification. Rain gloomed the windows of the doctor's office in the War-burton Hospital, way out near the end of Brick Street. It was the afternoon after the fire, which had, inci-dentally, burned all of the hotel, leaving nothing but a cellarful of black ash. A remarkably thorough fire. Dr Mannix was telling Mr Wooly about the patient. He had already stated that her name was Jennifer Broome, that she said she had lived until recently in Cagne-sur-Mer, which is, of course, a town on the French Riviera, that her lineage was English and American, that on the Eng-lish side she was related to certain county families, that her condition was, well, the good doctor paused and peered closely at Mr Wooly, as if that bewildered indi-vidual might be concealing some essential fact. He said, "Her condition, Mr Wooly, is extraordinary. It is won-derful. When," he asked, "and why did you take her clothes off?"

Mr Wooly summed up the rebuttal in two words. "I didn't," he said. "They were burned off. She came right through a sea of flame, Doctor."

The doctor slightly shook his head. "The human eye,"

he said with infuriating condescension, "plays tricks on us, Mr Wooly. That woman came through no sea of flame, I assure you."

Mr Wooly began thoroughly to dislike this doctor. "I was there, Doctor Mannix," said Mr Wooly.

"Oh, I know you were there. Good lord, Mr Wooly, the whole town knows that." He smiled genially, one old bastard to another.

"And you, may I remind you, were not."

"Thank God!" smiled the doctor. "We medical men, you know, have to be careful. I mean to say we cannot frequent such places as the Monroe. Not openly at least. But, there, what you thought you saw, Mr Wooly, you really didn't; and this I know, Mr Wooly, because if she walked through the fiery furnace, as you phrase it——"

"I said 'sea of flame.'" Mr Wooly looked out the gloomy window. The expression on his smooth, clean face was reticent. He was thinking that, having given this hospital ten thousand a year before, he'd see himself in Hoboken before he'd give it another cent.

"I judge an event by its effects," the doctor was saying in a tone that suggested he thought Mr Wooly judged an event by numerology or the study of tea leaves. "The skin of Miss Jennifer Broome is intact, spotless, unmarked in any part by fire. There is, however, a small pink mark on her right shoulder. It looks like"—he searched for a word, peering into Mr Wooly's soul with his distant little eyes—"like a bite," he said at last. "Not a mosquito bite," he added. "Tell me, Mr Wooly, how long have you known Miss Broome?"

"I never set eye on her before my arrival at the head of the stairs." Mr Wooly went on with dignity: "And as for the bite, if that is what it is, I do not bite."

Dr Mannix laughed genially. "Barking dogs!" he said, wagging his head. The old wag.

It came to Mr Wooly that before last night Dr Mannix would never have had the effrontery to cross-examine him like this. He was not through, either. "Then, I take it," he went on, "she is a new rather than an old flame." He appreciated that one and slapped Mr Wooly a stinging slap on the knee. "You're a deep one," said Dr Mannix. "Who would ever have thought it?"

"Who would ever have thought what?"

Dr Mannix winked. "Sly dog," he said. He added out of a spasm of inspiration, "Hot dog! Ha, ha, ha." Now Mr Wooly began to understand that since none had seen him go into the hotel—the crowd had not started to gather until just before he and Miss Broome had made their remarkable exit, which was paradoxically the most effective entrance ever made in Warburton—that many must have supposed that something had been up between Miss Broome and himself. Now indignantly, but in meticulous detail, he explained everything to the good doctor. The doctor, himself remembering, no doubt, the little matter of ten grand last year, feeling he had gone too far, now began to listen with a mask of respectful interest. . . . After that Mr Wooly went up to the women's floor and knocked on the door he had been told was Miss Broome's.

Her voice in there sang out, "Who is it?" Her voice pierced him. He did not like it, recognizing that it was like a cat's voice, high and clear, with a suggestion of back-fence whine or hum about it—a violin voice. No, he didn't like it, but as in his bed last night the thought of her set his heart going too fast, and his knees felt faint.

"It's me," he said, like a man bewitched, instead of saying, "Mr Wooly," or something sensible like that.

"Oh," she sighed, "come in, come in."

Most women look better in bed than up and around. The principal reason for this, of course, is that while in bed—to the casual visitor at least—most of them is covered up. Another reason is that if they have any hair at all it looks as if it were more, spread out that way on a pillow. Moreover, even though it be the color of dust, the contrast of the snowy pillow works a mitigating illusion. . . . And the most graceless of women can lie on her back as gracefully as the next one. It is a natural talent.

But when a woman has a great glory of lustrous dark hair and slanting eyes, half closed, the pupils a clear yellow light in shadow, a mouth curved in a short, catlike smile, mirthless as a cat's, cruel and passionate, small teeth flashing in a smile of pure joy, a hand, white as snow, reaching eagerly . . .

"Ah, Mr Wooly, you have come!"

His palm leaped above hers, refusing its contact; he grasped the tips of her fingers with the tips of his, bowed slightly from the waist. Formality, he had decided, was the line for this meeting, cold formality and a deliberate, well-bred avoidance of any mention of last night's contretemps.

"Miss Broome, I believe?"

She looked at him, astonished. Had he been a man who had ever even slightly sensed the thought of another, Mr

Wooly would have now seen in the slight drawing together of her magnificent long eyebrows, the slight freez-
ing of her smile, that she was not only astonished, but
displeased.

She said in a level tone of voice, the accent very May-
fair, very acid: "Well I'll be goddammed."

"I beg your pardon?"

She turned as formal as he: "Won't you . . . sit
down?"

"Thank you." He sat on the edge of a straight chair.
The room was narrow. He was necessarily close to her
bed. Her dark little head on the snowy pillow turned
toward him.

"May I present myself? T. Wallace Wooly."

"May you present yourself? Why not? How do you
do?" She touched his cheek, and the heat of her palm
struck into him; his skin remembered it. "Must we . . .
be so formal?" she asked. "After all, I owe my life to you.
It is yours, Mr Wooly. I am yours. And you come here,
aloof as some bank president with the wrong customer
or the ambassador from China. But that was not what I
expected. In the eyes of all of Warburton who am I now?"
She touched her breast with her finger tips.

Like pomegranates, Mr Wooly thought.

His thought was confused. Caution whispered in it,
good sense, but also something else—a sympathy for this
poor victim—and through all the mixture ran isolated
classical tags like "pomegranates" (hard, unedible, seedy
things, as a matter of fact) and a question: "Quo Vadis?"
which meant in Latin: "Where do you go from here?" or
something like that. And the "Sabines"? What about the

Sabines? He remembered the big picture of the Sabine
women in a book of engravings. One of them was lying
down looking sideways, a dark one. The Rape of the Sabines, that was the title of the picture, and since it had
no more to do with his present situation than Nero's
party in *Quo Vadis*—what a party!—why should he think
about it? Where were his usual cool and disciplined
thoughts? Routed, running away, a psychic Caporetta, by
Jove, and merely because his cheek remembered the touch
of her palm. All this time he was looking at her. When-
ever, slowly, she opened her heavy lids her yellow eyes met
his. Then the light gave way to darkness all around the
focus of his fascinated eyes, and in the world there was
only the clear yellow gleam.

At this moment, in the midst of this strange silence, in
came a crisp and cheery nurse, blue blouse, starched white
apron and winged cap—like the angel of the Annuncia-
tion, like the providential Saint Bernard to the prostrate
Alpinist. She bore a wide tray with a varied and plentiful
lunch and several newspapers. She chirped and smiled, arranged the bed table, clinking the dishes, saying "darling"
and "dearie," impersonally efficient, or pretending to be,
feasting her cynical pale eyes on the pretty voluptuary in
her bed and at the famous, stiff-necked, righteous Mr
Wooly. You can't ever really tell, she was thinking to herself; those small men, they say . . . Isn't she the hot one
though? Look at the hungry way she looks at him . . .
and so on, inventing useless tasks so she might linger in the
atmosphere of expensive lechery she imagined here, until
Mr Wooly, making his eyes like two polished horse chest-
nuts, gave her the glare that sent her flying.

Food regularized the situation. Mr Wooly's thoughts re-formed, accepted discipline, as he watched Jennifer eat. She ate like an aristocrat, that is, with a dainty sensuality, like a well-mannered, dainty-pawed wolf. She ate oysters, gazing at each before taking it into herself; she ate a bowl of pink shrimps, a steak, black-skinned, gory within. Oc-casionally she smiled at Mr Wooly, offered some of the steak, which she praised, and did not notice that he shud-dered.

She said rather unnecessarily: "I really feel perfectly well. I'll leave this place tomorrow."

"Where will you go?"

She looked sad, shoving the table from her. "I don't know."

He noticed the glisten of food on her white hands, drew in his breath with shock as she wiped them on the sheet. He noticed now that the dark and lustrous hair grew low on her forehead, a bit too low, in fact, that the long brows were joined to the hairline by the shadow of fine, fuzzy hairs growing there. Now she definitely re-pelled him.

Jennifer licked her lips. "I was hungry." She sighed and, suddenly pathetic again: "What am I to do? How can I stay in Warburton, Mr Wooly?"

"Why not?"

"Why not?" She picked up the Warburton *Evening Sun,* the town's only newspaper, pointed a long sharp finger at a front-page picture. Mr Wooly leaned for-ward to see. He saw himself, popeyed, upon his left shoulder something—a pair of limbs, quite bare—though his face tended directly toward the lens that had caught

him, the pupils of his wide eyes nestled in their left corners.

"The caption," Miss Broome said, "is 'The Bottom of
the Stair.'"

"They've misspelled stair," Mr Wooly said. "They've
spelled it 's-t-a-r-e.' How stupid of them." He continued

to look at the picture. It was no credit to him—or to her
—aesthetically or socially.

"How can I face them now?" Lady Jennifer asked.

"Well, you can't go on like this," said Mr Wooly, gazing at the picture. "I mean, forever not facing them.
That's no way to meet people."

She began to cry. Like a child. It pierced him to the
heart.

CHAPTER V

Hell Breaks Loose, at Last

MR WOOLY, preparing for dinner after a devastating day, talked to Bentley. Bentley arranged a pair of pants over his right forearm. He slightly bent forward, achieving an expression of intelligent and intense interest merely by arching his red eyebrows. He had a broad face, mostly cheeks, tallowed over by that stunned, eye-glazed expression achieved only by many years of economic security, plus confidence in an endless future of the same. Having decided in his own mind what the master wanted him to say, he now proceeded to say it:

"In my opinion, sir, she put fire to that 'otel 'erself, knowing you to be the honorary fire chief, sir, and did the foul deed only to meet hup with you, sir! Lady! Lady, my eye. I should 'ave her hinvestigated. I should 'ave 'er 'ole pahst probed hinto, I should."

"The authorities here, in New York and in Washington have been apprised of the facts," Mr Wooly said coldly.

"Yes sir. I only meant to say, sir . . ."

"She is a very, very lonely girl, Bentley."

Bentley diminished. He pulled hurt silence over himself. One minute the master railed against this female, but say one sensible word and he'd be on top of you. Bentley was going screwy himself.

"And is it her fault that she is in love with me, Bentley?"

"Are you sure, sir, that she is in love with you?"

Mr Wooly frowned into the mirror. He saw the arched eyebrows and the moonface of his servant over one shoulder. He turned to face it. "Do you mean to infer that no one could be? Why should I be denied this sentimental, emotional tribute that is often not withheld from the lowest, the most insignificant? Have I warts on my face, Bentley? Is my spine loathsomely deformed? Tell me, Bentley, where is there sure sign of my leprosy? Where is my goiter?"

This was too much for the butler. His eyebrows disappeared into the upstanding thicket of his pale hair. "Goiter?" he made plaintive echo. "I didn't know you had one, sir. There's Mrs Wooly's mandolin, I know where that is. It is . . ."

"Silence!" shouted Mr Wooly. There was silence. "This evening," Mr Wooly said, "I am to have a final meeting with Miss Broome. And I tell you, I shall not be penalized for a generous, a heroic impulse, as if it were some felony; do you understand?" His tone changed, became suspicious. "She was ready to leave the hospital but she did not. Why? Because she had no clothes. No clothes, no passport, no money, nothing. All burned." Then, voice clearing: "Did she cry? Not a tear! She laughed over the phone. She told me it was like being born again. She said, 'Call me baby.' What a woman, Bentley!"

"A wonderful woman," Bentley said.

"But who paid for the clothes, the incidentals, hats, purses, goodness knows what—the baggage?"

"A baggage!" said Bentley, stamping his foot. "You're right, sir!"

"Silence!" angrily, but soon Mr Wooly smiled again.

"I took my secretary with me to help with the purchases. Bentley, I don't remember purchasing garments for Mrs Wooly before she passed on." He spoke in the hushed and solemn tone he always assumed when mentioning her.

"Mrs Wooly did 'er own shopping, sir, and yours, too, as I remember," Bentley said.

"Ah, this, this was an interesting experience, Bentley. One buys, you know, not only the superficial or exterior garments, as it were . . ." He sighed and again was torn by harsher thoughts. "A transparent confidence game, Bentley! I shall not be taken in. I shall tell her to clear out—and she *will* clear out!"

"Yes sir, and good riddance, sir."

"That will do, Bentley! You may go."

Bentley canted toward the door with the gait of one who has just fallen off a runaway merry-go-round. He halted, wavering, at another shout from his master. "A moment! You understand that she is dining with me— here!"

"Here?"

"Here."

"Tonight?"

"Tonight." Mr Wooly ground his teeth together. "*I'll put her in her place,*" he muttered.

"How many places, sir?"

"What, you blockhead?"

"How many for dinner, sir?"

"The two of us, and flowers . . . anemones, a huge bowl of them. They grow," he murmured to himself, "in the fields above Cagne-sur-Mer. They will be a surprise for her."

"A bowl of enemies," Bentley said submissively.

"Anemones."

"Enemas," groaned Bentley, and his fat figure faded sadly away.

Mr Wooly, left alone, gazed at the reflection of himself in his dinner coat. A small compact man with large, crazy brown eyes. He looked, this evening, rather older than his thirty-eight years. The lines that a habitual, self-righteous smile had made from his straight, pointed nose were deeper but seemed lost, and he really wore no single expression. He had never been so uncertain, never so torn between desire and good sense, and he had not yet fixed his face for his sad new state. Much and, at the same time, very little is known about that portion of Mr Wooly's life extending from the death of his wife in 1928 to the present. He had lived a life which was for the most part about as private at that of a polar bear in a zoo. He was sustained moreover by his faith, by the need to set an example to other members of the Men's Bible Class, yet he was a vital creature; he had depths; the desires that must have been suppressed, forced down flat like springs, were pushing for their release. Grinning, leering jack-in-the-boxes were popping open all over the poor man's soul. As he strode back and forth on the yellow Chinese rug of the drawing room downstairs the prick of a thought, a memory, would send him jumping sideways like a skittish horse. There is truth in old catch phrases. He muttered: "The very devil to pay!" and "Hell's broken loose!"

He was acting like a fool. But he well knew it. So he

was not wholly a fool. Plain as the nose on Bentley's moon-face he saw that the most sinister thing about this woman was her lack of background, her detached and orphaned state—no relatives, no properties, no documents, not a sign of these but her own story. It was her story that the day before the fire she had gone to a bank in Manhattan and drawn out her funds and from a safe-deposit box a coffer of jewelry, as well as her passport and a file of correspondence. Everything, of course, had been burned.

"She's a liar," Mr Wooly said to himself, "an abject liar. She probably comes from Flatbush."

She had been living for years in Europe, here and there. That was her cunning story. Yes, Europe. That desert. Europe was a place to come from. Poor old Europe wouldn't testify against one. For instance, the château she had owned north of Paris, near Chantilly—the government had taken that for taxes. As for the family seat in Little West Snifflehurst, Hants, the family seat had been so kicked by recent adversities that it was in tatters —a blushing shame.

"She's a liar," Mr Wooly said aloud.

Bentley, arranging glassware on the Louis Quinze dresser, said, "Yes sir," which was another mistake.

"Silence!" shouted Mr Wooly.

The door gong sounded. She had arrived.

For a time she was invisible while the quaking Bentley took her furs. She entered the drawing room, paused to gaze calmly about her with her slanting eyes, her small cat's smile, while Mr Wooly didn't say what he had planned to say. For a time he didn't say anything. He didn't because she was gowned in midnight-blue chiffon velvet, her heavy, lustrous hair in a complicated, intimidating pile on top of her head. There were no shoulder straps on her gown. It stayed up, what there was of it above her waist, but he couldn't imagine why.

The whining, piercing voice said: "Good evening!"

"You have come," he said stupidly, unnecessarily.

"Did you doubt me?"

"If you think," he said, trying to whip himself into a righteous anger, "that by getting yourself up as if . . ."

As he spoke she drew close to him, stopped his mouth with hers. Bentley, turning from his work to face them, gasped. He quaked and paled; he backed away. That kiss continued. It was like . . . But to watch a kiss, to describe one, is to serve only to make you respect and envy the Japanese, who focus *their* tenderest attention upon the nape of the little necks of their darlings, thus avoiding their eyes, as well as their noses and the whole odd face-pressing business. Mr Wooly, of course, did not see that kiss. He experienced it, and as for describing it, he would never have attempted that. When at last she drew away from him, as her arms and his dropped, he reached backward for the wall, leaned against it, slid slowly downward toward a chair that happened not to be there. Arriving at the floor, his torso wavered upright but for a moment, then he lay down while she, less affected, wandered about the room, admiring—or checking over—its elegant contents.

Presently Mr Wooly regained his feet but not his wits. Bentley, fearing the worst and showing it with every quiver and quake of his fat self, served them. They ate; they drank ice water; they conversed politely. They

admired the anemones. Eating did not interest Mr Wooly.
He put down a forkful of escarolle and rested his chin
on his hand. He watched his lady eat, wondered at the
smooth pallor of all skin. How *did* the blue velvet stay up?

"It's pasted on," she said demurely, though he had not
spoken. "Darling, you have such lovely big brown eyes."

"I see through you," he said quietly, intensely.

She blushed with pleasure. "Darling," she repeated.

"What is it about me," he wondered impersonally,
"that so charms people? I often wonder."

"You are so modest," she said, and she added a jarring
note: "But the food you serve. What is this?"

"Nuts," he said.

She gave him a quick and searching look. "I beg your
pardon?"

"It's made of nuts and whole wheat and ground carrots, molded in the form of a cutlet."

She gazed at it, frowning with disgust, as a hungry cat
might gaze at a plate of sliced cucumbers. Bentley quaked
over the silver on the dresser. She spoke to him. "The
wine, Bentley," she said.

Bentley gazed round-eyed at his master.

His master spoke: "Wine? I never serve it. We are dry,"
he explained.

"Not as dry as I am, I'll wager," she said, putting her
small sharp teeth to the edge of her glass of ice water,
sipping it.

After the floating island they had a brown health
beverage in demitasse cups in the Chinese west room, and
after that Jennifer proposed exploring the house.

Oh, she had her nerve. There was no doubt about that.

She had that with her always. After all, she had invited
herself here tonight; she had sneered at his food, sipped
his excellent ice water with an upper lip that drew back
and quivered as if offended cat whiskers sprouted from it.
Now she proposed to inspect his house.

*Mr Wooly said: "Oh, come, it is time for you to go, my
nameless, pushing friend. Time for you to turn to some
other softer victim. I am a multimillionaire, at least what
passes for a multimillionaire in this part of New York. I
am a widower. I am a wonderful catch for such an, an, ah
—adventuress—that's the word—and so you are, with
your faceless family, your addressless past . . . your
orphaned present. You wish to make an inventory of my
personal property? No, thank you, just the same!"*

But all this Mr Wooly only said to himself. What he
said aloud was as follows: "Bernard Doodle designed the
house, with my help, of course. I think he did rather a
good job of it. The main hall is . . . That? That is a portrait of Mrs Wooly. She died while visiting a favorite
aunt in Grand Rapids, an eccentric lady who . . ." He
went off into details and anecdotes which would have
been boring even if Jennifer had known this aunt.

Jennifer interrupted. "When?"

Mr Wooley pawed the air. "When what?"

"When did she . . ."

"Pass on?"

"Pass on."

"1928."

Jennifer nodded her lustrous, dark coiffeur. She looked
sideways at her host. "Ah," she purred, gazing again at
the oil painting of Mrs Wooly—a blue-eyed, rich-off

woman in rimless, gold-chained eyeglasses, an inexperienced mouth, a bland and stunned expression.

"I am psychic," Jennifer said. "Mrs Wooly's favorite dish was a fruit salad with whipped cream."

"You *are* psychic," Mr Wooly said, beaming, and he added, looking sad: "Poor Sadie. Ah, Sadie, I have been true to you!"

Jennifer put her hot, hard palm on the wrist and he slightly jumped. "Shall we go upstairs?"

Up they went.

The billiard room, the dark-paneled library, the other rooms, had not greatly interested her. She looked. She said nothing. They came to his room, that Napoleonic magnificence. "This," he said, "is my room," and opened the door a crack. She put her satin foot in it. *"Yours?"*

She went in. After all, he couldn't crush her foot.

He explained the window brocades, the needle point that covered one wall, the fireplace, imported from Spain, every carved stone numbered, and so forth. The bed, he told her, had belonged to an ancestor, a collateral ancestor.

"How much collateral?" Jennifer asked.

"I mean he was not in the direct line."

Jennifer gazed at the enormous bed, her interest undisguised. She found and turned the switch of the rose-colored reading light. She found and touched the button that released the yellow satin horizontal covering of the mirror that roofed the bed. The yellow satin flew toward the foot. Twisting her neck, Jennifer saw herself on the ceiling, so to speak.

Beyond the windows, which were long and opened as doors, was a balcony extending over the columned porch on the south side of the house. There was a moon, a half-melted golden lump, heavy in the sky. And a moist, half-cool breeze fingering its way along through foliage and through her dark and lustrous locks. It was freighted with the odor of lawn and of the tea roses down by the fountain, three floors below.

There was on one wall another photograph of Mrs Wooly, a full face, the eyes focused directly at whomever might look that way. Mr Wooly did. He remembered again his long loyalty. The room was shadowy, his visitor invisible in a corner, and he felt how Jennifer, that alien, invaded and disturbed it. A self-defensive anger glimmered in his soul. He knew all at once what he should do. The windows were open. He and Jennifer drifted out to the roofless balcony and stood by the low stone rail.

"Jennifer," he said, "I have something to say to you."

"Yes, Wallace," she sighed, using his middle name for the first time and not knowing his first.

"It is this. I can never marry again."

There was a pause of heavy silence.

"Never," said Mr Wooly, feeling certain triumph. "After Mrs Wooly I could never . . . love another."

She had bowed her head. A strange sound came from her throat. She hid her face in her hands.

Mr Wooly realized with horror that she was moaning. This poor, friendless little woman. It was terrible. What followed was worse.

"You cast me aside, don't you?" she moaned.

What could he say?

"Now, I have nothing to live for. O God, I wish I were dead."

"Please, please don't say that," Mr Wooly said. "It is wrong. Your life is not yours to take."

"I will not wait for death," she moaned.

Before he knew what she meant by that Jennifer had jumped lightly to the stone balustrade. "Farewell," she said. "Farewell, Mr Wooly," and even while his palsied limbs strove to bring him closer to her she threw herself off, head down. There was a hideous crashing and tearing in the great elm tree which spread its boughs just beneath the balcony. Then there was silence, a deathly silence that filled everything.

Mr Wooly sank to his knees. He dared not look over the balustrade. "Jennifer," he cried. "I have killed you. Now that you are gone I know that I love you. I love you. Ah God, for a miracle so that you might live and we might have married. Jennifer, my love . . ." and so on, over and over, as if at last he really had lost his mind.

He was profoundly, terribly frightened, and yet over his fevered thoughts ran a comforting thought: I will be true to you, he thought.

There are professionals and there are amateurs in all lines of human endeavor. Mr Wooly was a professional insurance man, a professional after-dinner orator, an amateur Christian (or perhaps here his standing was ambiguous), and also he was a professional true lover. He had been faithful to the shadow of the shadow of Mrs Wooly; now he glimpsed an opportunity to be faithful to another nothing bearing the name of Jennifer. He spoke his thoughts aloud, and even while he spoke them he felt a hand upon his shoulder. It burned through the fabric, the padding, the cambric shirt, till it spoke to his very skin. A very real hand.

"Mr Wooly!" said a tense, a singing, albeit nasal voice.

He dared to look up. It was not her ghost. It was Jennifer herself. The blue velvet was in tatters; it hardly existed below her waist. Its upper front, however, unhung, unfastened, miraculously remained. . . . Mr Wooly gazed at her, his eyes like those of a moribund horse.

"Forgive me," he sighed.

Jennifer put her burning palms, one to each of Mr Wooly's cheeks. She said, she whispered, that the elm tree and under the elm a sturdy catalpa tree had received her in their arms, stripping her very nearly bare naked but sufficiently modifying her headlong rush toward the hard earth. The skirt part of the blue velvet was gone, and no wonder, and her stockings . . . but not her golden slippers. . . .

"Jennifer," Mr Wooly said. "Jennifer." And then he heard himself saying: "Will you marry me?"

She seemed to think. She bowed her head. "Yes, Mr Wooly," she said, and there was an incisive click in her voice, as if invisible handcuffs were being locked. "Tomorrow." Here her body went limp; again he had to carry the wench. He took her into his bedroom and across it to its massive door. She moved slightly then. "Where are you taking me?"

"Home," he said, contriving to press a button to summon Bentley.

"Put me to bed, darling," she said and added: "You won't need Bentley."

What could he, as a fundamentally kind and chivalrous

man, do but obey the poor lady? He gave the portrait of
Mrs Wooly an imploring look: the painted gleam behind
the painted drooping eyeglasses did not, however, soften.

He begged her forgiveness with an agonized, beseeching
roll of his big brown eyes and a shrug of his weighted

shoulders. He parted the blue brocade curtains of that
bed, deposited the half-naked Jennifer and snapped on
the soft, rosy glow of the reading light.

"My shoes," sighed the lady. He understood that she
meant him to take them off. They were of gilded kid,

and he thought—a little madly—that golden kid was as
pagan as ever the golden calf had been, and all the while
within himself the tides of his soul dizzily alternated from
ebb to flood, seeking an equilibrium that had for so many
years been his. He hated this interloper with all his being.
He humbly kissed her silken toe. She sighed and softly
laughed. "What a bed!" she sighed. "We shall live in it,
sleep and eat and take our exercise. A Madison Square
Garden of a bed, built for wrestling matches. . . . Hand
in hand we shall pace up and down in it. We shall hang a
white sheet at the end and give motion-picture shows for
our friends; we shall have twelve children, my little husband, and they shall all sleep down there in that corner
while we curl up in this, you wicked little man, you, you
poseur, you and your righteousness! You vegetarian victim. Look at me, Wallace, observe me well. . . . Doth
flesh still revolt you?"

He dared now to observe her as she directed, studying the pale smoothness and perfection of her skin, so
much of which was visible through the tatters of her
gown. But there was not a scratch anywhere to be seen,
a fascinating, an incredible, fact. He redoubled his
studies. "Not one," he said. "But that is impossible." She
languidly agreed. It was impossible, but there it was; or,
rather, there it wasn't. All that gravity pull, that headlong rush downward from the third floor, all those sharp
branches and twigs like fingernails clawing, and not a
scratch!

"Don't," she said, and her sleepy voice was like F-sharp
plucked on the violin and permitted to hum, "don't fret
your little head, my darling. It is late. It is time for bed.

You in that corner, I in this. Is there a telephone, or shall
we communicate by yodels? You might come over and see
me sometime, at that!" Mr Wooly said nothing. Trembling all over, with longing, with loathing, he undressed,
turned Mrs Wooly to the wall.

It was the least he could do for her.

Bentley arrived at his usual time in the morning. He
knocked and at once, as usual, he came in. He paused
then, holding aloft the tray with its usual little silver tea-
pot, its cup. Mr Wooly had always had a spot of tea before rising in the morning. Bentley gazed and emitted a
little moan. Mr Wooly had said last night he would put
her in her place. Was this it? Bentley's worst apprehensions had been fulfilled. She spoke, and her tone was that
of the mistress of the house.

"Put it down there, Bentley," she said.

He bobbled and quavered, his eyebrows like frantic
caterpillars. He risked a frightened question: "Where is
Mr Wooly, may I ask?"

"Certainly you may ask, Bentley."

"I do ask, madame, if you please."

"Mr Wooly," she said, flattening a pillow to reveal his
pale countenance, "is in a swoon."

And so he was, paralyzed, with a small remembering
grin on his face, a rosy smudge of lipstick on his ear.

CHAPTER VI

The Strumpet Vine

IN THE RESTAURANT where Mr Wooly and his gentle, long-legged secretary were lunching on various starches and a great deal of health-stimulating greenery there was music. It muttered and moaned steadily from a hole in some distant corner, having been piped from Manhattan. It was blind music, and though it was supposed to please and to cheer it seemed sad to Betty Jackson. She was hungry, hungry for love; the longing bound her limbs, made them heavy; and hungry, too, for food. She could have gone on eating this rabbity food until her very nose trembled and her ears grew long; still she'd be hungry. Not that she criticized Mr Wooly, who had been talking for an hour and was still at it. No, if he wanted her to be a vegetarian, then a vegetarian she would be, without question. She cupped her round and adorable chin in her left palm and gazed upon him. She looked at his lips, and a flush crept up her cheeks; her eyes darkened.

Mr Wooly, ticking off the names of those who would attend his wedding, looked everywhere but into Betty Jackson's face. He was talking against time, against silence and thought, talking loudly, boastfully. For the fiftieth time he told her what a happy man he was.

She sighed. She felt so sorry for him she could have cried. "Why are you laughing at me?" he asked.

48

"I am not laughing. I would never laugh at you, Mr Wooly. Oh, this is not funny." She put her hand across the table, touched his arm. "Don't do this," she said softly. "Don't marry her."

His face twitched as if she had struck it. He said in a hoarse whisper: "It is too late, too late," and with that he covered his face with trembling fingers. "Too late."

"You do not love her, poor Mr Wooly."

But now he recovered his poise. He spoke harshly: "You do not understand," he said. "Your pity is misdirected, impertinent."

All she could see was that he was unhappy, terribly unhappy, and in the secrecy of her pure and loving heart she did swift and lethal things to Miss Jennifer Broome, who was, she thought, a dark and evil cat.

Now it was time to go. Swanson drove first to the boardinghouse.

"Good-by."

Mr Wooly patted her hand. He laughed hysterically. If a goat laughed that would be a similar sound. A thin bleat.

She put her long arms around him. "Come to Betty," she said, "when you need me. Good-by."

She was his mother, his beloved. She *was* not! He was going crazy. As the car sped away he was deciding to fire Betty Jackson tomorrow or, anyway, the day after tomorrow.

But the day after tomorrow there was a small but fashionable wedding at the First Church, and the night of the day after that was the night he saw the true face of his wife—and then . . .

There is little to be told of the wedding. The bride cynically—for what right had she?—wore virginal white, carried white roses. She concealed her avid, slanted eyes, looking down. The bridegroom held his chin up, and his large brown eyes rolled.

"The old boy," said Mr Simpson, who was there, "looks like he's about to canter off with a loud neigh."

This was heard by Sara, Mr Wooly's fifteen-year-old daughter, a slender, personable creature and no fool.

"She'd hop on and ride him if he did," Sara whispered. "Holding on with all her claws."

"But isn't she pretty?" whispered a boy cousin.

"Poor Pop," sighed Sara.

"About as vegetarian," said this boy cousin, "as a weasel, though."

"Pop goes for weasel," Sara agreed. "Who'd have thought it?"

"But beautiful," insisted the cousin, and Mr Simpson, next to him, could only sigh, "Ah."

Bride and bridegroom now faced Dr Fergus Peyton, the tall, hollow-cheeked pastor. There were no interruptions.

Bride and bridegroom, the dozen guests, went directly to the Wooly residence and partook of a healthful, if not very stimulating, collation. Everybody there had their private opinions about the new Mrs Wooly, but none could deny that she deported herself as every inch a lady.

Little Sara was shocked and concerned to share her father with a stranger, and the boy cousin darkly hinted that Mr Wooly had quite given away his true nature, marrying such a hot number as Jennifer obviously was.

As for Bentley, the butler, his comment to an upstairs maid named Hortense was that today she entered here as the "mistress of the 'ouse instead of the mahster.

"She'll ruddy well burn 'im to hashes," he added.

Jennifer went out of her way to win the friendship of the children. With the precocious boy cousin, moreover, she achieved something, awakened an interest so that after she had kissed him he gazed at her with a new expression on his homely, lecherous little face, but with Sara she got nowhere. The very young little woman looked into the yellow eyes of the older woman without a blink and with no hint of dawning affection.

"You are a pretty little thing," said the new Mrs Wooly. "Swanson will drive you back to New Rochelle this very evening." New Rochelle was where Sara's school was.

Mr T. Wallace Wooly himself moved about like a man in a trance. He was looking ahead a bit, and it took his breath away. He'd been in a wall-eyed trance ever since that first night. He was a walking conflagration, poor fellow.

Late in the afternoon, at Sara's suggestion, he and she went for a ride along their wood road, the girl on a small black horse, Wooly on an old bay mare named Rummy, a gentle, stupid creature, an equine grandma, who had been young in the last days of the first Mrs Wooly and very like that lady, to tell the truth.

"Don't feel that anything has changed," Mr Wooly told his daughter as they came out of the shadows of the wood, returning to the house. "Jennifer is a lady—lovely, cultured. She will be a good mother to you."

"Yes, Dad," said Sara.

"Of course she is different," said Mr Wooly.

"That is true," said Sara. They reined up for her last look at the big old house under the elms.

"How is your algebra coming along?" asked Mr Wooly.

"All right," she said. "I mean it's lousy. Are you happy, Dad?"

"What? What do you mean, asking me such a thing? Am I happy? On my wedding day? I am as happy as a lark."

"Are you sure?"

That was too much. "Am I sure? Confound it, girl, how do I know how happy a lark is? I've never seen a lark, much less asked him a question. Maybe this whole business about a lark staggering around forever in the throes of some tiresome happiness is just a myth. But then a myth," Mr Wooly added a little wildly, "may be as good as a smile. Ha, ha."

"I've never seen you just this way," Sara said sadly.

"You've never seen me on my wedding day, girl," Mr Wooly snapped.

"Don't go on calling me 'girl' like somebody in Dickens or something."

"Well, Miss Wooly, it's true, isn't it, that you've never seen me on my wedding day before? You certainly didn't attend my first one. And as for larks—well, I was just going to say that 'love laughs at lark myths.' Ha, ha."

"Oh, poor Dad," said Sara. "You're on edge."

"Ha, ha," said Mr Wooly.

"You seem bewitched."

"And why not, Sara? Is she not bewitching?"

They walked their horses into the stables. Swanson

came out of darkness. He gazed over melancholy whiskers, with restrained but utterly disapproving eyes, at his employer. His expression, the most maddening expression known to the human physiognomy, said that he was more hurt than angry. . . .

Mr Wooly dismounted and met the same sort of expression on his daughter's face. He was prey then to a brief convulsion during which he met and defeated an impulse very alien to his essentially dignified nature, that of kicking first Swanson in the pants and then, rather harder, his daughter. At this moment he met the large, beautiful eyes of old Bay Rummy, his first wife's favorite, and in them the distracted man thought he read the same expression. It was too much. He stepped back and gave her that hitherto repressed kick right in the middle. "There," said Mr Wooly, dusting his gloved hands, one against the other, "you—*horse!*"

All Rummy said was "Oof," but she put her soul in it. She meant it. Whatever her thoughts she kept them to herself. They were obviously not friendly thoughts. She was both hurt and angry now.

Swanson drove Sara away early in the evening. Old Bentley wet his fat cheeks with tears to see her go. And Jennifer was so gentle and so charming that, watching her, a mist came to Mr Wooly's eyes. "How," he said to himself, "I have misjudged this little woman!"

After being left alone—*enfin seul*, as Mr Wooly tenderly put it—they walked for a little while, her hand on his arm, through the living room, the library, finally to the wide south veranda where gravely they paced and gravely they discussed a happy future. She was delighted and delightful. It did not occur to Mr Wooly that she might be delighted because of the artistic satisfaction derived from a well-acted part or perhaps even because she was inwardly tasting her triumph—over him. In any case, when he murmured something about the lateness of the hour and of being tired Jennifer whispered in his ear, her hot breath tickling it, that so was she tired, so they mounted the curve of the main stair slowly, with a touching, Old World dignity.

It was Jennifer's fancy that night to prepare herself in her own apartment, which adjoined his, with the aid of her maid Hortense, and to take her time and come in at last in a misty, billowy but very modest nightie and puffy mules, to run quickly, hair flying, and with a low, embarrassed little laugh jump into the big bed, where Mr Wooly had long been. It was as if she had forgotten that consummation is, after all, a singular proposition, but Mr Wooly was a one to be easily inclined toward such hypocritical self-deception.

She said breathily, "Now you, you stay right there in your own corner, Mr Wooly. Let us talk."

No other suggestion, or hardly any other, could have pleased him more. So they talked about the foreign situation and many other things, such as the fact that the house was not mortgaged, that the horse Rummy had been a colt when the first Mrs Wooly was alive, a special pet of hers, and had been kept out of respect for memory of her affection for it. Jennifer asked again about the enormous bed. The uncle Mr Wooly had inherited it from, Mr Wooly explained, had evidently been an early self-improver. Mr Wooly pulled the cord that stripped bare the vast mirror that roofed this bed. The rosy reading light was made to glow. Mr Wooly looked at his bride and smiled. "Ideal," he explained, "for training the facial muscles." He widened his smile, observing the change in the mirror above, frowned, looked horrified, opened his mouth wide in hortatory enthusiasm. "See?" he said. "Or you may engage in very helpful exercises." He raised one leg, lowered it, raised it, so vigorously he began to pant, and Jennifer anxiously urged him to rest lest he waste his strength. This he found quite agreeable, for he now noticed another talent of the bed's odd ceiling; in it one not only saw oneself but one's companion, and admirable as he had always found himself, Mr Wooly now found the contemplation of another—up there—was just as interesting, nay, more so.

"A solid bed," he sighed approvingly.

"A risky one," murmured Jennifer getting closer.

"What kind of risks?"

"Asterisks," she said.

*   *   *

He awoke and found her asleep in a far corner of the vast bed, quite uncovered. He covered her carefully. In her sleep she rejected the covers. He tried again. Odd of her. Like a pussycat, he thought, as he returned to the deeps of exhausted slumber. He was awakened again— this time, he knew, by the faraway mournful song of some night-struck tomcat. For once Mr Wooly had lost track of time. But it was still thick night outside his windows. He heard another noise—a large scratching and scraping noise. It was, to his horror, repeated. Mr

Wooly sat up, snapped on the light and gasped to see a hand, one single hand all by itself, on the sill of a window. It was his wife's hand. He knew that even from this distance. It was slender; it bore her ring. And a swift glance around told him she was no longer in his bed.

He called her name, using a hushed conspiratorial tone for some instinctive reason. The hand disappeared. In a moment he was there, thrusting his head out into the cool night air.

"Look here, Jennifer," he pleaded.

She looked up at him from a distance of about **three feet.**

"Where are you going?" he asked.

"I was just going out," she told him.

"But what are you standing on, my sweet?"

"This vine. I don't know what you call it."

"It is a trumpet vine," he said helpfully. "A very old trumpet vine, my great-grandfather planted it."

"Go back to bed," Jennifer urged him. "Don't stand there with your head sticking out like that, talking about your great-grandfather. It is the middle of the night. Tell me about your grandfather tomorrow morning at breakfast."

Obediently, considerately, he pulled his head indoors but thought of something.

"Jennifer?"

She looked up again, her narrow eyes gleaming in the dark. She was five feet farther down now. "What is it *now*, Mr Wooly?"

"Is it strong enough, darling?"

"What?"

"The trumpet vine."

"Of course it is. Go back to bed or you'll catch cold. If you must discuss the strumpet vine . . ."

"Trumpet," he said. "Oh, Jennifer, what a mistake!"

"Trump or strump!" she exclaimed.

"Ha, ha," laughed Mr Wooly; "that's very good, you know. I mean you could go on like that—crump, bump, lump, dump, frump, hump, sump, pump, clump, jump— why, it's practically inexhaustible, isn't it? Mump, rump— ha, ha—and they're all funny words."

"I don't think they are," Jennifer replied. "You chump!"

"How clever you are! I forgot that one," and then, pleading, "I want to come too."

"No, no! I'll be right back, dear. Go to bed now; think of all the work you have to do tomorrow."

"That's right, I have," he agreed. But unwillingly.

Mr Wooly went back to bed, not to sleep, however. He began to wonder about this business. He began to realize there were a lot of reasonable questions he might have asked besides the ones he had asked, such a question as: "Why not use the stairs?" for instance. He tried not to do so, but now began to think his wife more than a little strange. Warm as he was in his big bed, he shivered.

It may seem that our Mr Wooly, that pillar of the community, was acting in an extraordinarily eccentric fashion, blowing hot and cold about his new wife, averting his attention from certain of her traits, certain areas of her personality, even contriving to forget whole events, such as her dive off the balcony, her unsinged condition after the flames of the Hotel Monroe; yet he was, in fact, acting like many husbands, most husbands. They marry some camouflaged monster and there they are—married to it—so they do their best not to know too much about her, while she generally does her best to make the worst visible as neon signs on a country road. Yes, Mr Wooly shuddered in his bed. His own bed. He was wholly awake. He knew that what he dreaded most to hear was what he was waiting to hear—the scrape-scrape of Jennifer's ascent back up the trumpet vine. Or would she use the stairs, like a Christian?

She didn't. She came back through the window. As the

first faint promise of morning lightened its squares she crawled back in. Poor Wooly lay there, his eyes tight-closed, pretending to sleep, because he simply could not face up to the job of interviewing his bride about all this. He didn't know what to say to her, what to ask. He went on pretending to sleep. She was cold as a frog. He felt the chill creep from her to him through the bed. She drew nearer his warmth.

Outside cats yowled again, and a large bat, black as some cinder fluttering from an infernal conflagration, came in the open window and soundlessly fluttered but went out again. The town of Warburton woke up; the placidly affirmative statement of the milkman's horse filled the street a block away. Trucks rumbled and a rooster crowed; a train called over the hills. A bland and atheistic sun looked through the windows. Mr Wooly observed that his bride slept quietly beside him. Maybe she needed exercise. Wasn't that it? Mr Wooly decided to equip his games room, the ceiling of which was plenty high enough, with gymnastic rings and bars. At last he went back to sleep. . . .

CHAPTER VII

Brief Love Nest

THERE is symbolism everywhere, even in our mechanized time. George, the sleek young man who sat at the switchboard behind the receptionist's desk in the large semicircular lobby of T. Wallace Wooly, Inc., showed his teeth to Mrs T. Wallace Wooly, who was in gray squirrel, hat to match. George was not asking advice about his incisors, his molars; he was smiling because here before him for the first time was his boss's wife, the woman the boss slept with if the old so-and-so had that much gumption. George, who was nineteen and hadn't got far either in the business world or any other, looked at Jennifer's gray squirrel coat where it was open, at the dark brown silk underneath, the way the latter didn't lay flat. He said, "Oh" and "Oh, migosh," but not aloud; then, turning (she having greeted him with a slight smile), he plugged in a plug into the switchboard with a special verve, a distinct emphasis.

"Mrs Wooly is here," he said into the receiver.

In the sanctum Miss Jackson, pale as a ghost but prettier, said: "Mrs Wooly is here."

"Fudge!" said Mr Wooly moodily.

"Tell her to come in," said Betty.

In came Mrs Wooly.

She kissed her darling lightly on the left temple. She

looked all about and exclaimed, as wives always do, "So this is where you work!"

"No," said Mr Wooly, being a husband, "it's where we play ring-around-a-rosy."

"Really," exclaimed Mrs Wooly. "And how do you play ring-around-a-rosy? Is this Rosie? Or who is, or what is? Sounds interesting," she said.

"This is Miss Jackson."

"How do you do?" said Mrs Wooly, looking her over, far from friendly. "How clever you are! I was watching how your quick little fingers tap-tapped on your machine. Such nice hands. Let me see them."

Poor Miss Jackson, slightly flushing, offered her hands into custody. Mrs Wooly patted them. She smiled at her rival, and neither of them had the least delusion about her status. "Thank you," said Mrs Wooly and turned to her husband. "Darling," she began, "the check . . . you quite forgot it, you careless, careless man." She turned to Miss Jackson and explained: "I must do *so* much shopping! It's exhausting."

When she had departed with her check Mr Wooly for a time spun himself in his chair, round and round, very quietly. There was no sound except the sound of Miss Jackson's typing. She whipped a sheet from her machine. She read it over, and then there was a new sound. It brought Mr Wooly right up out of his chair. "Confound it," he cried, "what is it now?", man getting toward the end of his wits.

Miss Jackson was crying. It shook her all over. "Look," she said. "Just look at this."

Mr Wooly looked at the sheet she thrust toward him.

The typing was excellent, but it had one fault; it went the wrong way:

                                              ,ris raeD

D'cer tnatsni htnet eht fo sruoy

The whole letter went that way.

Mr Wooly studied it. "Why do you write in reverse?" he asked. "Do you think it is funny?"

"I couldn't help it," said Betty.

"You couldn't help it? Come, come. You're a fine, normal girl," said Mr Wooly; "of course you can help it. Just a momentary aberration," he said. "Come, let us try another letter."

Betty wiped her lovely eyes and tried, but the tap-tap-tapping had not continued for long before she collapsed forward on her machine.

"Calm yourself, calm yourself." Mr Wooly looked at the second letter and saw that it, too, was backward.

"It won't do, you know," he told her. "It simply won't do. I want my letters done in a forthright, forward-looking, conservative, normal sort of way. This is novel, Miss Jackson, but it won't help the reputation of T. Wallace Wooly, Inc. Now let us have the *right* kind of a letter, the old pure Betty Jackson brand. There's a little soldier. Come along now." He patted her head.

"Oh, you are so kind, Mr Wooly," Betty said. "So kind," and she began to type, but again she stopped.

"She has bewitched me," Betty sobbed against the smooth lapels of Mr Wooly's double-breasted gray suit. "She has bewitched me."

He pulled her to his lap. Could he do less? He could

do more, of course, but could he have done less? He whispered that it was a mere nothing, a slip of some sort, a notion, a whatname. . . . Psychiatrists, said Mr Wooly, probably knew all about it. Perhaps his wife had, accidentally, so to speak, hypnotized Betty; that was it, a fine word. Hypnotized, he repeated, not having the least idea what he was talking about but needing to talk.

But his secretary was one to look a fact in the face.

"What good am I now," Betty asked him, "if I cannot do your letters, except backward?"

"Tomorrow you will have recovered," Mr Wooly assured her.

"No, no, I will have to go somewhere, somewhere far, far away, Mr Wooly."

"But I need you," he said.

Betty Jackson was one of those who combined beauty and gentle fantasy with an element of hard realism.

"Need me—for what?" she wanted to know.

"For yourself," he said, saying exactly the right thing. "You must have a rest," he said. "And after that we shall see; we shall see. We will make you an executive, a vice-president, a consultant. . . . Just how you will function I don't know—but——"

"Please don't worry, Mr Wooly," she said in a low voice. "I'll know just by instinct."

Mr Wooly of T. Wallace Wooly, Inc., was not a man who deliberately begins a double life. He didn't like, didn't want, a double life. He was a victim of circumstances. He told himself so. But what could he do? Here was a poor, defenseless girl who had been victimized by his wife—robbed of her livelihood. Who wanted a secre-

tary who wrote everything backward? Not even a China-
man or a Hebrew scholar—and, anyway, Betty couldn't
write Chinese or any other right-to-left language. Leonardo da Vinci, he remembered from his high-school
studies, wrote backward, but where was Leonardo now?

Obviously the only thing, the only right and proper
thing, even though to the philistine, the snooper, it might
seem extremely improper, the only thing that there remained for him to do was to go rent her an apartment
or, better, a cottage in some pleasant but obscure part
of the town. Some place his wife would never find.

So that is what he did.

It was a small stucco-and-timber cottage with an attached garage into which a man who did not want himself or his car to be studied by nosy neighbors could drive
directly in.

Mr Wooly's home life had become very complicated.
He did not understand his wife, or rather he was beginning to understand her, which was a state that promised
even less serenity than that of his previous utter ignorance and bewilderment. He soon was in the habit of hurrying out to Betty's place just to talk about his wife. Her
habits were, he would say, not nearly as regular as his had
always been, though like his they were well established.

"For instance," he said to Betty one late afternoon,
"take her in bed."

"I don't want to take her in bed," Betty objected in
a voice and a manner that amazed him. "I find her difficult to take in any condition but especially difficult to
take in bed."

"I mean in the matter of sleeping," said Mr Wooly. "Don't go off at half cock like that."

"I don't, and anyway, I don't know what half cock means. It doesn't sound like a nice expression."

"You're being difficult on purpose," sighed Mr Wooly. "What's got into you lately?"

"Vitamins," Betty said moodily. "Old iron. Carrots, cucumbers and parsnips."

"Don't you like parsnips?"

"I don't even want to talk about them. And anyway," she added inconsistently, "we never talk about anything but That Woman."

Had Betty Jackson begun to change, now she had left her room in a boardinghouse to live in that stucco-and-timber cottage with the attached garage? Not a physical change—she was still a handsome, long-legged, slumberously voiced blonde—but an inner change? Now that she no longer took his dictation, no longer lived in the routine he prescribed, in his office, perhaps she would begin to dictate? A frightful thing seemed to be happening. She was turning into a wife, while his wife daily became less like a wife.

"All I was going to say," Mr Wooly persisted, "was that sometimes she sleeps in the barn. She gets up in the middle of the night and crawls down the trumpet vine and sleeps in the barn."

"You have already said that," Betty told him.

"We've got a goat," Mr Wooly went on, disregarding her interruption. "Last night a maid saw her riding it."

"Why shouldn't she ride the goat if she feels like it?

It's your goat, isn't it?—you just said it was—and so it is her goat too. She's your wife. You can't hold out goats."

"But she was riding it through the apple orchard. Very slowly."

"Where else would she ride it? Down the main street in broad daylight? That would attract an awful lot of attention. It would interfere with traffic. Give the woman some credit for sense. You complain too much," Betty complained. She was, it seemed, determined to be unreasonable, to take a hostile or critical attitude toward anything he might say, but Mr Wooly was too avid for comfort, for release from the new and queer twists his married life was taking, to leave well enough alone and start talking on some other topic—such a topic, for instance, as Miss Betty Jackson.

"It was a moonlit night," he went on, "and she passed from the black shadow of one apple tree to another. Under the moon she and the goat seemed all white, and she was talking to the goat."

"Everybody talks to goats," Betty objected. "Or horses or dogs. 'Here, doggy, doggy,' they say. 'Well, he's a nice old doggy-woggy. Feeling well, are you? That's fine.' And so on, they keep it up for hours, but people don't go around saying in hushed voices how they talked to their doggy. If she wants to talk to a goat why don't you let her talk to a goat?"

"I don't know what's the matter with you today," Mr Wooly said. "You're so touchy."

"How do you know? You haven't tried to touch me."

Mr Wooly sighed. He felt something like a man who is trying to drive a nail into a wall with his head. He had never heard of a Roscoe Tenowitz, who kept ten women crazy about him with never a slip, simply by taking care never to discuss another woman with any one of them. When this Roscoe talked to Mabel he always talked about Mabel. Simple. But Wooly, hardly giving a word to the lovely creature before him, talked on and on about his wife.

"Last night," he said, "I came home late from a meeting of the Warburton Neighborhood Association, where I made a short address, and a very telling, eloquent address it was, too, everybody assured me. Taking a turn in the lower garden before retiring, I chanced to look up at our roof. She was there."

"Who was there?" Betty asked. "Don't tell me you are still giving me the last five-star news of That Woman!"

"She was on the roof and she ducked behind the chimney when she saw me. But when I got to my room she was in bed, pretending to be sound asleep. I tell you, it upset me; it was uncanny."

"And I tell you," Betty told him, "that I don't want to spend the rest of my days listening to descriptions of how she 'sleeps' in your bed. I am beginning to believe that you are so madly in love with your own wife that you deliberately make up all these fantastic complaints just so that you may be able to come and torment me with endless conversations about her." Betty burst into tears, such a flood of tears that for a moment Mr Wooly could only sit in his corner of the blue sofa and gaze at the bowed golden-crowned head. Then his better nature, or at least his nature, got the upper hand. He took her in his arms.

The tear-wet kiss summed up a good deal of conversation that might have been used to explain just how Mr Wooly now felt about his wife. And that kiss was a first step, a long one, toward the pleasant couch by the living-room fire, and here their new understanding increased by leaps and bounds. . . .

He returned home very late. Rather than awaken his wife, whom he had a certain disinclination to face, anyway, he slept on the day bed in the games room across the hall. . . . In the morning he was awakened by a sight that he was never to forget. His wife, Jennifer, was gazing at him from a little distance. She was wearing gym shorts and was curiously tangled in the acrobatic rings

which hung down from the nickeled crossbars of the frame he had installed for her. She was doubled in a suspended sitting position, arms about her ankles, rings under her knees; she peered at him from between her knees, unblinking, absorbed.

He could not forbear an ugly start, which she did not seem to notice at all.

"Good morning," she said. "Where were you last night?"

He had thought she might ask that and had his answer ready. "Working," he said, knowing this was a lie, realizing with a sinking heart how when one grasps the hand of deceit one is likely to walk along with it for a long and tortuous journey.

"Where?" she asked him, grave as ever and not altering her batlike position.

"At the office."

For a moment she was silent. "Mr Wooly," she said, "you do not lie very well."

All this time he was lying there on his back under the one blanket, gazing at her, spellbound. And she was hanging like a bat.

"How is your little sheep, anyway?" she asked.

He feigned bewilderment by blinking.

"The dopey little, ordinary little, whiny-voiced blonde that used to work for you, Mr Wooly." Here she slipped down from her perch and stood before him briefly. "*You* know," she said. "Shall I scratch her eyes out of her head, Mr Wooly, or are you going to behave?"

"You have an evil and suspicious mind," he protested, not, however, with great strength of tone or manner.

She laughed out of her small red mouth and slipped to the floor. "I know who my lawfully wedded husband is," she told him, "and I intend to keep him, by hook and by crook, by all the powers I possess, Mr Wooly. You behave yourself or you will earnestly wish you had." She left. The big room was filled with an aghast echo of her impressive, her terrifying, little speech.

She had seemed to know all. But how? What intuition?

Mr Wooly got up as best he could and moaned as Bentley helped him with his toilet, moaned and sometimes shook his head to his dismal thoughts. But at breakfast he found Jennifer looking her prettiest and filled with worldly comments about the news she had been reading in the morning paper while waiting for him to appear.

When he left for the office she kissed him nicely. He accepted this with a smile, a contrived smile, for her kiss was far from welcome. It was hot and curiously dry; it burned his cheek evilly. Already he was estranged from his wife. She was not for him. How well he knew that now! But he waved and smiled his best as Swanson drove him out the curving drive, but he did not smile when Swanson turned his melancholy face toward him. Swanson's eyes were piercing.

"Yah," he said and nodded.

"Someday," thought Mr Wooly, "I'll not only fire him; I'll brain him."

Mr Wooly did not see Betty that day until around four o'clock when they met in Brookside Park, both having gone there in separate taxicabs. The sight of her delighted him; it refreshed his seared spirit; the trees were almost fully in leaf, and the sun was cheerful on the sloping lawns, the little brook. For an hour he was happy. So was she. While they were filled, both of them, with the memory of what had happened last night neither spoke of it. Nor did they speak of Mrs Wooly. They walked hand in hand. Sometimes they turned their faces to smile or to say, "Hello," as if every glance were a wholly new and unexpected meeting of their hearts.

As the sunlight thinned he grew mindful of their peril, reluctantly said they must part now. She, alas, by herself and he by himself. As it turned out this was as well, for it was his luck, when his cab was within a hop and a skip of the Central Firehouse, to hear the siren go. Two minutes later he was clambering up to the seat next to the driver of the hook and ladder. As they went tearing through the evening he forgot his troubles in a delightful public excitement that made him feel like his old self. As they streaked through red lights, careened around corners, Mr Wooly began to wonder where the fire was. Here was Rosebud Avenue, its long stretch of new stucco-and-timber cottages. They stopped.

The block was beautifully aglow with the flames that, he saw at once, were consuming Betty's cottage. The careless girl—what had she done? The flames came out of all its windows. The roof, very fancy with small dormer windows, collapsed a few minutes after their arrival. It was an extraordinarily definite sort of fire. It burned everything and wound up despite the tons of water the Warburton Fire Department pumped onto it, making a pot of flame of the cellar.

"Mr Wooly," said a young fireman, "I never seen such a fire. Whoever lived there must have been hoarding gasoline or celluloid or something. Nothing we could do even discouraged that fire. It was out to make that cottage disappear, seems like, and that's what it did. By the way," said this young fire fighter, "Mrs Wooly is here."

She was, indeed, down the street a little way, having watched everything with great interest, being able to look with ease over the heads of the crowd because she was on board old Rummy. When she saw her husband she waved her riding crop.

"Quite a little fire," she said cheerfully.

He was not at that moment at his most alert. "What's that?" he asked.

"I said it was something of a conflagration," his wife explained. "As an expert, a connoisseur in the arsonic and incendiary, I was expecting some critical appraisement from you."

"It was a definite sort of fire," he conceded.

"A forthright, unprocrastinating sort of fire, wouldn't you say?"

Mr Wooly, still in the grip of bewilderment and the embarrassed confusion consequent upon meeting his wife in front of this burned-out love nest, didn't know what he should say. His glance, wandering, met with an almost audible sound of collision the steady gaze of Rummy herself, a remembering sort of gaze. Rummy looked like a horse that was trying to decide whether to clip his ear off or to maneuver herself about until her rear artillery might be in position to do unto him several times what he had done unto her.

"Nice Rummy," Mr Wooly said. "Nice horsy."

Horsy just looked at him.

"Betty," said Mrs Wooly, "is over there at the edge of the crowd, poor dear. Does she live anywhere hereabouts?"

This question was not, Mr Wooly thought, sincerely phrased or spoken. It was not really a question at all. It was rather a sly dig, a jibe, a mean crack. Mr Wooly, staying well away from the horse's head, made no reply. His wife's next speech, spoken in a low tone as she leaned down toward him, was brief and earnest: "I've warned you," she said.

She wheeled Rummy about and cantered off, while Mr Wooly went in search of Betty. He found her still in the taxi, the clock of which was ticking on merrily enough. Betty was not merry.

He said what he could by way of comforting the bereaved woman, told her to go to a hotel, gave the driver necessary directions and went away from there, having made no mention of the very strange fact of his wife's presence.

CHAPTER VIII

Mr Wooly Learns All, or Almost

BY DARK BACK STREETS Mr Wooly made his way home.
Mr Wooly was not the first husband to go home furtively
through dark back streets, his hat well down over his eyes,
or the first husband whose apprehensions increased as the
distance between him and his wife was reduced; no, but
no other such husband had ever harbored such an obscure
and at the same time profound bewilderment. Other husbands have been afraid of their wives, afraid of their
voices, their fiendish psychological weapons, such as heart
attacks, suicidal seizures and the sheer noisy fire of outraged virtue, afraid, too, of their pitching arms or their
way with an iron skillet; but Mr Wooly, more deeply
stirred than these, was suffering from a chill of the soul.
He had goose pimples on his subconscious. . . . His wife
—there were no two ways about it—was a strange woman.
He had boasted that she was different. Ah, she was different, indeed. Too different! What he disliked most was not
understanding her, not really knowing her at all. She was
in his bed or out of it, a stranger to him. He did not like
the way she crept down the outer wall of their residence;
he simply did not like it. It gave him the creeps, himself.
And what sensible wife ever went out riding through
Warburton on a horse at night? He was so deep in his
gloomy criticism that he forgot to continue to put one

foot in front of the other and came to a full stop near a corner. A street light illumined the maple-shaded walk ahead. Mr Wooly murmured something to himself, disapprovingly shook his head from side to side.

A sharp and hostile voice broke into his reverie.

"Well?"

Mr Wooly blinked.

"What's the matter with the little bitch?" asked a big fat man, an elephant of a man.

"I beg your pardon?"

"I don't beg yours," said the disagreeable fellow. "She's got a right to, hasn't she?"

Mr Wooly, getting his eyes into focus with the actual and immediate world, now saw that the fat man had a black dog on a leash, a contorted, gasping little creature with a heavy mustache and beard. Its eyes at the moment were closed. It was, and had been, busy in a manner that deserved at the very least the courtesy of the averted glance rather than what had seemed to be the absorbed attention of Mr Wooly.

"A fine dog," said Mr Wooly, extemporizing.

"I give her pills," said the man, somewhat mollified. "I do my best."

"And so does she, it seems evident."

"That's where you make your mistake," laughed the man. "She don't. I hate her. And she knows it. She's my wife's. The last thing of an evening I have to take this out for a walk. Even before we start I'm tired. I'm thinking a block will be plenty. But what she is thinking, this horrid little mop here, is that a half mile is the least she'll settle for; see what I mean?"

"I think I do," said Mr Wooly, who had no interest whatever in the unattractive canine, much less the workings of its insides. He bowed to the man and then, as an afterthought, to the dog too. But the dog was still too occupied to pay anybody any heed.

"What I mean is," the surly behemoth insisted, "it always has to be like a deal. I'm in the auction business myself; see what I mean?"

"Yes, of course, I see what you mean. Don't go on tagging that unnecessary question onto every simple statement you make. There is nothing abstruse in what you are saying."

"What?"

"Never mind," Mr Wooly exclaimed. "Never *mind*."

"All I was saying is this: It's like a deal. I say so much down and so much a block, and Dawn Frigganza, that's her name, goddamn horrid little bitch, she holds out. She bargains. No first deposits, straight credit. I got bad feet," the fat man said, "and I don't enjoy long walks; see what I mean? They itch."

This was too much, a good deal too much. Mr Wooly addressed him with dignity but with rising, minatory stress to his voice: "You have itchy feet, do you? You stop me on a dark street, me, a total stranger, to tell me that you have itchy feet. Confound it, man, what do I care? Am I a foot specialist?"

"I don't know," said the fat man simply.

"Do I *look* like some quack corn doctor?"

"The light ain't too good," the fat man said. Suddenly he bellowed with rage. "Look! Look! See what you've done by your butting in? You've taken her mind off it entirely. Now I'll have to walk her some more. Why don't you go mind your own business? Why do you stand around here throwing big words at a peaceful citizen? I got a mind to . . ."

But Mr Wooly never learned what he had a mind to— Mr Wooly was hurrying onward.

He was not himself. He did not know who else he might be. But he was not himself, not T. Wallace Wooly hurrying along home, afoot, and through dark streets. His hat was so far over his eyes, his step so unchristian, that two slender young men raised their arms high above their heads at his approach, thinking he was a holdup man and that the glint of Mr Wooly's worry-glazed eye was the glint instead of felonious coercion. As it was, Mr Wooly strode on by the two, only wondering why they stood in such an odd pose. It seemed crazy; it seemed of a piece with a night that had gotten out of control entirely, a night in which, since natural laws were sagging, if not actually breaking apart, lots more might happen. From the corner of Rhododendron Road Mr Wooly saw that the gates to his drive were open. He hurried forward. From behind a tree trunk jumped a policeman. He seized Mr Wooly by the shoulder so violently Mr Wooly's hat fell off. "Now then," said the policeman, "now then, where do you think *you're* going?" Then he recognized Mr Wooly. Dropping his hands at once, he substituted friendly repartee for the several good swift sockos he was all tensed up to deliver. "Well, Mr Wooly," he said. "Excuse me, sir. Lovely night."

"It is not," said Mr Wooly.

"Taking a little constitutional, ha, ha?"

"Is it unconstitutional, ha, ha?" asked Mr Wooly bitterly. He saw what the fellow had in his hand. "Officer Connolly, what do you think you are up to, waving your revolver around in the middle of the night? Are you hunting?"

"Yes sir, in a way of speaking, Mr Wooly."

"What? Pheasants? With a pistol?"

"No sir, not pheasants. Don't think so."

"Are you sober, officer?"

"I thought I was, sir."

"What do you mean, you thought you were?" snapped Mr Wooly. It did him good to slang the fellow a bit, he knowing Mr Wooly could have him thrown off the force if he so minded.

"I mean I thought I was until I thought I saw what I thought I saw, sir. I was coming along the road down there, in the shadows like, and right there by the big oak where you can see through across the lawn to the south side of your house I saw something climbing down, climbing down, climbing down. . . ." He spoke this last very slowly and made foolish finger wiggles in Mr Wooly's face to make clear what he thought his repetitive phrase failed to make clear. "White," he whispered.

"White what?" Mr Wooly asked, his heart sinking with a great bump. "White dress?"

"White . . . limbs," the policeman said hoarsely. "So I took out my gun and I aimed—I'm a good shot, Mr Wooly, I got a medal for shooting once—so I aimed. And then . . ."

"And then?" prompted Mr Wooly.

"And then I didn't shoot because why?"

"How do I know?"

"Because I had an argument. With myself. I ast myself, 'What is that, Connolly?' I told myself, quick as a flash, 'What do you mean, what is that?' So I came back, 'What you think you was aiming at,' and I said it was a figure of a woman crawling down a wall, as nekkid as a, as a"—he sought manfully for just the right word—"as a poached egg," he finished triumphantly. "You ever see anything on a poached egg, Mr Wooly? No, you never did."

"Yes, I have. Toast, for example."

"Oh no!" exclaimed Connolly. "Toast goes under a poached egg, not *on* it."

"I've seen truffles on poached eggs."

"You mean trifles like?" said Connolly coaxingly.

"I do not, confound it all," exclaimed Mr Wooly. "I mean truffles and I won't be truffled with, I mean trifled with—confound it, who started this? I'm not interested in poached eggs!"

The big cop shook his head sadly. "All I was saying was that it was nekkid as a poached egg, crawling, crawling, crawling; see what I mean?"

"Don't start that!" exclaimed Mr Wooly.

"Start what?"

"Start saying 'see what I mean?'—every noodle in Warburton has taken to saying 'see what I mean?' Stop it, I say."

"First time I said it," Officer Connolly protested, but after a moment of hurt meditation he started again:

"So, continuing this here argument, or discussion, as you might say, I passed this remark to myself; I said: 'A nekkid woman is it, climbing down a wall? I don't believe it! That's what. I simply don't believe it, and if I'm right not believing it—where would you be *shooting* at it?'"

"Now, now wait a moment. With whom were you having this conversation; can you remember that?"

"I was talking to myself," said Connolly patiently. "So I said to myself: 'Where would you be, Connolly, if you started off shooting away at a moonbeam mooching around on the wall of the residence of Mr Wooly? Where would you be?' I says. 'You'd be in the soup for sure. You're drunk,' I said to myself. 'You haven't touched teeth to crock in two days, and you're boiled.' So the upshot of it all was I didn't shoot." He was silent a moment. "But it didn't look like no moonbeam," he said stubbornly, "so I stood here ready to bop anybody that might come sneaking around, and that was how I grabbed hold of you, Mr Wooly."

"Very odd, Connolly, very odd, indeed. Shooting at moonbeams, talking to yourself. But there, I'll say not a word about it, not a word."

"Thank you, thank you, Mr Wooly. Good night."

"Good night."

Mr Wooly went on down his own driveway but did not go up the front stair, continuing around the house, with some vague plan of looking over the lawn, the barnyard, before turning in.

A wild animal hurtling out of shadows with a sound like tearing canvas knocked him down near the fountain pool, but it was only Red, Swanson's setter, who now recognizing his victim, began at once to lick Mr Wooly's face. Mr Wooly got up, gasping, and went on, more certain than ever that the way for a sane, upright, prosperous citizen of Warburton to act was the normal way—regular hours, chauffeur-driven cars, wives that stayed abed of nights. . . . Oh, this night was raveled; it billowed like a punctured blimp in some infernal draft, threatening to part its moorings and go God knows where.

"Nice doggy," said Mr Wooly.

"A vegetarian," yawned the setter, "in spades."

So his yawn would have been understood by anyone understanding canine yawns. He accepted without thanks a pat on his head; he went back to his kennel.

Mr Wooly brushed the dust from his pants. It was at this moment that from away down the lane, beyond the stables, from the direction of the hen house, came the scream of a hen. A death scream. A hen may cluck, may cackle; it has a way of murmuring and growling a little, talking to itself; when it is angry it can yell; it only *screams* when it feels or sees the hand of death. It is a blatant, bloodcurdling sound, especially when it is unexpected, when it rips out of the deep silence of night.

Mr Wooly, straining his eyes for the marauder that was suggested by that scream, felt how like noodles his knees had become. He did not want to go down there. He wanted Swanson to go down there. Swanson evidently was sound asleep. So was his worthless setter. Rummy stamped slowly in her stall, but what could Rummy do? Mr Wooly himself certainly did not want to go down there, but as the silence continued he told himself that some sort of wild animal had penetrated that hen house, a weasel, perhaps, or a fox, in any case, something small and timorous, after all. With dragging step he went. The hen houses were dark. He heard low-toned gallinaceous conversation within. The first house, wherein lived his Cochin Chinas, he guessed as he entered, had been the house visited. In the glare of the electric bulb he had snapped on rows of the birds, half their feathers still in fright's disarray, stared at him. He saw a cock's feather on the cement floor and looked around for him. He wasn't there. As his reign was solitary—all these others being hens, one of whom must have let out that scream as she saw the harem's mainstay, its pivot, violently set upon— it became evident that he, and he alone, was the victim.

"Confound it," said Mr Wooly, for he was proud of that bird, who was of a good race and excellent points, a prize winner.

The hens, watching him, murmured, saying buck-buck . . . and wuck-wuck. . . . They seemed to be filled with contempt for him. They looked very like a meeting of the women's auxiliary of the Warburton Board of Trade. He thought as he returned their female gaze that though he had often heard women called hens he had never realized before how very apt the epithet was. And vice versa. "Ladies," he said, "ladies of Warburton, good evening."

"Bla," they uttered, deep in their throats, shifting their tails slightly. "The old wuck," they seemed to say quietly, eyes aglitter.

"I have been asked to come here this evening," Mr Wooly said, "to address you on the subject of thrift stamps."

He realized where he was. "A lot of *old women!*" He sneered at them. "A lot of gossipy old . . ." But here he went silent, for his eye had caught something else upon the cement floor. He picked it up. It was a mule, a bedroom slipper, that is, with a pink pompon on its toe. It was his wife's.

"Cluck," said a hen. "The cluck," echoed the others. Under their cynical eyes he turned the thing over and over in his hands, while a primeval, a jungle, shudder, beginning where his tail would have been rooted had he had a tail, crawled up his back. He put the slipper in his pocket. He turned out the light.

A few minutes later Bentley at the bottom of the dark main stair was saying very quietly as he peered upward: "Was that you, sir?"

"Yes, Bentley."

"You seemed to be in great 'aste. Is heverything hall right, sir?"

"Yes, yes, everything is all right," said his master, telling about as thorough a lie as could have been returned to the old fellow's honest question.

Mrs Wooly was not in their bed. He went through the door into her apartment, and she was not there. He could not tell whether his supernatural apprehensions were thereby increased or decreased. Which was worse, her presence or her absence? He decided to sleep again across the hall on the couch in the games room and went in there at once. He would lock his door. He would have some peace, he would. The rings and the bars he had installed for his wife's exercise gleamed their newness in the middle air of the big room. They made him think of how she had received that thoughtful gift. She had stared at first at his innocence and then laughed at his stupidity. He thought of her hanging like a bat.

There were no blankets in there. Mr Wooly went back

to his room to get some. He noticed at once that the door
to the bathroom was half open. The bathroom light was
on. He started toward the door and stopped. Jennifer
was in there, bent over the tub. She was wearing shorts
and a white cardigan sweater, open. Her hair was wild.
As he glimpsed her intent profile he saw how gaunt it

was; her hands were busy with the Cochin China rooster.
One held it on its back, throat extended; the other poised
one of his safety-razor blades. Her eyes looked upward
with the expression of one waiting, listening.

Downstairs the standing clock began softly to bong
midnight. Jennifer sliced the rooster's throat expertly,
with a tight-lipped smile, and the blood pumped out,
splashed her hands, her clothing. She was clumsily filling

a cup with blood. Now she dropped the rooster. She was talking to herself in a language he had never heard. Quickly unwrapping small packets of tissue paper which she brought from her sweater pocket, she added their contents to the cup of blood. With a toothbrush handle she stirred it all, and her voice continued saying strange words over and over.

A faint blue smoke rose now from the cup. She smiled. He heard her pleased exclamation, "Aha." She rinsed the toothbrush handle under the hot-water tap, shook it a little, replaced it, turning toward the mirror to do so, and thus her wild conspiratorial eye met the eye of her outraged husband. For a moment she looked at him through the mirror, then she spoke: "You ought to be ashamed, a man of your age—peeking!"

Without another word, as with modest dignity, she closed the door in his face—turned its lock.

At once and very quietly he ran down the stair and across into the library. That fraudulent, hypocritical reprimand had proved the last straw.

Above the great library fireplace there was, among other curious and antique weapons, a short-handled battle-ax. A few moments later Bentley, the cook, the maids, were awakened by the thunderous noise of the attack. Mr Wooly was chopping at the bathroom door, panting, sweating, doing his best against a barrier that was all heavy oak, so hard it turned the edge of the ax at once.

The servants gazed in from the hall.

When Mr Wooly paused for breath Bentley spoke in a quavering voice:

"If you wish to go to the bathroom," he said, "why not go across the hall?"

"My wife is in here," Mr Wooly explained.

"Oh."

"Don't say 'Oh' like that. She refuses to come out!"

"Perhaps she is not—ah—ready to come out."

"Ready or not!" yelled Mr Wooly, raising the ax again and bringing it crashing down. "She is an evil thing," Mr Wooly was heard to gasp. "A draggletailed harpy, a trull, a conspirator against the public and the natural order. Out with her!"

They thought he was mad. They ran away from there, and Bentley told Swanson. Swanson got his shotgun, came up by himself, the red setter sniffing, trembling, behind him. The bedroom door was closed now. He knocked. Mr Wooly in an exhausted voice called, "Who is it?" When he was told he ordered his chauffeur to go to hell, and at once.

Downstairs, after long consultation, it was decided that a policy of watchful waiting was best for the time being, a decision made easier by the unanimous sentiment that the new Mrs Wooly deserved a good swipe over the head with an ax more than anybody else in this world.

But in the morning there was Mrs Wooly and there was Mr Wooly, each at the proper end of the long table, having their breakfast, or pretending to have it, as natural as you please, though a bit silently. It was certainly not the place of anybody belowstairs to complain or to criticize the bedroom games of Master and Mistress.

Everything went on as usual.

Nobody but Mr Wooly knew that, having finally

chopped through the bathroom door, he had found a quite empty bathroom. He had looked in the blood-speckled tub, in the washbasin, the medicine chests, the linen closet, he even raised the lid of the —— but who wouldn't have? She wasn't there. Ah, but the window was open.

We return to the Wooly breakfast.

Mrs Wooly finished hers. She went over to invade the slight privacy Mr Wooly had managed behind his New York *Times;* she kissed him on the forehead, her lips dry and hot like two cinders, and she said softly: "You're such a darling! So passionate. So impulsive. . . ."

He did not answer this. He looked at the watch on his wrist. He said in a perfect impersonation of T. Wallace Wooly that if he did not start now he would be late at his office, and he went out and went away in his car.

"Swanson," he said, "do you speak Egyptian?"

"Eyiptian? No, I speak Swedish."

"That won't do. How about Arabic?"

"Swedish is very fine language," Swanson said. "We have many fine writers in Sweden."

"Confound them all," said Mr Wooly irritably. "Drive me around to the chief's office."

"What chief, sir?"

"The chief of the Navahos, of course."

Swanson turned to look. "Of police?" he asked.

Mr Wooly did not answer. If the world were going to turn on him—this was how he now looked at it—then he would turn on it. Swanson damn well knew he meant the chief of police. . . .

CHAPTER IX

Mr Wooly Takes the Defensive

THE NAME of Warburton's chief of police was George Williams. He was a tall, thin man, gray all over—suit, hair, eyes. He had little of the cop about him. His predecessor had had a bit too much. Williams' manner derived from his previous profession—that of teaching history in a well-known, rather fashionable boys' school. He was the sort of chief of police a town like Warburton occasionally hires after a spasm of reform, the reform in this case coming shortly after repeal, when suburbia with the clear and mistrustful eye of that physical and mental state known as hang-over found it no longer possible to ignore the fact that it was being largely governed by a gang whose interests too often ran counter to the interests of Warburton's own big shots. Our Mr Wooly, as a matter of fact, had played a prominent and oratorical part in the "cleanup." He felt confident when he told the young policeman in the outer office that he wanted to see Chief Williams he would see him. In this expectation he was not disappointed.

"Hello, George."

"Good morning, Mr Wooly. Here, sit down, sit down. Well, I am very pleased to see you here in my office. What do you think of it? Like the maps? I like maps. Once it was etchings, you know, dry points of Chartres Cathedral or the New York sky line. They gave just that extra, cultural tone to an executive's office; now maps are generally preferred. Art seems suspect, uncertain. But maps in chaotic times supply dignity, precision. One feels safer with a map, enemy of chaos. We crave the aloof and objective note. Ha, ha. Well, here I am at once giving you a lecture. And, oh yes, I have meant for a week now to call on you to extend my congratulations."

Mr Wooly, the chief had noticed, did not seem to be listening. "Congratulations?" Mr Wooly said, wonderingly.

"On your marriage. Very romantic of you, and heroic —I mean the rescue, of course. Not getting married. Ha, ha. Lovely woman, if I may say so, Mr Wooly."

"You may say so," moodily, "but *I* wouldn't. She isn't, you know. Far from it. Unlovely. Unnatural. That's the better word, I think. An unnatural creature, George."

George Williams was too astonished to speak. He gazed in his grave and genteel way upon Mr Wooly, whom he had long considered a great bore, a conceited little ass and now a proven, moralizing fraud. He had smiled with other worldly men in the Marlborough, his favorite bar, at how that providential fire had exposed to all who had sense enough to interpret events the real manner of life of the virtuous Wooly—miserly, to boot, keeping his mistress in a place like the Monroe Hotel, rich as he was! But facing him, the chief paid Mr Wooly the respect Mr Wooly was always paid and which he always accepted as sincere.

"Are there laws covering acts against nature?" Mr Wooly's manner was very grave.

"Yes indeed, exhibitionism, sadism, cannibalism, incest . . ."

"No, no." Mr Wooly impatiently shook his head. "Pooh," he said. "Pooh. They are trifling transgressions, natural as spring flowers by comparison."

Good God, what had the little man or his new wife been caught doing?

"By comparison with what?" asked the chief.

"Are there no laws against crimes that subvert the natural law?" asked Mr Wooly.

"Ah," exclaimed the scholarly chief, twining long fingers together, "the natural law! You don't mean black magic, for instance? Witchcraft?"

"But of course I do."

"Hex, not sex," the chief summed it up, "as it were."

"As it is."

"Indeed, there are laws!" Williams was happy to be on such familiar ground. "I've gone well into such history, as a matter of fact. Warburton has some special laws of its own, and still on its books. Warburton never went to the extremes Salem and other New England towns did, of course, during the witch terror of the seventeenth century; still we ducked a few, hanged one and stoned another ten miles along the old pike before she croaked."

"And a good thing too," bugled Mr Wooly in his best community voice. "A straightforward, American way of dealing with the pest! Chief Williams, I've come to you to swear out a warrant."

"For the arrest of whom?"

"A witch."

"Which witch?" the chief asked him gravely.

"What do you mean witch-witch? Look here, George, I'm in earnest."

"I see that you are, Mr Wooly. That is what concerns me. I, too, am in earnest, and I ask you, which witch? The name, if you please. I can't go arresting nameless, unlocated persons."

"My wife, of course," said Mr Wooly.

The chief thought it over. He was puzzled. He was about convinced that the civic leader before him had gone right off his apple. To the chief, Mr Wooly looked like a man doing a mental St Vitus's dance very close to the edge. Like a man who had been spurring a nightmare, with protracted and, no doubt, well-deserved whips and jingles. He decided to go along with him, however, providing what he could by way of soothing balm for the balmy.

"Is she a practicing witch?" he asked Mr Wooly.

"On the contrary, an expert."

"You don't understand me. I mean, does she make money at it?"

"She made me," Mr Wooly said simply.

Chief Williams sighed and gazed down along his scholarly nose at his scholarly hands. "Let me ask another question. Has she used the mails?"

"The males? That, I think, is none of your business."

"Oh, come, please be frank."

"I have reason to believe I was not her first."

"To defraud, I mean," the chief added, a slight flush coming into his lean cheeks and a faint stir of hysteria into his viscera.

"Why else would she be after us?"

"Wait a moment," groaned the chief. "I beg you wait a moment. This can be all straightened out. I am trying to discover if your wife has used the post office of the United States."

"What other would she use? There isn't any other I know of. Not in this country."

"Please! Has she ever offered for a price to teach witchcraft or to accomplish certain things, the paralyzing of a mother-in-law's jaws, for example, or the seduction of some young motion-picture beauty by a lonely elevator boy with a bad case of acne? Does she tell fortunes for a price, sell love philters, contract to get needy scoundrels personal audiences with the Black One himself?"

"Not that I know of," Mr Wooly said.

"Why then do you think your wife is of the evil sorority? That's my question. Explain your evidence."

"Very well," said Mr Wooly. He began to pace the floor, hands clasped behind him. "And may I ask that you do not interrupt, do not bring in extraneous and evidently quite fictitious persons, such as that elevator boy with the bad case of acne? That can only confuse the matter. I am surprised that you, the chief of police of Warburton, should indulge in sheer fancy during a serious conference on recent crime in our community. Now then . . ."

Mr Wooly described in detail the fire at the Hotel Monroe and everything that followed, concluding with the horrid scene in the bath.

Chief Williams, as he had been requested, listened throughout in respectful silence. At last Mr Wooly began to relate the events of the night previous, to describe in detail and rather well (the chief thought) his moment of blinding comprehension of his wife's true nature.

"I am not a professor of history," Mr Wooly explained to the ex-professor of history, "nor am I *any kind* of professor." He contrived to say the word in such a way as subtlely to imply that he would rather be found dead in the nameless muck of Canarsie Creek than be a professor. "I am only a businessman, a practical, humdrum businessman, servant of the people of our community. That is all I am. I do not have second sight or a poet's inspiration," he went on, piling up his humilities like wreaths of golden laurel leaves, one upon another. He began to glow under this pleasant self-castigation. "However, I am not completely illiterate. No, I can, after all, sign my name and do simple ciphers! I am respected, envied, in this community and far beyond its confines. I accept social and political burdens. The people are grateful. But busy as I have always been, the books in the world are not closed to me, not all. I am a religious man. I have read somewhat in ecclesiastical history. I mean to say that to me the ways of witches are not wholly unknown, though I had never seen one before. But when I saw my wife engaged in that vile midnight spell, I knew at once she was a witch, a creature of evil power. That is all. You will now direct me in whatever I must do to swear out a warrant for her arrest. . . ."

Chief George Williams had raised one elegant foot upon his desk. He carefully placed the tips of his fingers together, slightly, delicately, tested the palps against each other. He puckered his lips in a silent whistle. As he did so he raised his grave, genteel eyes so that the whites showed clear underneath the pupils which were leveled directly into the focus of Mr Wooly's. Thus carefully adjusted, Chief Williams slowly shook his head.

"The Hotel Monroe burns down," he said softly. "But *she* is not burned. Very well. She falls into a tree, is unhurt." He went on listing all the strange actions. Her

"bewitching" of Betty Jackson's pretty fingers so that all her typewriting thereafter went backward, the burning of Betty's cottage, the climbing of walls, the doing in of the thoroughbred Cochin China.

"There is no law against climbing a trumpet vine," said Chief Williams reasonably, "not if the vine grows on your own house." And with similarly cool reasoning he disposed of all other charges. There was no proof she had set those fires, no proof whatever; as for Betty's failure as a secretary, "Ts, ts, ts, ts," said George Williams. "A jury would be all on the side of the wife in such a matter. They'd say if she's no good as a secretary what do you hire her for? What *is* she good at?"

Mr Wooly was not to be put off.

"But, George, this hideous midnight business with the rooster . . . There's a ceremony everybody has heard of. *There we have her!*"

George looked wholly unconvinced. He tapped his finger tips softly together. "I remember," he said, "an insomniac colleague of mine. Lectured on existential philosophy, you know, the one that holds that our nearest, most intimate experience is ontological—that our own existence is at once proof of our existence and also a clear, though wordless, earnest of the meaning of meaning. . . ."

"Yes, yes," Mr Wooly said. "Go on, go on."

"Well, this chap lived next door to a woman who had New Hampshire Reds. Fine birds, a bit bigger than the Rhode Island Reds. Every early morning just before dawn, which was when this chap had been asleep for a half-hour or so after tossing and squirming all the early hours away, this woman's New Hampshire Red cock would let go with his conceited yell for the sun to come up. One night my colleague went down and wrang, or wrung, its neck for it. He was apprehended, tried by jury."

"I hope this is pertinent," grumbled Mr Wooly.

"It is, I assure you. Well, this colleague of mine made his own defense. He declared the rooster had no sense of time, anyway, that for all his practice at it he would always miss the sunrise by from half to a whole hour. He said his crowing, therefore, had no social utility. It was, he claimed, pure self-indulgence and, worse than that, a disturbance of the peace under the meaning of the law, a kind of chronic misdemeanor. In conclusion he declared in so many words that he was glad he had silenced the pest. What happened?"

"Great Scott!" exclaimed Mr Wooly. "Don't you know?"

"Of course I know. He was cheered. He was acquitted."

Mr Wooly, seated in a wooden armchair, wore a congested, brooding look upon his face. He closed his big eyes.

"Why, don't you see?" went on the chief in his quiet, reasonable voice, "people are likely to say, 'Well, maybe she was hungry. Nothing in the icebox, so she went out to the hen house. Maybe she felt empty, had a midnight craving. Who doesn't?' "

"Craving for what?" Mr Wooly impatiently exclaimed. "For my prize Cochin China cock?"

"It's conceivable," said the chief.

"And the icebox is always filled, anyway. What nonsense," Mr Wooly shouted.

"I'm not opposing you," the chief said. "I am merely pointing out the possible legal aspects. . . ."

"She wasn't in the kitchen, remember; she was in the bathroom."

"You are inclined to split hairs," the chief told him.

"Chickens!" said Mr Wooly, running off the trolley again. "Nobody was talking about hares or rabbits or kangaroos or duck-billed platypuses."

Chief Williams smiled in a friendly way. "Busses," he said.

"Busses? Where? How did busses get into this, George? Don't you think you're inclined to get excited and incoherent? I don't remember any mention of rabbits or busses or anything of that nature."

"I meant to say duck-billed platybusses. You mentioned them first, I believe. Just threw them in to make your point."

"Did I make it?" asked Mr Wooly.

"You crapped," Williams said with that roguish smile ex-professors use; but seeing how his joke effected Mr Wooly—the little man's face had turned quite purple—he hastened to explain: "That's a dice joke," he said.

"Didn't sound nice to me," said Mr Wooly, who figured the chief must have a cold.

"And suppose, God forbid," the chief hypothecated, "suppose she testified that a little hot rooster's blood was exceedingly beneficial to the complexion when carefully applied just before retiring? Wouldn't that sound reasonable? Wouldn't that convince any married man—or any woman, for that matter? Worse of all, she might thereby start a vogue."

There was a considerable silence, broken at last by Mr Wooly. "Your answer, I take it, is no. You refuse me that protection any and every citizen is entitled to?"

"You must see that I have no alternative. You might go to the district attorney if I have failed to convince you. My advice is that you keep a close watch upon your wife, being always ready to pounce upon any real evidence."

A very discouraged Mr Wooly rose to his feet, started slowly for the door. It was a low moment in his life, perhaps the lowest. As his hand descended upon the knob Chief Williams, coming along to bow him out, had an idea: "There are tests, of course," he said. Mr Wooly turned with a last hope bringing a dim light to his shadowed, quenched face, that large-eyed, usually Napoleonic visage, now so troubled.

"Tests? What sort of tests?"

"You immerse them in boiling water. If she doesn't scream she is, of course, an unnatural creature, plain as day."

"She'd scream," Mr Wooly said.

"But the screaming might only prove how cunningly she played her role of injured innocence and thus would also serve as proof that she was a witch. Of course if she cooked . . ."

"Oh, now you're getting far off," sighed Mr Wooly. "She wouldn't even think of it. She hasn't put her nose in the kitchen since we were married. . . ."

"I mean if her flesh cooked in the boiling water. You say she walked through flames, was clothed in them and was in no part of her singed, scalded or the slightest degree broiled. Well, I'm saying if under this test she cooked that would prove she wasn't a witch. Of course the disadvantage here is that she'd be cooked."

"That's no disadvantage," Mr Wooly interrupted. "She'd be *cooked!*" But he shook his head, and the light faded from his eyes. "Before you cook your wife you have to catch her," he pointed out. "That would be more difficult than you think."

"Well," said Chief Williams, "in all the other tests, the one with needles, the water test, in all of them you'd have to catch her first."

"Thank you," Mr Wooly said listlessly.

"Don't mention it."

"I won't."

"Let me know developments, will you?"

"If there are any," Mr Wooly said with pessimism. His car and Swanson received him, smoothed him away through the neat thoroughfares of Warburton to the offices of T. Wallace Wooly, Inc., and there Mr Wooly went through the motions of being the big executive. Late in the afternoon he told Betty Jackson over the phone that he would be busy this evening, for it was the evening for him to address the Men's Bible Class. She was disappointed but did not complain. "You're my darling," she said. A darling herself, if there ever was one.

Mr Wooly, as it has been delicately hinted in these pages, had been a fathead of the first water, though it wasn't water he had on his brain but self-satisfaction. Nevertheless, it was no reflection upon the First Episcopal Church of Warburton that therein Mr Wooly felt at home. No, that church was not exclusively a home for fatheads. It was home to all sorts of people, including fatheads, which is something else. It was smallish, of an English Gothic style, built of old brick and cut stone. Its dusky interior was shot through with the jeweled rays from a small rose window. Day still lingered in the streets as Mr Wooly entered the church after a quick solitary supper at the Downtown Club (some macaroni and cheese, a salad built upon a foundation of a pineapple slice and a raspberry jello in a very pretty formation for dessert). The cool evening that already inhabited the interior of the church was a surprise—a pleasant one. A few candles burned upon the altar. There was no one else there. Mr Wooly sat down to rest.

Religion with Mr Wooly was indistinguishable from certain other feelings, such as the gratification enjoyed from applause for one of his long speeches about thrift or civic betterment, also the feeling associated with the moment a new and important client took his fountain pen to sign on the dotted line; above all, with the sensation of elegant boredom he associated with memories of the first Mrs Wooly.

He had made many a speech to businessmen and to youth organizations about down-to-earth religion. It is to be feared that he had been only too successful in getting it there.

Now as calm and comfort lightly wafted around him from candle and rose window the cool silence, he thought, "How homelike," and then was fearful of heavenly displeasure at this simple, relaxed comfort being enjoyed in His church.

Mr Wooly decided to say the Lord's Prayer, quickly, as people of another superstition touch wood or say pins and needles. But he could not remember the Lord's Prayer. What was the matter with him? He tried. Nope! While his tired mind went in search of the dispersed words his ear heard the gathering of young men in the room adjacent—the Bible Study Class.

This would never do. He went in there and took his place at the head of a long table whereat already were

seated fourteen or fifteen Warburtonians—most of them
in their thirties, a half dozen of whom worked for Mr
Wooly and who counted these evenings as necessary evils,
like overtime of some sort, the rest bank clerks, managers
of chain stores, and so forth. They greeted Mr Wooly
with a special kind of respect, this being a church affair,
their smiles of a different sort of hyprocisy than the
smiles they used in their various jobs. Boredom hovered,
an invisible and choking cloud. There was no reality here,
as usual, but now as Mr Wooly began to talk muscles
tensed against yawns relaxed; eyes glazed with unchurchly
reverie brightened and searched Mr Wooly's. He was talking about evil spirits and devils and hell-fire, piling one
biblical quotation upon another to support his thesis that
these were not figures of speech or yet something that
merely *had* been true. . . .

He brought these horrors up to date, sent malevolent
little fiends tracking Warburton's bland streets on their
infernal embassies. He cracked open the smooth security
of Warburton's suburban daze, its "modernity."

Eternal perils flowed in.

Fears inherited from ancient days stirred within the
deeps of the dull young men, and in sublime paradox their
world brightened in beauty, for there can be no argument
about the efficacy of the light of hell. Its glint and reflection is revealing. It enhances. Without it how would virtue be visible?

In the midst of this, just as Mr Wooly had the Gadarene
swine tossing themselves into the drink, his voice ceased.
He struck his forehead with his left palm; he said, "The
Lord's Prayer—of course, of course!" answering a thought

that had burst upward like a Veery light in his brain, and he said, "Gentlemen, I am sorry. I cannot continue. I have . . ." He floundered for an excuse, could think of none but: "a headache, a terrible headache!" He looked at one of them. "Thomas, will you carry on?" And then he made an exit that resembled headlong flight. But it was, instead, the first stage of all-out attack.

The Lord's Prayer. He would use that! And to hell, so to speak, with the police!

CHAPTER X

They Let Anybody Live in Miami

JENNIFER WOOLY knew she had gone too far.

She had been careless. She wanted to stay right where she was, so she decided to reform—temporarily—and thus win back the blind adoration of that fathead, her husband.

While Mr Wooly had spent the day interviewing police chiefs and history and God, Mrs Wooly had spent the day having a permanent, a facial, vigorous massages, had consulted with milliners, modistes, furriers; she had bought eight pairs of shoes, and so on. She had even listened to a program of chamber music at the Civic Center. She felt almost exactly like a wife, and so when at about nine-thirty o'clock in the evening she heard the wheels of Mr Wooly's taxi on the gravel before the front door she skipped into the library—his favorite room downstairs—and propped herself on the sage-green brocade of the couch, a book of Longfellow's poems open in her hand. She was a picture. She waited, full of confidence, and when she heard Mr Wooly asking Bentley where Mrs Wooly was she smiled a little to herself. He was seeking her. He needed her.

He came in to her at once, a short, taut man in a dark double-breasted suit, brown hair neat, big brown eyes rather wild. He went at once to the same token-hung fireplace wall from which he had taken the battle-ax just last night, but this time he took down (she did not know this until he turned and faced her) a long Mexican cattle whip made from a bull's pizzle, well tanned, of course and unrecognizable as such, with a plaited thong. Having it firmly in his grasp, he swiftly turned upon his wife and, before she could do more than sit up on the couch, thrust a small leather-bound prayer book into her hands. Then he snapped his horrid weapon and said in a loud, strong voice:

"It is open at the Lord's Prayer; read it, my beauty; read it or I shall flog you into shreds!"

There, indeed, was a picture for you! The beautifully gowned, slant-eyed little wife, the husband doubling his stature by this towering rage, the Bible open in her nerveless, unwilling grasp, the Bible—in his righteous hand the black leather whip, curling and swishing. He raised it as she let the silence lengthen, and it sang a terrible, shrill song above the clear green velvet of her gown.

"Read it!" he cried, prompting her with: "Our Father Who art in heaven . . ."

She was pale now; she was terrified. But at sight of her terror Mr Wooly only cried out the louder: "Read it!"

"Heaven in art Who Father our," she said. With that he stepped back two steps, his arms wide, like a ringmaster in some circus, a trainer of wild animals (and was he not?), and he said: "Warlock! Witch! Gray old woman of evil! I have found you out. Continue: Hallowed be Thy name . . ."

"Name Thy be hallowed," she quavered for, being a

witch, she could only say it backward, the way of the
Black Mass.

When she had said it through she fell back exhausted,
utterly helpless before him.

He dropped his whip and pulled up a chair.

"How about Miami?" he said, thus beginning what was
certainly the most difficult selling talk he had ever attempted. "They let anybody live in Miami," he said. "You
must understand that you must leave here at once and
never return. How about Hollywood? You would like
Hollywood," he said. "You belong in Hollywood. Or
Chicago? But no—first Reno—it is a very attractive
town, they tell me, fraught with evil, and there you could

obtain your divorce." And he went on, bringing a greater degree of coherence to his argument as he proceeded, outlining the advantages of this place and that—the advantages, that is, considered from the infernal angle rather than that of civic betterment, clean politics and thrift.

She heard him through. She gazed at him.

She saw that he was adamant. "O.K.," she said. "You win—so far." She was pondering how to get good and even with him. "You are such a self-righteous little ass," she said. "You think you have lived, that you have learned. You haven't learned anything. I realize, little Sahib of Suburbia, that I was overly careless, that now you know at last who I am, and why I married such a small, porcine, self-important windbag as you, Mr Wooly. As a springboard, as something to walk upon, you were not impossible, but as anything else . . . I'll be glad to be rid of you." She slid off the couch and herself took the center-of-the-rug position, began to pace, but with a far more graceful, more feline movement than his. "I'll take the nine forty-five. Oh, I'll leave you!" she shouted. (Her voice carried clear out to the kitchen steps where Mr Connolly loitered. He had heard many wives. He shook his big head and said to Hortense, the maid: "There they go, at it again!") "But before I leave," Mrs Wooly shouted, "I'll damn well put my mark on you, Mr Wooly!" She grinned like the fiend she was at thought of a horrible revenge: *"I'll curse you with ears!"*

Mr Wooly involuntarily felt of his ears, which were of medium size, expecting to find they had sprouted. They hadn't, not palpably, at least.

When he looked up his wife was gone. She had run upstairs. Not many minutes later, while Mr Wooly still lingered, stunned, yet in the face of new fears clinging to a sense of triumph, she ran downstairs again in a neat dark-toned tweed *tailleur* and a mink coat. Swanson, already summoned by the upstairs telephone, was waiting out front. Thus Mrs Wooly departed. Watching from the library window, her husband again felt thoughtfully of his ears.

Bentley came in. He put the Mexican cattle whip back on its brackets.

"Stop talking to yourself," Mr Wooly said.

"I beg your pardon, sir. I did not know I was talking to myself."

"Certainly you were," Mr Wooly snapped. "Muttering away like an old woman! There you start again. Stop it, I say!"

Bentley, who hadn't said or muttered a word, withdrew, trembling in every limb. He was indignant and a little frightened.

CHAPTER XI

Cross Marks the Spot

AFTER PACING the library for a time Mr Wooly went upstairs. He felt as restless up there, prescribed some exercise for himself. He jumped a foot when the phone rang in the games room. He was at the moment rowing the rowing machine, hoping thus to weary himself so as to be able to sleep. The receiver was within reach. He picked it up, speaking into it as he drifted, so to speak. The voice at the other end was Swanson's, and its tone was not joyful or triumphant.

"It's about Mrs Wooly," he began.

"Yes?"

"She's gone, sir."

"I knew that, Swanson. Did she catch the nine forty-five?"

"She yumped out."

"Of the train?"

"How could she? We missed it."

"Where is she?"

"I don't know. All I know is that when I yumped out at the station and opened the door for Mrs Wooly she wasn't there. Nothing was there. It was yust empty."

Mr Wooly felt a wave of discouragement, a sort of backwash, just as he had supposed he was safely on the strand. Swanson was waiting.

"Mrs Wooly," said Mr Wooly, "is a very active woman, Swanson. She had simply stepped out of the opposite door as you got down. Don't worry. I'm sure she made the nine forty-five."

"No, by gumps, she didn't. I walked all over the nine forty-five. Shall I notify the police?"

"Good gracious, no."

But as he hung up, Mr Wooly wondered why he had said no to such a sensible suggestion. . . .

He tried to sleep.

Something was looking at him! He got up, went across to their bedroom, and something was looking at him there too. But what? He turned round time and again, first slowly, then quickly, to catch whatever it was in the act. He realized what was looking at him. Windows! That was all. Windows! His own windows. Each one stared; each one asked the same question: "Will it be through me, across this sill, *she* slithers while you lie helpless in your bed?"

Mr Wooly rang for Bentley, and together they checked over every window lock on three floors. They buttoned up the house tighter than a fortyish man in the dinner jacket he hasn't worn for eight months. And all through this defensive operation Bentley kept talking to himself in a low, blurred voice. . . .

"Stop it, Bentley!" said Mr Wooly.

"Stop what?"

"That infernal muttering to yourself. What's the matter with you?"

" 'E's gone potty at last," muttered Bentley, "and no wonder, after all he stood from the bohemian sort of wench he married!"

Mr Wooly couldn't believe his ears. He stared at his butler.

"I am not muttering," muttered Bentley. " 'E's 'earing things!" And then in a slightly clearer tone: "I'm sorry, sir, I was hunconscious of any muttering, as you call hit!"

At once the blurred murmur began again. "I'm over-wrought," Mr Wooly told himself, which was certainly true. He had so many other things to think of, to listen for, that he gave up trying to catch Bentley in the act of this outrageous new habit, finally wished him a curt good night. Bentley was getting old; that was it. Even Bentleys get old, thought Mr Wooly.

Nothing much more happened that night except fire. As Mr Wooly later dimly remembered, he had climbed out of his bed, wherein he'd found no sleep, slipped on his Jaeger's camel's-hair robe, his red leather slippers, and gone quietly out of the darkened house to speak to Offi-cer Connolly, whose shadow was going back and forth before the main gates. Connolly saw him coming, paused. The night brooded; clouds covered the firmament. Con-nolly said, "Here he comes agin, barging out of his house in the middle of the night; now what the devil is the little man up to?"

Of course it was impossible that Officer Connolly could say anything of the sort. Why should he? Mr Wooly, coming along like a Trappist monk, poked a finger in one ear and then the other. A sort of buzzing in his head. That was it. That and his confounded imagination work-ing overtime. But why should he imagine "little"? He was no giant, Mr Wooly, but surely the effect he gave was of height, was it not?

He wished Officer Connolly a good evening. He told him if this night, too, he thought he saw something crawling up the wall of the house or moving about on the roof, let him then draw his weapon and shoot, taking great care to shoot straight.

"Is he kidding me now; is it a trap?" asked the policeman.

"What's that?"

"I said maybe it was a moonbeam, or maybe it was all in me eye. And look at the little man's face now," went on Officer Connolly softly to himself. "By God, he looks scared to death or I don't know faces. If I had as much gold as he's got sunk I'd be nervous meself!"

"And maybe it was no moonbeam," Mr Wooly said, again pressing his ears. "Today I observed the vine broken in several places." That sounded fairly technical. But Connolly said: "It's a lie; I can see it as he tells me. I wonder why now!"

"How dare you say such a thing? You must be drunk, Connolly."

The policeman fell back a step. The light above the gates shone on his face. He looked utterly amazed and scared too. "I didn't open me head," he explained.

"Didn't you? Are you sure?"

"Of course I'm sure." And again the low murmur, "Why shouldn't I be sure? What's eating little Mr Big here?"

While he said that, or seemed to say that, Mr Wooly had been watching his mouth. It had remained closed. It wasn't likely Connolly had learned to talk out of his ears or his pores. Mr Wooly began to sweat. He didn't like hearing what wasn't. He didn't like it at all. "I'm sorry," he said. "I've something of an earache, I think, a buzzing. Very bothersome. Good night."

He started back for the house.

He hadn't reached the door when the fire siren in town let go with a wild whoop. Connolly called in a big voice: "Look at that now." Over the treetops in the west an infernal glow appeared and began to grow at once.

"There's a terrible fire!" Connolly shouted. "A beauty, Mr Wooly."

Fire, gasping and snarling with its utter greed, ate at the vitals of the little church; the jungle growth of its flames thrust out of one window, then another. The flames stood tall in the night, red-pronged, bright as molten brass, and they bowed to the east, with an infernal grace bowed, at the suggestion of a capricious wind, to the west, pointed again straight at God Almighty, roaring and spitting a brief but fearful defiance of order, of right.

Worshipful, in a great half circle the citizens stood, each face a mask of fascination and respect, shadowed, painted by the ruddy glow as for the theater. Just before them, in glinting black coats and hats, ran the firemen, chorus to this tragedy, dragging water-filled, brass-nozzled cobras, shouting. Among these, just such a rubber coat and hat upon him, was our Mr Wooly. Under his fireman's coat sagged the bottom of his camel's-hair robe, upon his feet his red bedroom slippers, for he had come here in a hurry after Policeman Connolly's shout. In hope of rescuing God knows what, a splinter of that rose window, perhaps, he wanted to walk straight into the fiery furnace by the front door which stood staring open, but others grasped him, shouted no, no, that there he would find only painful death. He pulled himself free and ran. It was the sight of his wife stopped him dead, rocked him back on his heels.

Now in front of this church, in its triangular front yard, stood two tulip trees of considerable age and unusual girth for this species. As it happened, only yesterday they had burst into their wonderful bloom, already wilting under the unnatural heat from the conflagration. Beside these tulip trees stood Mrs T. Wallace Wooly in her new mink coat. Her wicked slanted eyes were more Chinese tonight than ever, and her small red mouth was half open in a laugh of pure pleasure at sight of fire, which she loved, and now at sight of her husband, whom

she didn't. His plight changed the quality of her lecherous cachinnation; her eyebrows shot up, and her mouth
opened wider, showing her little teeth back to the middle
molars; she pointed a finger sharp as a thorn at her husband and sneeringly laughed. It was a dreadful sight. In
this moment Mr Wooly knew better than ever before
that he had married a creature of the darkest regions of
this universe, a woman of evil all compact. His skin
moved and contracted with revulsions at unbidden memories of his intimacies with her, with "it"—as if she had
indeed been a cat and yet had been to him what she had
been. . . . She stood in the great heat and the dreadful
glare, rejoicing in the death of the little church.

The crowd raised its voice.

The chief of Warburton's fire department came running to shout at the honorary chief of Warburton's fire
department that the roof was threatened. The rafters
had burned through on one side. Hardly had he reached
Mr Wooly, forcing him back and away a step or two, before the west wall did indeed begin to go. The roof slates
with a great clatter rained to the ground. The façade
itself wavered and with it the small stone cross up there.

"Look out," cried a voice. The red brick, the cut stone,
came apart, fell in a heap. The stone cross left its peak,
curved wide in the air, turning over slowly twice and
made first contact with the small head of Mrs T. Wallace
Wooly, second contact with the trampled lawn beside
the tulip trees.

Mrs Wooly, with no outcry, had fallen to her knees in
a more prayerful attitude than any she had ever assumed
before. Her lifeblood poured into the fur of her coat and

even upon the ground. As she died she fell sideways and lay, knees a little bent.

Firemen stooped over her. "She is dead," said one.

"Thank God," said her husband.

"But she is dead," said the chief.

"I know it," Mr Wooly replied. "I know it because the buzzing in my ears has ceased. She put it there. It's been driving me crazy. When she died it went with her. It must have."

They gazed at the man, shaking their heads. What a dreadful shock to him, they thought.

Later, having led him back to his car, Mr Wooly was assured by the chief that he, the chief, would see to everything, would inform Sanford Digges, the mortician, would see that the body of Mrs Wooly be brought out to the Wooly residence.

"Not that," whispered Mr Wooly, immediately distraught. "Have her taken to the funeral parlor. I don't want her home."

"Very well," agreed the chief but plainly he did not like that. Nor did he like what he heard as Mr Wooly's car moved away. It was the sound of Mr Wooly whistling. "Whistling," he told his wife later, "as cheerful as you please. It was a scandal."

"The poor man," said the chief's wife, "he was hysterical from grief!"

CHAPTER XII

The Happy Mortician Is Shocked

SANFORD DIGGES was essentially a cheerful and merry soul. After all, for him death was good news. When he said good morning to Schultz, the plumber whose shop adjoined the funeral parlors, Digges always thought about Schultz's inevitable funeral. He would make a better-looking corpse than a live plumber, Digges thought, and he'd need an oversize casket. Boy, he'd pay for that! Digges even played with the idea of forgetting and going back for all sorts of tools during the course of Mr Schultz's funeral—a puncture and no spare for the hearse, for instance, no ropes to lower down, for another, and so on—delay after delay, all at so much an hour, after the manner in which Schultz had installed the bathrooms in the Digges residence. Digges had a clear and calculating eye. When he walked along Brick Street he'd measure his fellow citizens with his eye, and at the same time he would be smoothing out their faces, so ill adapted for the most part for the vicissitudes of this life, with injections of embalming fluid and warm paraffin, improving pallid cheeks further with a delicate application of rosy paint and powder. The fact that the timorous and the evaders, those silly citizens who wanted to believe they'd live forever, met the measuring Digges eye with a certain modest reluctance did not detract from his simple pleasure.

In appearance Sanford Digges was no presidential candidate. Far from it. His face seemed made of tallow that had been fingered until it was gray; he had somber, opaque eyes and a long cold nose. No one felt his nose to test its temperature, but everybody knew at first glance that the Digges nose was a cold one. It looked cold, chilled to the cartilage. His thin lips never lost their downward curve. He had the face of a man who had cried himself to sleep every night since his birth, but his heart was light, his spirits as light as only the spirit of the man who has found his vocation and dearly loves it. He particularly enjoyed burying wives.

In the best manner of his profession he received Mr T. Wallace Wooly on the afternoon of the next day after the destruction of the church by a fire whose origin could only be guessed at—rats gnawing matches in the belfry, a short circuit of electric wires; such were the guesses.

"I will not burden you with an expression of my deep sympathy," Mr Digges told Mr Wooly in a grief-stricken voice. "I only wish to say that we shall miss her, all of us; she was a beautiful and a good woman. I know that you will bear your loss, Mr Wooly, with the fortitude that is so characteristic of your whole career; and, after all, you do have the comfort of our Christian faith; you know that she is in a better world."

"I hope not," said Mr Wooly.

Mr Digges decided that he had not heard aright. He went on with his lugubrious act: "Perhaps it will be too great a trial for you to discuss with me now certain . . . ah . . . necessary details. Perhaps you could delegate all that to someone near and dear to you or even leave it to me."

"What details?" asked Mr Wooly, who did seem singularly matter-of-fact and wholly untearful, Digges noticed.

"Ah, the dimensions, so to speak, the quality, the sort, the quality of, ah, her last resting place."

"You mean the box?"

"The casket," sighed Digges. "Or perhaps you had planned cremation. There are many who have preferred it."

"How do you know?"

"I mean the relatives, of course."

"No," Mr Wooly said. "She liked fire too well."

"But then, it seems to me, it would be ideal."

"Does it? But heaven knows what might result if you shoved that one into a good hot fire! No, thank you— we'll bury her in the wet, cold ground."

Mr Digges did something for the first time. He shuddered.

A mortician like Mr Digges, with a face of habitual grief, masking a merry, practical heart, can be upset only by one sort of client, the sort Mr Wooly was proving to be. Mr Digges was upset. He was at a loss for words. He decided to go straight to business and began to talk up a velvet-lined casket with solid silver handles that could be had for a mere $1875, a casket, Mr Wooly gathered, with all the comforts of home, which would, moreover, rest within a solid lead casket. Thus would she be guarded forever, or almost, from something Mr Digges called natural seepage. Even as he expounded the advantages of his most expensive number Mr Digges observed that the widower before him was not paying his whole attention. Mr Digges paused.

"Mr Digges," said Mr Wooly, "the problem before us is not what kind of a box, or casket, she is encased in before her burial; no, the problem is the location of her burial. For a certain reason I would like to bury Mrs Wooly's remains at a corner—that is, at the intersection of two streets—and I wish that you would make certain that a stake, say something two by two, of ash or oak, with a long point, the point, you understand, to be carefully and accurately but firmly driven through her heart."

Mr Digges held desperately to his usual expression of righteous but humble melancholy.

Mr Wooly gazed at him with rising distaste. Mr Wooly subtly had changed since first we saw him. It was not that as a businessman he had matured, but as a man. You cannot sleep with a warlock for weeks on end—or sideways, for that matter—and remain the same. It is simple as chemistry. Thus it was that now he watched Mr Digges instead of the case being that Mr Digges watched him.

"Well?" said Mr Wooly, rather aggressively.

"Under the macadam?" breathed Digges.

"They don't need to be paved. Of course they must be well traveled."

"There aren't any well-traveled but unpaved roads," Mr Digges stated, "not in this state."

"Not any at all?"

"None. Of course a man of your position and influence might have the pavement pulled up, the electric-light cables, the sewer, the water mains, all detoured to the side of some appropriate intersection for the burial of Mrs Wooly, but you will have to consult with the appropriate authorities. There's bat-eared Reilly, the street commissioner; you might go talk to him. You find him this time of day in the Marlborough Bar."

Mr Wooly's heart sank as he thought of the sardonic, practical Reilly. "Would I have to go to him?"

"Of course," said the mortician. "And the City Council, no doubt. Rather unusual, you know. If you ask me, I think they'd say no." He added after a moment, "At the least."

Two days later Mrs T. Wallace Wooly was buried formally, normally and unstaked, in the Wooly family plot in Cloudy Lawn Cemetery on the side of the smooth hill to the north of Warburton. She was buried, indeed, a few feet from the first Mrs T. Wallace Wooly. Two dozen limousines followed the hearse; there was a mountain of flowers. Dr Fergus Peyton, pastor of the destroyed church, had delivered a eulogy over the casket in the smaller auditorium of the Civic Center, where the ceremony was held. He said the prayer at the edge of Jennifer's grave. The grave was deep; the stone to be placed on top of it was large, weighed more than a ton, yet Mr Wooly did not feel easy about any of it. Having discovered the truth of the Black Mass and the Lord's Prayer in reverse, he was, of course, more than a little disposed to believe other details of the ancient lore, such as the detail concerning the best manner in which to bury a witch. Lay her among Christians, unstaked, and she would wander. That was the old wisdom. Mr Wooly was afraid that it was true.

After the ceremony he was exhausted. He had not eaten anything but a small bowl of corn flakes with sliced bananas since the day before yesterday! He went to his office and phoned Betty Jackson at her hotel. She wasn't in. As a matter of fact, she had gone all by herself to the cemetery to watch the sad pomp and circumstance from a respectful distance and, seeing the bowed figure she identified as Mr Wooly, tears of sympathy had coursed down her cheeks. He was disproportionately discouraged to hear she was out. Not knowing her only thought was for him, yet dreading scandal, she must avoid him, he felt alone and abandoned and did not know what to do.

His office manager, Simpson, a bald-headed man whose stomach swung close to his knees, came in with a folder under his arm.

"Chief?" he asked with unctuous humility. "A word?" He was told to come in.

"A dark day," Simpson said, "but a man of your stamina, chief!!" He sat down. Distinctly, but in a lower, somewhat muffled tone, Mr Wooly heard him say: "Boy, don't he look awful. Old bastard, running around like a young rooster. Too many women, old boy; that's what's taken it out of you, you stuffed double-breasted suit, you. Lookit how he sits there with a face all lengthened out by a fake grief, the hypocrite. As if I didn't know all about Betty! All I hope is he doesn't haul off and hand me one of those boring, highfalutin pep talks. However,

here goes, I'll have to ask him for the dope on this Creelman file."

Toward the end of this Mr Wooly slowly lifted his
head and gazed into the face of his office manager. He
noticed that while his ears received the low-toned, somewhat muffled words from Simpson, that worthy's lips
were quite closed. A dreadful suspicion took hold of Mr
Wooly. He said, keeping his large brown eyes on this
office manager's unattractive face: "Simpson, the Creelman file is your headache!"

Simpson turned green; his eyes pushed out and lay
upon their lower lids, an effect so trying that Mr Wooly
turned his face away.

"How did you know it was the Creelman file?" Simpson demanded to know in a strangled voice, and he added

in that other tone: "Christ, the sanctimonious old bastard's turned mind reader!"

"I am afraid I have," said Mr Wooly. "You may go,
Simpson. And if anybody asks for me tell them I have
gone home, that I am not well. You'll be telling the truth
for once," he added.

In the street a murmur as vast and as constant as the
sea flowed over him, filling his ears. It had come back—
that "buzzing in his ears"—but tenfold. The oceanic
sound rose and fell. It was like the murmur of an enormous multitude of folk all talking to themselves. The
trouble with it was the same as the trouble with the ocean,
with a running stream or waterfall—it really hadn't any
meaning but just itself; it ran on and on, and you felt
that it would run on and on; not weary in itself, yet it
seemed a weary thing because it could not stop. Appalled,
our Mr Wooly stood near the entrance of his offices, on
the shore, so to speak, of the traffic. He remembered his
wife's curse. But she was dead, and the curse had died
with her—the murmur and the mutter, the sharper,
nearer words, that had filled his ears had ceased with her
death. But now it had all returned, and more. Had she
returned?

Some stranger, a man of middle age and not of striking
appearance, approached, eyes front, step confident and,
as it were, honest; yet as he approached he seemed to be
making a speech, the words sounding louder and louder.
". . . and leave my house and never darken its door
again, *you self-indulgent, utterly selfish, virtuous old
double chin. So I'm your son-in-law, admitted, but I tell
you here and now* I'VE HAD ENOUGH, AND IF IT

MUST COME TO A CHOICE BETWEEN HAVING YOU MOOCHING ON ME or not having Matilda, my wife, then I say . . . you can get the hell out. . . . Ah, what's the use? I'll never, never . . ." The pitiful harangue died away as the man himself receded from the vicinity of Mr Wooly.

Mr Wooly sighed. He called a taxi, told the taxi to take him to the Warburton Hospital, settled back, hoping for surcease in motion, as how many other Americans before him!

The driver, a frog-eyed youth with slanting knife scar on his cheek, said, "Yes sir," passed a remark or two about the quality of the day and then, receiving no encouragement to conversation, settled back to drive his car. At once, as if from the back of his unattractive head, words came. A radio not rightly tuned in, slightly distorted, yet all of it understandable, worse luck. The youth's words were not quotable, having to do with a broad with whom he had spent the night. There were words, scraps of remembered conversation of an appalling sort, but long silences which, uneasily, Mr Wooly guessed were taken up more with remembered scenes than with words. . . . The coarse fellow was living that night over again. Being by himself in the task, he was unhampered by any pudeur, none whatsoever. Mr Wooly, before they reached the hospital drive, felt that he knew much too much about that broad and her reddish hair, her legs, her this, her that, the way she drank her gin and what she did *then!* He put his fingers in his ears and discovered that this made no difference whatsoever. Whether he would or not, it seemed, he must learn. The "sounds," indeed, seemed to come into his consciousness by a more direct route than all those passages and sounding drums in his ears. . . .

As he paid off his driver he avoided the fellow's eyes. He hoped he would never see him again. He went into the hospital and was told Dr Mannix would see him at once.

CHAPTER XIII

The Antidote

DR FRANK MANNIX, he of the blue jaw and the glasses like bottle bottoms, observed the approach of Mr Wooly, noting the dark circles under his eyes, and thought, "Kidney trouble." Further studying that face of tragedy, the high frown, he capped this. "Probably inflammation of the bladder," he said to himself. He was astonished to see Mr Wooly stop midway as if some invisible person had handed him one on the button.

"Doctor Mannix," said Mr Wooly, speaking carefully, avoiding the medico's little eyes, "I am in a bad way."

"Sit down, Mr Wooly," said Dr Mannix.

To Mr Wooly it seemed that the doctor, as everyone else, said things with his mouth and then went into an audible soliloquy without moving his lips. Mr Wooly did not want to hear this soliloquy. To drown it out he hummed. He began to sing, picking his song at random—anything, just so he could drown out that queer muttering sound. He sang a song that had been popular when he was about five years old. He had learned it from the morning-glory horn of his father's gramophone; it went like this:

> *"Baby dear, listen here,*
> *I'm afraid to go home in the dark,*
> *Every day the papers say*
> *Another robbery in the park. . . ."*

As he sang this he strove to make the doctor feel that everything was all right. He signaled the doctor, waggling the fingers of one hand at him, pointed at a chair and sat down.

"*I'm all alone in the Y.M.C.A.*
Singing just like a lark. . . ."

Dr Frank Mannix listened, watched. He was a tough old doctor. Being called "baby dear" didn't mean a thing but a symptom to him.

"Ha, ha," laughed Mr Wooly. It was the most unconvincing try at a laugh that Dr Mannix had ever heard.

"I sing so that I won't hear your thoughts, Doctor. Droll, what? Ha, ha, Doctor, I hear the thoughts of people around me. I can't help it. Everything people think I hear. It's awful. It is destroying me. The taxi driver slept with a broad last night. Now he's driving around deliberately thinking it over. There I was, practically in bed with both of them. Disgusting, no? You should hear the sound of the people thinking; it isn't an encouraging sound, Doctor; it goes on and on; it gives me a terrible feeling to know that all those minds go on working all the time. From birth to death, Doctor, they talk and they talk and they talk. What in the name of God is the sense of that, Doctor? It's like the wind in the forest; it's like listening to the awful sound the planets must make as they whirl senselessly through endless nothing. . . . Tell me, Doctor Mannix, you are a man of experience; what is a broad, anyway."

"A female," Dr Mannix said briefly.

"What kind of a female, a broad one?"

"Any kind, I think; any female, except only your nearest and dearest—your sister, your wife." Dr Mannix leaned forward. "When," he asked, "did this delusion seize upon you, Mr Wooly?"

"It's no delusion, Doctor."

The doctor smiled the infuriating smile of the expert who knows more about what one feels and thinks than one does oneself. "Isn't it?" he asked, his little split-pea eyes dancing behind those thick spectacles. "Isn't it? You are in a bad way if you really believe it, old chap." They looked at each other. Mr Wooly heard the doctor's thought: "Next thing, he'll be jumping out of windows, the horrid, complacent little moneygrubber. These businessmen with their nerves, their ulcers, their deliberate self-delusionments. I wish to God I didn't have to toady to the larcenous little insect."

All this Mr Wooly heard, but by now he was too tired, too woebegone, to be shocked by anything. He had learned so much so rapidly.

Aloud the doctor said, using, Mr Wooly observed, his mouth to speak the words, not this other system of personal broadcasting: "Mr Wooly, you are near to a nervous breakdown. You've been overworking and, in addition to that, your personal tragedy." His lips closed. The other tone said: "I wonder if it's financial. By Jesus, I'll wager he's overextended himself on the street and is ruined!"

Mr Wooly raised a weary head. "My affairs, by the way," he said in a subdued voice, "are in good shape, Doctor. I mention this in passing. Matter of fact, I'm financially in better condition than I have ever been."

He smiled a ghastly smile: "I mean to say I'll be able to pay your bill, you know."

Dr Mannix had the grace to look a bit embarrassed. "Oh, the thought never crossed my mind."

"Yes, it did," said Mr Wooly.

"Have you been drinking?" Dr Mannix asked. "I mean a good deal, slipping away to your closet or the bathroom or any safe corner and taking a shot? You'll have to stop that, you know. Solitary drinking is definitely dangerous. It is a form of suicide, Mr Wooly. The reason the solitary drinker drinks is a suppressed desire to escape this world, to die. And your type is often . . ."

"I don't drink," Mr Wooly said. The doctor's suspicion had profoundly shocked him. "I have never tasted alcohol in any form, not in my whole life."

Dr Mannix, still startled by Mr Wooly's "good guess" at reading his thought, anxious to maintain his doctor's pretense of omniscience, exclaimed: "Then for God's sake, try it! Take a little. Relax. Man, you are overwrought because you never relax. What you need more than anything in this world is a drink or two! No, no, don't shake your head. I know what I am talking about. You have a buzzing in your ears. You delude yourself into a belief that you are hearing the thoughts of others. Good God, man, do you think you are the first overwrought businessman to get such a notion into his so-called brain? I beg your pardon—brain. Certainly not! I have some excellent bourbon in the cupboard. You sit there a moment. I'll get a glass. I'll get two glasses." He jumped up and fairly ran across his office, returned to his desk and in a twinkling had poured out two measures of whisky, added to them the fizzing contents of a bottle of soda water, which he had also found in the cupboard. "There," he cried, "drink it down."

"No, thank you," Mr Wooly said.

"It is my prescription!" Dr Mannix told him sternly. Still Mr Wooly said no.

"But for my sake, try it." In the end the doctor won.

"In that case . . ." Hesitantly Mr Wooly raised the glass. "It is my first, you know," he said in a sad virgin's voice and he raised the glass; he drained it.

Mr Wooly's chronicler had seen this pleasant moment from afar. He has yearned toward it, feeling how all the appropriate words bloomed within him. Now observe Mr Wooly. His face contracts; his large brown eyes are tightly closed in spasmodic wrinkles. "Oh, gracious," he whispers as the strange flavor outrages his palate; and then the heat of it, striking out in all directions in little warming rivulets that seem to seek every corner of his corporeal envelope. No, the words, after all, fail.

Mr Wooly sat as if listening to what was going on within his own depths.

"And another?" said Dr Mannix, who was in a state himself.

Mr Wooly drank that one too. He squirmed and gasped and made a poisoned face. Then after a little he gazed into the doctor's expectant little eyes. He smiled, Mr Wooly did, for the first time in a long time. He smiled a smile that was more like the dawn of a beautiful day than anything else. Tears of pure joy glistened in his big brown eyes. "Doctor," he sighed, "it has stopped; that tidal, aerodynamic buzz and murmur and roar has died away; I am alone again inside myself. How about another?"

But Dr Mannix (who, after all, was a man of some conscience) shook his head. "You have had your prescription."

"But how blessedly quiet it is!" murmured Mr Wooly. "How lovely." And to himself he made a promise: "I'll go across the street—to the Marlborough." That is where he went as soon as he had left the doctor.

The Marlborough was a bar that Mr Wooly had done his best from time to time to close up. Today as he entered its warmly lighted, commodious interior he was very glad he had been unsuccessful. He smiled upon the bartender, a very clean individual. Mr Wooly noticed with approval his coat, his apron, of a snowy impeccability.

"How do you do?" said Mr Wooly with a courteous smile. "We have not met before, I think."

The bartender, a recent and unwilling exile from Manhattan, whose opinion of Warburton was nothing to write to the Chamber of Commerce about and who had never seen or even heard of Warburton's leading citizen, directed an unemotional blue eye upon Mr Wooly. The bartender did not speak; he merely gazed. His whole posture, the tilt of his red nose, the set of his jaw, asked a question, and the question was: "Who the hell *is* this pompous little swearword?"

Mr Wooly tried again: "I hope I'm not intruding?"

At last, and with great dignity, the bartender spoke: "Whatever it is, Jack, the answer is no."

"What?" asked the astonished Mr Wooly. Dimly he

realized that he had entered another world. This man, he
saw (our Mr Wooly, after all, though suffering from a
long course of miseducation, was essentially no fool; the
doors of his mind might stick, might creak, still they
could be opened), was no mere waiter, no lackey: he was
a personage, in a sense a priest busy at the altar of his
deity, the deity being, of course, that fat and disorderly
and irrepressible fellow, that ultimate rebel against routine and enduring responsibility, the laughing old slob,
Bacchus. He served, this bartender did, but you did not
whistle him to heel. He served, yet he whom he served, in
a certain sense, was less than the servant. "I beg your
pardon?" Mr Wooly said anxiously.

"Whatever you are selling is what I don't want any
of." The man barely opened his mouth to speak the
words, disturbing no other of his facial muscles at all.

"I am not selling anything," Mr Wooly said, feeling
wounded. "I came in here not to sell but to buy. If I
may, please."

"What?"

"An alcohol beverage."

"We don't sell jelly beans," the bartender said.

"I don't like jelly beans," Mr Wooly told him. "I
never did. Even when I was a little bit of a shaver and
the other children in Doctor Fillinches' school doted on
jelly beans, I refused them. Stupid flavor. And they got
stuck in your teeth. Remember?"

"No."

"I put one up my nose once," said Mr Wooly conver-
sationally.

The bartender met his eye. He was silent.

"Well, that's neither here nor there now," Mr Wooly said. "Now let me have a drink, please."

"What's the gag?"

"Gag?"

"You stand there," said this bartender, carefully placing one elbow on the bar and with the hand of that arm supporting his chin, "you stand there with your double talk. I'm not laughing, see?"

"I thought this was a place where one *got* drinks."

"Did you really?"

"I'm not asking you to *give* me a drink, you know." He put a five-dollar bill on the bar.

"That's nice of you," the bartender said insincerely. He took a deep breath. "What kind of a drink? Would you mind loosening up to the degree necessary for the communication of that bit of information, Mr Big?"

Why was the fellow so cold, so hostile? Mr Wooly felt very uncomfortable. "My name isn't Big," he said. "It is Wooly." He extended a friendly, a beseeching, hand over the bar. The bartender looked at it. Presently Mr Wooly withdrew the hand and hid its scorn-scorched contours in his pants pocket.

"I would like to purchase," he said gently, "an alcoholic, an intoxicating, drink, brown or rather amber in color, pungently flavored." He tapped his lips, thinking hard. The bartender doubled his right hand into a fist, lusting for a good swift poke at one of Mr Wooly's large brown eyes.

"I think it is called blurping or burping, or something. That's what he called it. Doctor Mannix, I mean to say. He prescribed it, you see. I take it medicinally."

" 'Blurping,' " sneered the bartender. " 'Blurping.' "
At the end of his patience with this solemn practical
joker, he did an outrageous thing, an act out of nightmare, suitable to the end of the world, the breaking up of
all values, all certainties. He reached across the bar slowly
and took Mr Wooly's nose between his thumb and index
finger. He wobbled it. As he wobbled it he spoke between
clinched teeth.

"You," he said, "horrid," pronouncing these sounds
with great care, "little"—he turned the nose again as if it
were a screw; he licked his lips and seemed to consider—
"cutup!" Still he held to Mr Wooly's nose so that Mr
Wooly leaned across the bar, striving to mitigate the
tension. "You come in here with your little prepared
joke, as if life were not difficult enough, with my bills,
my wife, my new boil, my taxes. You come in here all
primed up to kid me, do you? Because you have five dollars in your pants you think you can bait me. Torture me
with your nonsense. What do you really want? Speak!"

"I'd speak," Mr Wooly said, "ib youb lebgobe by
dose."

The bartender let go of it.

"Burden," said Mr Wooly earnestly; "that was the
nabe of it. Please hurry." (The murmer was rising again
in his poor head. He could even overlook the outrage to
his nose; his need was so urgent. He wanted only to be
left alone with himself, insulated from the incessant beat
of the thoughts of his fellows.)

The bartender, though hot tempered, was at bottom a
kind man. He already regretted his hasty action. "You
mean bourbon? Is that it?" He poured Mr Wooly a

double one. Mr Wooly did not know the *mœurs* of this
new world, yet he took a chance and did the right thing.
"How about you?" he asked. "Will you have one at the
same time?"

Mr Wooly's nose shone rosily. His eyes shone also, of-
fering friendship.

"Thank you," said the bartender, pouring it out for
himself. They drank together. He looked at Mr Wooly
and said in a humane tone: "I'm new to this town. Do
you live here?"

"Oh yes." Silence, blessed, sacred silence, had returned
to Mr Wooly's mind. "Here, will you measure out another
one of these? And one for yourself, too, if you'll accept it."

"I'll accept it," said the bartender. "I am sorry I pulled
your nose. I never did anything like that before in all my
life."

"All's well that end's swell," Mr Wooly said. "Ha, ha,
get it? Yours looks a bit swollen itself."

"Beginning of a boil, I'm afraid. Gets me down. I'm
sorta irritable, if you've noticed."

"I have," Mr Wooly said. "Usually, you know, it
wouldn't have been all right. Far from it. But today—
well—even today I didn't really like to have my nose
twisted. But now I look at everything rather differently.
I've had an experience that very few men have had. I've
been forced to listen in on people's brains. Hear everything they think, unless I'm full of this."

"God sakes," said the bartender, "how do you do that?"

"It just came unnaturally," Mr Wooly explained.

"Can it be taught?"

"I wouldn't know how. Only thing I learned about it was that so long's I'm a bit dizzy from the effects of this, ah, medicine, I can't listen in any more. As now. The peace and quiet is lovely. Best thing in the world."

"Should think it would be interesting, listening in."

"You'd think so, but it's awful."

"How do people's brains sound?"

"Messy," Mr Wooly said. "Egotistic—and messy."

"Look, will you sober up and come out to my house with me tonight and tune in on my wife? Not letting on, you understand—just tapping her wires, so to speak, and giving me the dope?"

"What dope?"

"Whatever she's thinking; whatever don't come out in her conversation. I'll pay you well."

"You wouldn't like it," Mr Wooly said. "Mind you, I'm not casting aspersions on your wife—I'm just saying you wouldn't like it." Mr Wooly tried resting his elbow on the bar after the manner of the bartender but missed the edge by an inch and nearly fell into the brass cuspidor. He laughed at himself. He felt fine. It was all strange and new to Mr Wooly, yet from some deep instinct, some region of human universality within himself, he picked out the appropriate words. "Woops," he said. "There I go!" And he whistled a soft exclamation. "Pour it forth," he said, holding everything.

People were coming into the Marlborough now. Betty Jackson came in with a friend, an older woman. They sat on a stool at one end of the bar. Betty did not at first know that her Mr Wooly was at the other end. George

Williams, the scholarly reform chief of police, strolled in; after him a half dozen or so businessmen and newspaper reporters from a trial that was going on in Judge Gilead's court across the street. Then Sanford Digges, the mortician, his appraising eyes seeking among them, quick for future assignments, and Bat-Ears Reilly, himself, followed by Mr Simpson, the Wooly office manager, wobbling on his short legs. It was, Mr Wooly realized, though he did not examine them individually, a pleasant crowd, a superior crowd, indeed, friendly, intelligent. When Betty saw Mr Wooly her little mouth made a red O of astonishment. She could hardly believe her eyes—Mr Wooly in here? What was up? Was he out to have the place raided, perhaps? Surely he would be deeply disappointed to find her there, though she had only come because of her need to drown her loneliness at being cast off from him by his tragedy. Presently she, as well as the others, realized that Mr Wooly, the teetotaler, was there for the same reason that they were. Dr Mannix strolled in, and even bearded Judge Gilead himself. All soon realized that Mr Wooly was not today trying to reform anything or anybody. On the contrary.

Mr Wooly observed a beige-colored, double-breasted vest, pearl-buttoned, decorated with loops of heavy gold chain. It was fancy, Mr Wooly thought. It was admirable. So was its wearer, who happened to be Bat-Ears himself.

"Ha ya?" Mr Wooly said to him.

"Mr Wooly!" said the street commissioner with no little respect in his voice, a note that was not lost on the bartender, who now clearly began to see that all these, the most important people in Warburton, looked up to Mr Wooly, not down.

"Was coming around to see you, Reilly," Mr Wooly went on. "Little matter of street work. Too late now."

"Anything you might suggest," said Reilly, who knew which side his bread was buttered on better than most. He barged up to be alongside of Mr Wooly. "Didn't know you indulged," he said.

Mr Wooly, who was feeling his liquor, slowly blinked. His cheeks as well as his recently twisted nose were rosy. He hiccuped and held tighter to the bar. "Stormy night," he observed. "Big wind, big waves. Woops, down we go! And up we come! Indulge?" he echoed belatedly. "Don't like that word, Reilly. 'S entirely uncalled for."

"I beg your pardon," Reilly said.

" 'S medicine, 's what," Mr Wooly stated.

The bartender was now trying to look like a man who has never, could never, pull the nose of a rich and in-fluential customer. He beamed around on everybody. His attitude to Mr Wooly was that of a rookie hanging about just for a chance to salute the generalissimo.

"Jim knows you, I see," Reilly said, pleasantly making conversation. Jim was the bartender's name.

"Knows me!" exclaimed Mr Wooly. "I'll say he nosed me. He nosed me very well indeed."

Jim, the bartender, turned pale. What, he wondered, had come over him to do such a thing to this gentleman?

Mr Wooly smiled. " 'S all a mishunnerstan'ing," he gen-erously explained. "Right, Jim?"

"Absolutely," said Jim with a great sigh of relief. "This one, Mr Reilly," Jim said, "is on the house."

It was a mistake.

Jim started with unpleasant surprise at the expression that now took possession of Mr Wooly's face.

"What house?" asked Mr Wooly.

"This one," said Jim.

"Want it inside!" Mr Wooly told him coldly. "Wan̄t everything inside. Nothing on the house." His voice rose a bit. "And *nobody* on the house either. Not even my wife, unnerstand?"

Jim didn't. Neither did Reilly, of course, nor Dr Mannix, who now joined them.

"What kind of a talk izhitt, annyway?" Mr Wooly wanted to know. He waved others aside. "You casting 'spersions?" He turned to Reilly: "He's casting 'spersions on my wife."

"Let's all be friends," urged Reilly.

"Wait a moment," Mr Wooly said drunkenly, confusedly angry. Suddenly he reached across the bar and took a firm grip on the bartender's inflamed nose. He gave it a hearty downward yank, nodded his head sternly. "There!" he said.

It hurt, and the bartender kept his eyes tight-closed, getting over it.

"Let's all be friends," Reilly repeated.

Mr Wooly's anger had gone as swiftly as it had come. "We *are* friends!" Tears came into his eyes. "Bes' friends. I din' mean anything by that. Jus' playing a game. Regular game. Wanna see it? Now watch; he takes holda my nose. Go ahead, Jim, take a good hold of it."

"I don't wanta," Jim protested. He was apprehensive now. Chief Williams, leaning over his scotch and soda, said: "Go ahead, Jim," which was close to being a command. Jim took hold of Mr Wooly's nose. "Dow," said Mr Wooly, "I dake 'old o' Jib's ol' dose, like that. Dow I zkeez and Jib skweez. Firs' man says Uncle's a digger baby. Dough," he exclaimed, meaning "Go."

Everybody in the Marlborough was interested. (Betty having repeatedly signaled to Mr Wooly and getting no reply, simply because he couldn't see the length of the bar, had gone away with her friend.)

"What is it?" asked Judge Gilead, stroking his divided beard.

"New game," Reilly said.

"Endurance test," Sanford Digges elaborated.

"An old, old game," ad libbed the scholarly chief of police. "Imported from Egypt."

"Oh," said the bystanders, immensely impressed. One, gazing into the bulging, tear-filled eyes of Jim, the bartender, and then into Mr Wooly's, said, "Wanna bet?"

"Certainly," said Reilly, who never refused a bet.

"A dollar on Jim," said the stranger.

"Taken," said Reilly, who knew about the incipient boil on one side of poor Jim's nose. "I wouldn't say a word of criticism against my old friend Jim there, but I think maybe Wooly's got the greater heart for this sort of thing."

Other bets were made. Silence descended upon the Marlborough, a silence disturbed only by the determined, stubborn sound of the contestants' breathing, the gritting of their teeth as they squeezed with might and main. The audience sensed now that here were two men of character, neither of them a quitter. Their attentive faces

were solemn, yet their interest was objective and courteous; not one of them seemed tempted to intervene in
what was, while rather unusual, none of their business.
Only Bat-Ears seemed to have some difficulty with his
own face. It swelled and turned purple. He rested it
finally on the bar. Strange sounds struggled out of his
bulk. Reilly, essentially a vulgar fellow, was laughing. He
was enjoying himself as he hadn't enjoyed himself since
his wife's sister's black wool underdrawers had fallen
around her feet while she was singing, "I would I were
a tender apple blossom" before a Civic Center audience.

Jim was sweating profusely. He had done his best. He
could do no more. He was afraid, indeed, that the vise-
like, slowly twisting grip of little Mr Wooly might remove his inflamed nose entirely. He knew his nose wasn't
pretty, but he wanted to keep it. Faced with a choice

between honor or his nose, he decided for the latter. He gasped; his moral collapse seemed coincident with a general physical softening; he sagged; he gasped: "Uncle, oh, Jesus, Uncle." The contest was over.

Bat-Ears collected his bets. He spent some of the winnings for further portions of bourbon. Never had the Marlborough been gayer. All there were friends, regardless of race, creed or Dun & Bradstreet, and while congratulations were showered upon Mr Wooly, the winner, it was generally recognized that Jim had put up a good fight and deserved no word of condemnation, not even from those several who had lost money on him. . . .

Well, one minute there was Mr Wooly, the center of the merriment, the next there he was, alone in his own bedroom!

It was improbable that the process was any sort of instantaneous magical transit. Perhaps Dr Mannix, uneasy at the swift success, if you could call it that, of his "prescription," had there and then decided to see him home and in bed; or it may have been that Bat-Ears did this, or both of them together; in any case, except for a memory of swirling fog in which at least two faces, like free balloons, bobbed up and down and swam away into invisibility, only to swim back in again, Mr Wooly had not and never obtained any clear knowledge of the manner of his home-coming. Wakening in his bed, reading the time on his wrist and not knowing whether that alignment of the hands told of midnight or the high noon of some black doomsday, Mr Wooly rang for Bentley. When Bentley entered he peered into his face for some clue. Bentley's expression was the expression of a man who has decided against any expression whatsoever. He said it was midnight. "Hintoxicated," said Bentley's mind clearly. "The poor little man, 'e's hintoxicated. . . ."

So it had returned, that cursed faculty! "Bentley," said Mr Wooly, "bring me a bottle of bourbon whisky and some ice and a siphon."

"What?" cried Bentley.

"You heard me."

"At this time of night? Where shall I get it?" asked Bentley, and then his thought, sounding simultaneously, of course, in Mr Wooly's mind, went on: "Good thing he doesn't know that I have a bit of Irish in my second bureau drawer!" Aloud, with his vocal cords, he said: "It is midnight; everything is closed, sir."

"Not your second bureau drawer," said Mr Wooly,

pleased for once to find a practical use for the curse fastened upon him. "Or if it is closed open it, stingy pig!"

"God Almighty," exclaimed Bentley. "There isn't any whisky in my bureau."

"Go get it," said Mr Wooly sternly.

"Yes sir." He went, a beaten, frightened man, and soon returned. With two quick ones Wooly won back to that solitude which many a poet, as ignorant, alas, as he was talented, has bewailed, little appreciating the horrors of its alternative.

CHAPTER XIV

The Haunted Horse

NOW FULLY AWAKE and no longer troubled at the mystery of how he got home, Mr Wooly telephoned Betty Jackson's hotel but was told she had gone to visit her aunt in Perth Amboy. He was too lonely to remain there in his bedroom. He did not want to see his late wife's pale face gleam like a smear of phosphorescence on his window-pane as he constantly half expected. Who could he talk to? Where was their companionship? He thought of telephoning his daughter; it was too late, and what would he say to her? He decided to go out and talk to Rummy, the mare. She, he decided, though a markedly stupid horse, would be better than no living thing. He picked up Bentley's bottle of Irish by its neck and went down the broad main stairs, out the western portico and so around by sweet-blooming plum and quince to the stables. He snapped on the fifty-watt Mazda there, heard the horses sigh, heard the goat stir on her high heels, and the ass. "Hello, goat," said Mr Wooly, remembering with a slight shiver how once the goat had been ridden under the moon by his wife.

But Rummy turned her big head and gazed at Mr Wooly with lovely eyes.

"Sweetheart!" he said to her. "How's horsy?" She wagged her head till her mane flew like a hula skirt. She struck the boards of the floor with heavy feet, signaling some platitude or other. "I'm lonely," Mr Wooly told her. "I'm lonely!"

Swanson, who lived above the adjoining garage, here made a racket on his outside stairs, running to see what was up. He paused in the stable doorway.

"Yah, so now what?" he irritably asked his employer.

"I'm talking to Rummy here. I'm lonely," Mr Wooly said. "Have you decided that I'm not to talk to my own horse?"

Swanson only stared. It occurred to him that his master was tight, but since he knew this was impossible, having never happened before, he rejected the thought to wonder about the man's sanity. Suddenly Mr Wooly realized he was no longer afraid of his father's chauffeur. "Go soak your head," he shouted. "Or boil it. It looks boiled already. Old potato face! Old bumpy potato face! It comes out here and it caves in there." Mr Wooly demonstrated on his own face, making a ferocious expression with it.

Swanson was amazed; he was profoundly hurt. He felt of his chin. "I need a shave, maybe?" he said, beseeching a crumb of comfort from the madman before him.

"Shaving wouldn't help that old potato face," Mr Wooly said, shaking his head slowly. "You could peel it, and it wouldn't help much; it's the fundamental contours of your face that are all wrong. If a man has a face he should have a face, not an old potato, with horrible holes in it, old black fungus eyes, old cellar sprout for a nose, and do you know what your old mouth is?"

"Don't tell me," Swanson begged. "Yust keep it to yourself, Mr Wooly."

"I will not," Mr Wooly said indignantly. "If I feel like speaking the truth, what right have you to stop me? I started to tell you what your mouth is, so I will continue. Your mouth is a hole for a potato worm, Swanson. What's on your old nose, Swanson?" Swanson felt his nose. "Your hand," Wooly said with a heartless laugh.

Swanson moaned distinctly.

"If I had that nose," Mr Wooly went on, greatly encouraged not only by the woebegone expression of his victim but also by the wide yellow-toothed smile of the attentive horse, whose eyes rolled from the face of one man to the face of the other. "If I had that nose I would not fondle it, I can tell you. I wouldn't touch it with a ten-foot pole."

"Yeesus," poor Swanson said.

"You may go," Mr Wooly told him.

"I may go." Swanson wagged his big head. "I go. Where?"

"Where? To pot, that's where old potatoes go."

Swanson moved one foot. He began to turn.

"Go to bed," commanded Mr Wooly.

"With this face?" sighed poor Swanson. "How would you like to go to bed with it?"

"Don't ask horrible questions. Take it away! You can't leave it here. And don't cry."

"I yust can't help it," Swanson sniffled. "One day is it Mr Wooly I work for; the next thing, boom, bang, yumping Yeesus, here comes a complete stranger!" Swanson oozed out; he was gone. Little did he know how soon he would be avenged!

Mr Wooly looked into the neck of the bottle of Irish

he had wangled from Bentley. He realized it was high time
for another dose of medicine and took it straight, which
nearly strangled him. When he got through coughing he
rested his arms and his head on the edge of the stall.
Funny things certainly were happening. All of a sudden
he had turned on Swanson. *Swanson!* "Must have had it
in for Swanson for a long time," he told himself dreamily.
"Old potato," he repeated to himself, smiling. That was
a good one!

Rummy, the horse, in the meantime was acting
strangely. She was carefully turning her big body around
until she could stand crosswise in her stall; she slowly extended her neck. Because she was again smiling that
yellow-toothed smile there was something strange and un-
horselike on her long face, in her wild, rolling eye. Her
black and hairless muzzle quivered all over itself. It was
plain now that the "smile" was no such a thing; it was a
sneer, a ferocious grimace. The powerful teeth approached
Mr Wooly's unsuspecting arm. Rummy opened her mouth
wide as a lion's. But now Mr Wooly chanced to glance up.
For a split second only man and beast stared into each
other's so-dissimilar faces, and then as Mr Wooly leaped
back and away, Rummy did her lightning best to bite his
arm off. She missed.

Again they stared, she with undisguised and homicidal
hatred, he with slowly dawning suspicion. "Rummy!"
he whispered. "What's got into you?"

Odd, unhorsy sounds struggled in the long throat. In
that brown, oval-pupiled eye seemed to gleam a nature
not equine.

"Jennifer?" asked Mr Wooly.

The horse blinked, calmed her lashing tail, turned from him, and seeing her thus, head busy in her manger, he had to doubt his daring conjecture. Here before him was a horse, an old, stupid horse; that was all. Instead of trying to bite his arm off she had merely been laughing a reminiscent laugh at his excellent witticisms about Swanson. He had grievously misjudged the poor old thing. He said as much to her, even patted her neck.

He said: "Oh, dear old Rummy, how I miss Betty! There was the wife for me, you know. I see it all now. What a fool, I, to wed that unclean trull—that evil brunette. Oh, horse, you should see Betty, her golden hair, the fairness of her lovely skin. The soft grace of her long legs. An angel," sighed Mr Wooly, "a haloed angel."

He who had not emitted a sob or dropped a tear since his memory held suddenly felt a deep desire to cry, so he did, between his sobs taking another swallow of his fiery medicine.

"Bear with my grief," he implored the silent horse.

"For a week Betty has refused to see me. Why? Oh, why? Oh, not that I blame her; who am I to blame such a wonderful woman?" The tears dried on his cheeks; he began to pace the stable floor, talking. He returned to and enlarged upon his preference for blondes over brunettes, explaining, this in detail, explaining further just why this particular blonde's virtues and loveliness provided such a startling contrast to the vices and the horrid, shallow prettiness of a particular brunette—to wit, the late Mrs Wooly. He was eloquent. He said that Mrs Wooly's teeth were sharp as bat's teeth, that her eyes were reptilian. Lost in his exegesis, he became careless. At one point, in midsentence, he strayed close to the open end of Rummy's stall—too close. That was the opportunity the old mare needed. With deadly purpose and wonderful accuracy, tilting herself forward on her front feet, she let go with the hind ones, connecting squarely with the rear of poor Mr Wooly, who thereupon at once left terra firma and literally flew through the open door to land with a long, rasping slide upon the harsh gravel.

Mr Swanson, brooding before his mirror in his bedroom atop the garage, heard the shrill neigh that rang triumphantly from Rummy's throat. Mr Swanson continued to brood over his face. He was doing his best to see his profile; he bared his teeth. He tried a dignified frown, a smile. The smile depressed him. It almost

frightened him with its fringe of wiry mustache. The poor man was in the position of having been sold something he didn't want. In a word, his face. He had been sold an old potato face by the persuasive and bitter eloquence of Mr Wooly. Before this he had had a face—not Greta Garbo's, of course, even though they were of the same race—but still a face that hadn't troubled him much, a face even that he had had a certain affection for. Now he saw it as Mr Wooly had instructed him to see it. . . .

Through his window, borne on the gentle nocturnal breeze, came a different music, a sound more resigned than the battle cry of Rummy. Sad music. Hearing this, Swanson turned an ear. Sounded, he thought, like Mr Wooly moaning. Must be Mr Wooly? In a bad and painful way? Swanson returned to the reflection of his face and brooded some more. The moans were repeated. With deliberation, a stretch and a yawn, Swanson got up at last and went down the outside stairs, a step at a time. There were no more moans, but the prone and crumpled figure of our hero was plainly visible in the shaft of the light of the stable door.

Swanson went over and looked at Mr Wooly.

"Why," he asked, "are you sleeping there on the gravel?"

"Ohhhhhhhh," moaned Mr Wooly.

"Hard, I should think," Swanson said, "and lumpy."

"I'm dying," Mr Wooly told him.

"Yumping Yeesus!"

"I've been murdered."

"You're dead and you talk to me? What kind of a tale is that?"

"A mortally injured one, Swanson. Don't stand there jabbering and gibbering. . . ."

"Yabbering and yibbering," complained Swanson. "All I say is I yust want to help you. . . . Can you walk?"

"Ohhhhh," moaned Mr Wooly.

"You been drinking," Swanson told the prone man. "You yust took a drop too much." This made him think of the first joke he had ever thought of. "A hard drop," he said with a snort of appreciative laughter.

"Swanson," groaned Mr Wooly, "it was Rummy."

"A fine, strong horse," Swanson said. "A spirited horse, by Yeesus."

But now he moved and went into the house, awakening Bentley, Cook, the upstairs maid. When she came out, rather surprisingly, Officer Connolly came out with her. Together they all got Mr Wooly upstairs and into his bed, arranging him thereon face downward.

They stood around, saying sympathetic words. But, knocked cold sober by his trying experience, Mr Wooly began to hear their thoughts, and these for the most part had a certain objective coolness about them. Swanson's were downright cynical. "Yustice, it comes," thought that one. "Right smack where he could best take it," thought Connolly. "He's sorta built to be kicked there." For a man who had never doubted that his own good opinion of himself was shared by all those about him, Mr Wooly was being dragged through the aching shadow of terrible experience. Already his curiosity about what others might think had been more than satiated. He didn't care. He didn't want to know. He didn't even want to learn, as he now did by his mental wireless, that Hortense, the maid, and Connolly had been in her bed. He tried to make his own thinking loud and so escape the intrusion of theirs.

Despite his blinding, face-down position in that bed, the cruel throbbing of his bottom, he faced a fact, a terrible, staring fact. Jennifer. She was in the old mare. That was why her curse still held. Knowing her as he did, Mr Wooly could easily surmise how it had come about. Unstaked, covered with Christian earth, with only run-of-the-mill, orthodox spells said over her by the Reverend Fergus Peyton, she had torn herself free of her somewhat bunged-up corpse and then with all the fury and the stubborn malevolence of her nature had aimed herself straight at the Wooly residence or rather at a habitation within the corporeal envelope of, say—yes, of course—of Hortense, the upstairs maid, who would be in such an excellent position relative to Mr Wooly for the convenience of further devilish plans. Evidently Jennifer had missed her aim: doubtless because Hortense was at just that time too occupied by Officer Connolly, and her mind, too, by thoughts of him. So Jennifer had caromed off the upstairs maid into the pocket provided by the stupid and empty-minded old horse. And there she was! There must have been a time while Jennifer was struggling out of that inadequate Christian trap in the Cloudy Lawn Cemetery that her curse on him had subsided. But now with her proximity in the stables, it was back at work in full force. That he so well and clearly understood all this did not, however, help Mr Wooly to be resigned to his fate. He was a deeply troubled widower, Mr Wooly.

Not before the first pale fingers of the dawn, as the old tales have it (without ever specifying how many fingers the dawn might have), did Mr Wooly achieve the blessed state of slumber, and then it was not blessed, but loud and confused with galloping nightmares.

CHAPTER XV

The Flapping Woo-hoos and Their Cure

EVERY worth-while skill in this world must be learned by many attempts and maintained by constant practice, even though the learner be vibrant with natural talent. This is particularly so of the skill or skills necessary for the endurance of hang-overs. The timorous, the mediocre, who for the first time is shaken by an acheful pulsation, who for the first time meditates with haggard visage a pit of despair which before his excessive sinning was merely the pit of his stomach, who feels for the first time that It, faceless, imponderable, but enormously threatening, lurks just south of his shoulder blades, while in ambush around the nearest corner, be it of his bedroom door or of a thoroughfare, lies some such anonymous Disaster as a personified revelation of the essential, ugly horror of this thing we call life—such a tyro, stranger to perseverance, to brilliance, is likely to refuse the bargain right there and at once and never again try the pleasure, the personal enhancement of the lilting tilt. He may not be a complete dullard. He may be able to understand that here on this earth you get nothing for nothing; he may merely object that what came after was in his opinion too great a price for what he got the night before. Success, in a word, is not for him.

To succeed in the endurance of hang-overs one must

try and try again. The first fact about a hang-over is the worst. There is no cure for it. It must be gone through. The speeding train may dislike and dread the tunnel, but if there be a tunnel ahead, then eventually the train must go into it, for a certain measure of time maintain itself in the dreary dark and the unnatural air before it again achieves the sun. In sober truth there is no cure, finally no avoidance, of the earned hang-over; this is a law, but there is always the possibility of postponement.

A first-day hang-over, treated at birth with "some of the same," evaporates, or seems to, giving place often, especially with determined and skillful persons, to a condition even better than that of the previous night. The second morning, however, brings the second-day hang-over. One might guess that this would be twice as bad as a first-day hang-over. One would be in error. The second is about twenty per cent worse than the first-day sort. Again a postponement may be effected, and even a fourth, fifth or sixth postponement, but all the time the bill is rising, slowly, of course, but rising, until it can be expressed only in the largest denominations. Beginning with the brown whimpers, it mounts step by step, from the huddle and mutters to the whips and jingles to the flapping woo-hoos, and worse and worse, until is reached a nameless hang-over that is variously described, sometime as a state of—but never mind; let us not think of it!

The best way with a hang-over, as with a maid, is to meet it fairly and frankly and take it. Its life is brief: it rises and dies with the day; dusk is its shroud. Lay it down. Let tomorrow's hang-over be a new one. The pusillanimous, the niggardly, the irrational, object that then all one's days march under the shadow and the woe of hang-overs. But how bright the night's thereof!

Our Mr Wooly, innocent, without the slightest education in such things, awoke with his first hang-over. If it could have been separated from him and exhibited in a cage in some children's zoo it would have spoiled the lives of all his little visitors, making bigots of them, persuading them in a way never to be forgotten that liquor was poison and Bacchus the devil himself.

Fortunately for the tots, unfortunately for poor Mr Wooly, it could not be separated from him. . . . He had awakened by degrees. While the ache in his bottom was a grievous one, so was the ache in his head. His head seemed unusually large also. He did not know where it stopped, really. Lying there staring into darkness, he did not know which ache was his head. Here was a problem to be approached coolly, to be solved by deliberate and careful thought. No time for panic, Mr Wooly said to himself. No. He winked his eyes, willed this act, and the lids obeyed. But where were his lids? It was a unique but terrible situation in which to find oneself—this inability to tell his head from his—his other ache. He devoutedly hoped that they had not during the night changed their places. If that had happened what would he do? Mr Wooly had not been wholly deprived of an imagination, and the spectacle he thought up to represent himself terrified him. Where would he wear his hat? He moaned slightly. He could have discovered the straight of himself at once by testing the joints of his arms, which seemed located somewhere about midway between his aches. These were not, after all, universal joints, unless they, too, had changed during the night, so by bending them he might find some clue as to their true location as well as the relation of other parts of him to them. But he did not want to move his arms. He was afraid they would fall off.

Mr Wooly felt fragile. He felt fried on both sides. His feeble brain gave up the jigsaw puzzle he seemed to have become, dismissed it as beyond its effort. He dozed, motionless, and thought his mouth was the subway at Forty-second Street. Downtown trains roared along his left molars, uptown along his right; when they struck his bridgework they thundered over, heedless of their danger. He dreamed that he awakened, dreamed that he opened his eyes to look up at himself in the mirror that roofed his enormous bed. At once he closed his eyes again, for what he dreamed he saw up there was an alligator, stark naked. Then he did wake up and discovered the darkness surrounding him was not the night but the pillow. He twisted and looked; daylight stabbed one eyeball as he peeled it. He knew at once where his head was; it was behind that eyeball. And south of his head, all in proper sequence, yet all in disorder, lay his hot throat, his heaving bosom and that wide consternation which was his middle. He moaned.

In a second there was Bentley, saying, "Shall I bring you some nice breakfast, sir?"

"No, no, no," groaned Mr Wooly. "Don't mention such a thing. Never mention it to me again. As long as I live—which won't be long. Something awful has happened to me, Bentley. I am poisoned from head to foot. Bring a doctor, for mercy's sake, a doctor." His voice sank to a whisper.

He heard the mumble and mutter of Bentley's scattered, ignoble thoughts: " 'Ow he takes on. Poison, me eye. Not what *you* were a-drinking of, Mr Wooly, not my Irish whisky isn't poison!" Aloud he said: "Doctor Mannix is 'ere, sir. 'E's in the drawing room, sir." And off went Bentley to be succeeded in a minute or two by Dr Mannix.

Dr Mannix said: "Good morning!"

Mr Wooly groaned. A long, desolate groan.

Dr Mannix sat down, pressed the bridge of his thick spectacles with his forefinger. He began to think, and what he thought was at once communicated to Mr Wooly's aching head.

"What a hang-over," thought Dr Mannix without a trace of sympathy in his mental tone. "Wonder what a hang-over feels like when you've put off having one all your life the way he has. Maybe it will teach him a little humility—horrid, strutting little prig that he's been all these years. God, doesn't he look awful? Makes my optic nerve throb just to think of his! Wonder what his motor nerve feels like; bet his stomach's full of butterflies and an electric fan to keep 'em moving against his tripes! My, my—what a human man will do to give himself permission to go have a bust. But it took this little fathead to invent a witchwife persecuting him with old medieval curses. What an ignoble, shameful, stinking little mess his mind must be to cook up such a self-delusion as that!"

"Not delusion—objective fact," groaned Mr Wooly. He couldn't help interrupting. He had had very close to enough of that soliloquy. He said as much, groaning and grasping between the words: "I never did like soliloquies,

not even Shakespeare's. Couldn't ever believe in them;
always wanted to throw something at the confounded
nuisance standing up there talking to himself. Now you
come in here, and I have to listen to your conceited
babble!"

"I haven't said a word, Mr Wooly," said Dr Mannix
with cold dignity. "I have just been sitting here thinking."

"And I have to listen in, don't I?"

"Nonsense!"

"Wish it were," moaned poor Mr Wooly. "You thought
butterflies in my stomach. Right? Well, I'll tell you they
don't feel like butterflies; they feel like bats. I've got
bats in my belly. That's what! Not butterflies. And all that
about self-delusion!" He paused.

Dr Mannix, aloof, tight-lipped, waited, his thoughts
beginning at once: "Good guesswork, but not difficult.
How he clings to his delusion! There you are, you souse!
T. Wallace Wooly! Wonder what the T. stands for?
Teetotaler? Tub thumper? Tosh?"

Mr Wooly spoke. "Ten-Eyck," he said.

"Ten-Eyck?" echoed the medical man. "What's that?"

"What the T. stands for," said Mr Wooly. "My first
name. Very old New York name."

Now at last the scientific mind of Dr Mannix had been
given pause. He *had* been wondering what the T. stood
for. Maybe he had unconsciously said it aloud?

"Your mouth was closed," Mr Wooly told him, more
awake than he had been and, while still as sick as ever,
able to take a bit of malicious satisfaction out of this.

"It is impossible," Dr Mannix said, "and therefore it isn't true."

"Think of a number," sneered Mr Wooly. "Put your hand over your mouth, turn your back."

Dr Mannix did so.

"Seven," said Mr Wooly, and then: "Seven hundred and sixty-nine million, 372 thousand, 627. How's that? Guesswork?"

Dr Mannix turned to face him again. He found his handkerchief and used it on his wrinkled brow. He polished his glasses. Mr Wooly heard his consternated thinking, ragged thoughts running around in disorder, piling on top of each other. Mr Wooly said: "I'm listening in, you know. I'm telling you nothing cuts me off, disconnects me, but ardent spirits—in sufficient quantities." His stomach shook at this overt mention of last night's invader, and Mr Wooly, his waxen cheeks blushing a clear green, swallowed, swallowed again, gasped and was, so to speak, still there at the helm.

Dr Mannix faced an ugly decision. If he gave in, if he believed in this unnatural horror, he would never be the same, nor would his world; the foundations of the latter were crumbling and sliding under his feet.

Here a light knock on the door, which was then opened by the upstairs maid, Hortense, a small brunette in uniform. Should she straighten up the room now or later?

Dr Mannix, squinting, examined her. His thought came clearly to Mr Wooly: "Nice mammaries; slight glandular fullness in the neck, but how white and soft; like to put my nose under ear. . . . Wonder what her . . ."

Mr Wooly, revolted, wanting to hear no more, defended

himself with song: "Oh, say, can you see, by the dawn's early light, what so proudly we hailed at the twilight's last gleaming? The rockets' red glare . . ." While he sang he waved Hortense away. She only stared. He paused to shout, "Go away." She went suddenly. Mr Wooly subsided.

"Nice what?" asked Mr Wooly of Dr Mannix. "What about her ear? You wonder what her what is? You lecherous, foul-minded old"—he searched for a word to blow the man down—"old mud-turtle neck."

Dr Mannix looked wounded, but he also looked downright embarrassed. "Get out of my mind," he yelled suddenly, "and stay out!"

"I know too much about your mind already," Mr Wooly said. "I don't want to be in the dirty place. I *want* to get out of it."

"How much do you know about it?"

"I said too much. You're a loose thinker, Doctor," he said, knowing that Dr Mannix would suspect from these words that he, Mr Wooly, had listened in on his inmost secrets. The nature of these, as yet really veiled from Mr Wooly, was, nevertheless, suggested by the horrified expression on Dr Mannix' face. "Doctor," Mr Wooly said, ruthlessly pressing his advantage home, "I want a long cold glass of what you'd prescribe for yourself if you felt as I do. And I want it now!"

Dr Mannix got up, breathing hard, trembling.

"At once, Mr Wooly," he said.

He went away. In five minutes Bentley tiptoed in, accompanied by a sound as of silver tambourines and xylophones. . . . These and the sounds of his breathing

and his incoherent thoughts drew near, departed, while
Mr Wooly kept his eyes closed in a pretense of sleep, for
he wanted no more of either God's daylight or of con-
verse with his fellow man.

He opened one eye. Bottles, glasses, ice. He closed his
eye again. It came over him in a wave of panic that it was
beyond his ability even to touch any of it, let alone get
it down inside himself. But, he argued, he must be brave;
he must somehow prove his self-control. Had this not
been his aspiration all these years—to do the right thing,
even though difficult, even though seemingly impossible?
Was he, T. Wallace Wooly, to quail before an ordeal, any
ordeal, even this one—if it were for his own good? With
this great and noble thought he opened his eye again;
with rigid arm forced to obedience by his inexorable
will power he extended a trembling hand until it grasped
the one tall glass Dr Mannix had himself prepared. It was
very cold, and that sensation Mr Wooly found was not
disagreeable. His hand, the arm from which it grew,
transported the tall cold glass nearer to Mr Wooly's burning lips. Nearer still. With closed eyes he sipped.

Now Dr Mannix had taken Mr Wooly at his word, and
he had poured into the tall glass an inch and one half of
brandy (Bentley's); into this he had added "t.f.," as the
prescriptions say, meaning "to fill," chilled champagne
(Bentley's), very dry. Nothing else; no bits of salad, no
garbage peels—nothing. Poor Mr Wooly's fevered lips
and throat, expecting the harsh outrage of straight whisky
—so little did he know!—were pleasantly—nay, raptur-
ously—surprised; and it was not long before all the glass
was gone and he was preparing himself another and simi-

lar dose, following the penciled prescription thoughtfully laid upon the tray by the doctor. Before he had swallowed more than two swallows from this second, his mind,
like a satisfied octopus, withdrew its tentacles, curling
them under itself as a kitten its paws; his mind rested,
satisfied with its own cave, ignorant of other caves and
thankful for this solitude, this ignorance.

Dr Mannix stuck his head in the door.

"Come in," cried Mr Wooly, "come in, my old friend."
And he added: "It's gone. It's cured. I'm myself again.
Come sit here, and perhaps you'll forgive me if I err in
this—I know nothing about such things—perhaps you
will yourself partake of some of your remarkably effective, therapeutic, stimulating prescription."

"You do not err," said Dr Mannix. And when he had
partaken he thought what a splendid chap this Mr Wooly
was, indeed, that is, with a couple of drinks in him. Born
sober, born six drinks short, poor old chap, thought the
doctor, and this thought which might not have bothered
Mr Wooly, after all, was not communicated to Mr Wooly.
His mind was at sea, pleasantly at sea, and the shores were
nowhere in sight.

And now, having cured the one, Dr Mannix turned his
attention to that other ache, removing coverlet, blanket
and sheet.

"Remarkable," he exclaimed almost reverently.

"What is?" asked Mr Wooly, who lay, of course, face
down.

"Symmetrical," cried Dr Mannix. "The old girl can
aim; one hoof there and one hoof there. Perfect distribu-
tion. And *what* color. I would like to take a Kodachrome

of this, Mr Wooly. It's the most beautiful and the biggest bruise I have ever seen in all my professional experience."

"How about your unprofessional experience?" Mr Wooly asked him.

Dr Mannix was too busy to reply.

Here the maid again entered, her soft knock having been disregarded. Hearing the door close, Mr Wooly asked with some modest apprehension: "Is that Hortense?"

Dr Mannix twisted his neck to look at her where she stood deftly rearranging things on the dresser top. "Seems quite relaxed," Dr Mannix said and added as he poulticed and bandaged with surgeon's gauze, "But what language, Mr Wooly. Heh, heh."

"What language?" asked Mr Wooly.

"How little we've known you, Ten-Eyck," said Dr Mannix dreamily. "May I call you Eyck or Ikie?"

"Call me early," said Mr Wooly, "for I'm the queen of the May."

"You boys!" said Hortense, waving at them modestly.

"What she doing, Doctor?"

"Dusting, with a duster."

"I don't want to be dusted," said Mr Wooly. "I'm beginning to listen in again."

Dr Mannix, who couldn't keep his eyes off Hortense, hastened to the task of concoction.

"Ask Hortense, the poor little drudge, if she doesn't want some," suggested Mr Wooly.

"Oh, that's her *name!*" cried Dr Mannix.

"You're so kind and thoughtful, Mr Wooly," said Hortense.

So they all had one. After a while Hortense, who, of course, had remained respectfully standing, was urged to sit down. She sat down on Dr Mannix' knee.

They talked about various subjects. Mr Wooly talked about Mr Wooly; Dr Mannix talked about Dr Mannix, and Hortense talked about Hortense. Between their frank and cheerful statements they drank brandy-and-champagne highballs. "Lovely people," said Mr Wooly to his new friends, "handsome, intelligent, loyal!"

"You never looked better," Dr Mannix assured him.

"Whose birthday is it?" asked Mr Wooly. Nobody knew; it wasn't theirs. "What day is it?"

"Second of May," Dr Mannix said.

"Shoot!" exclaimed Mr Wooly. "Confound it! We missed May Day, poor old May Day, just let go by without any celebration."

"That's shameful," said Dr Mannix.

But Hortense did not despair. "It's never," she said, "too late to celebrate."

"Celebrate, celebrate," sang Dr Mannix, catching tune and rhythm at once. He got up and began a little shuffling dance:

"It's never too late to celebrate, celebrate, celebrate.
It's never too late to take a mate,
So early on May Day morning. . . ."

Hortense looked at her master. "Can you stand up?" she asked him.

"I can try," said Mr Wooly, finishing his glass. And he

did. He could stand, but not like a soldier; he was half
doubled over, but he did not want to be left out of the
dance. They all joined hands and did a skipping run, as a
kind of tryout, while Mr Wooly furnished the second
verse:

"*It must have been something that we ate, that we ate,
   that we ate.
Must have been something that we ate
Swirly in the morning.*"

   "That's *wonderful*," screamed Hortense and kissed
them both, one after another. "Come on now, round we
go in a ring. . . ."
   "Your turn," said Dr Mannix, so she sang:

"*When Wooly's bottom met its fate, met its fate, met its
   fate,
When Wooly's bottom met its fate, 'twas from his
   horsy's fate. . . .*"

   "Oh, darling," exclaimed Dr Mannix, "you are brilliant.
Perfect Hibernian dialect! She *is* brilliant," he said to Mr
Wooly. "A lovely girl," he cried. "Full of bounce and
jounce and jiggle," he said, gazing at her, but not her
face: "Round we go," he cried.
   "It's never too late to celebrate. . . ."
Bentley, who had knocked several times, now opened
the door. He said: " 'Ere is the nurse, sir; she 'as just
this minute harrived; says Doctor Mannix sent for her.
. . . She . . ." But he could not go on. He could not re-
treat either or, decently, close the door, as he should have.

He stood there, petrified, staring at the scene before him.

According to some seasoned observers, the world is in flux. "The crux of the matter," as Dr Spingargle wrote, "is flux." Values are being transvalued; civilization is going down on an escalator out of control—holding on, but to what? Everything's wild, and the players are all plastered. Day after tomorrow, say these pleasant fellows, the least ruined of man's structures may be Stonehenge and the Pyramids. If that is so—and who are we to argue about it?—it may be that the vast *dégringolade* began, or at least its last and decisive phase began, with just this scene that old Bentley gazed upon. Here was womanhood, science and capitalism skipping round and round in a circle, mad and bad as so many goats!

They paused. Mr Wooly's back was to the door and to his butler. At his butler's back was a female figure, dimmed by the shadows of the hall beyond. Mr Wooly's pajama top, of a modest beige hue, reached midway between hip and knee. That is, it did in front, but in the rear, because of the extensive poulticing and bandaging Dr Mannix had deemed necessary for his injuries, the pajama top hiked or scrooged up to accommodate this unusual swelling. Also, Mr Wooly could not stand erect. He stood bent forward like a gnome, a wicked, bibulous gnome. He looked distorted and depraved, and because he, unlike his playmates, did not see that an audience had appeared, he alone went on singing:

> "*I'll never go back at any rate, any rate, any rate.*
> *I'll never go back to a sober state*
> *Swirly in the morning!*"

He expected a hand for that but was disappointed.
" 'S matter with you two?" he asked plaintively. "Sweetie
face," he said to Hortense, putting one arm on her pleasant shoulders, "don't be mis'ble. Come on now, once

more around." They only stared over his head. The party
was dead. It had rigor mortis. Slowly, unwillingly, he
turned around.

There was Bentley. He didn't waste time on Bentley.
Beside Bentley, in a nurse's cap and uniform, stood Betty
Jackson.

"Oh," said Betty Jackson. And this remark she repeated: "Oh."

Hortense decided to do something smart. She wove away from there and picked up from a table the feather

duster she'd been using before the party started. But her heart wasn't in this transparent pretense. She couldn't keep her mind on it. She had to come back to watch what was happening. Rejoining Dr Mannix, she absent-mindedly dusted his bald head. He giggled because it tickled.

"Don't do that," he said, "you saucy minx." Seeing all

the astonished and woebegone faces before and beside him, the zany went off into a series of tight, strangled giggles in a tenor voice, until he had to take his thick glasses off his red nose to wipe them, and then, of course, he couldn't see anything but a few blurs.

"I see," said Betty Jackson, finding her voice again. "So this is it!"

"So this is what?" asked Mr Wooly, staggering slightly and grabbing hold of the doctor to save himself. He should have right there, he knew, said something reassuring to the girl, something to win her confidence, bring her into the gay little circle. He should have told Bentley to go away and then offered her a chair and urged one of those good, long concoctions upon her. Alas, he could only stare, his head on one side, his odd legs coming down out of his scrooged-up pajama top. He looked like a bird but not a successful or happy bird. He blinked, hiccuped. In the heavy silence the loud click resounded. At the same time his head shot straight up until his neck was twice its normal length. " 'Scuse me," he said with a placating one-sided smile.

"Oh," said Betty Jackson again.

Here Hortense decided to participate in this curious conversation. "How are you, dearie?" asked Hortense. "Won't you come in?" Saying this, she bowed slightly. It was a mistake; the bow changed the center of her specific gravity and she slanted with a hurry of little steps until she fetched up against the bed. She fell forward on it, said, " 'S all right, all right," and went to sleep.

Bentley here remembered who he was. He withdrew.

"You don't even speak to me," Betty said.

Mr Wooly couldn't. His words were gone. He put one bare foot on the arch of its brother. He blinked and scratched the side of his right knee slowly.

"Oh, oh," said Betty and, covering her suddenly streaming eyes with a small handkerchief, she, also, withdrew; she faded away from there, was gone.

CHAPTER XVI

Conference Belowstairs

THE KITCHEN of the Wooly residence looked like a surgery. Mass murders could have taken place in that kitchen day after day, and what with the capacious sinks, the washing machines, the garbage choppers and liquefiers never a trace need have been left. The stove looked like a refrigerator, and the refrigerator, sunk into the wall, was so large you could have gone in there with an armchair to read your newspaper and so caught a nice case of pneumonia. Cook, whose name was Ferguson, was a sturdy, whiskery woman with black hair and a low mind. Bella, her assistant, was thin and young and manless. She had opinions. She and Cook and Bentley, the fatcheeked butler, sat around a metal-legged table that looked like something for a morgue, a high-class morgue, and discussed recent events that had so altered the atmosphere of the world of Wooly. From time to time they glanced over at Hortense, who drooped on a chair in a corner, forcing black coffee into herself.

"He's changed," Cook said. "Everything has changed. Everything happens so quick now. She was hardly more than a bride. She dies, and he has her under the ground in less than two days. It don't seem decent."

"She couldn't go under too quick for me," Bentley declared. "But you're bloody well right abaht 'ow quick things last these days. Take 'is drinking, for hinstance."

"I couldn't," Cook said. "Not that I can't do my share, Bentley, but I couldn't take his. He puts his head in like a horse and pulls it in. I never see anybody drink the way Mr Wooly drinks. Not even Tennyson, my husband, who used to spend his week ends at Bellevue."

"Is that," Bella asked, "beside the sea?"

"When you're there," Cook explained, "you're beside yourself."

"No balmy breezes stirring in the oaks?" Bella asked wistfully.

"Only balmy soaks," Cook said, "sneezing in the stir."

"As it were," rhymed Bentley.

Bella, listened with both ears and her mouth, still didn't

quite understand. "Is it exclusive?" asked the poor girl.

"Very abusive," Cook assured her. Cook rarely smiled, and as Bella never knew if talk were true or false, sad or funny, except by examining the expression of the face of the talker, she was in a chronic state of bewilderment in this kitchen. However, since she was quite certain that this was no fault of hers, that she alone was privy to the truth while the others were too blind and dumb to get it, she didn't suffer.

"She drug him down," Bella declared. "He was a fine, decent man, and she drug him down. She put a spell on him with her wickedness, and she drug him down."

Bentley sipped his whisky and milk. "Hif you ahsk me," Bentley said grandly, " 'e wanted to be. What I want to know is 'oo peached? Hit was one of you three females did, I'll be bound."

"Peached?" echoed Cook.

"Abaht the Irish whisky in my drawers."

"Oh, poo," Cook said.

"Poo, is it?"

"Poo and pish and peanuts! And what do I know about your drawers?" Cook wanted to know.

"Yes, I wonder," Hortense said, somewhat muzzily, though by now her expanded and frazzled personality was pulling itself together. She could hold her head up now.

"Oh, you do?" Cook's voice was dangerous. "Well, there isn't much I need to know about you, my girl."

"No?"

"No. I already know too much. You and that ordinary, plain, overweight policeman. Ugh!"

"You mean Mr Connolly?"

"How many policemen do you take to bed with you?" Cook asked her.

"Nah, nah," Bentley said soothingly and drank the rest of his whisky and milk. "Nah, nah, gels."

"Oh, I don't mind her, Bentley," Hortense said sweetly, and added: "Do you know what he said about you, Cook? Oh, ha, ha, ha, it was very funny."

"Nah, nah," repeated Bentley.

"And as for your drawers," Cook said hastily, "you upper-class English don't wear drawers except in winter."

Hortense was so interested her grasp on the bread knife relaxed. "Don't they? What do you know!"

"Of course they don't," Cook said while Bentley fidgeted in his chair, getting ready to explode. "Don't you know the old hymn that goes like this:

> "Oh, the British lawds set sail
> To fight their country's wars
> And everyone used his shirttail
> To serve as underdrawers.

"They wear these long shirttails fore and aft," Cook explained, "and tie them together in between."

"It's a base libel," Bentley shouted, purple in the face.

"What do you know!" Hortense breathed. "Like diapers, what?"

"My husband Tennyson used to sing the Wipers verse of this here hymn. Wipers was in the war, you know. It went like this:

> "The English lawds at Wipers
> A-fighting for the Cause

All wore shirttail diapers
Instead of underdrawers."

"Hit's houtrageous," shouted Bentley. "Of course they wore drawers, and so do I."

"Don't believe it," Hortense said.

"Neither do I," Cook agreed.

"Let's see 'em," Hortense suggested.

"I will not," Bentley said.

"Stand up in the corner there and show us. Come on, down with them, Bentley. Don't be so old fashioned. I was raised modern," Hortense said. "My mother was a militant suffragette, a real bust-up idealist. She used to say: 'Down with the pants. Up with the skirts!' A regular war cry!"

"What? What kind of a war was that?" Bella asked.

Hortense looked at her. "What kind of what was who?"

Bella seemed to ponder this odd interrogation. "Who?" she asked.

"Yes, who?" demanded Hortense. "Who?"

You could see Bella had lost the drift. "Who?" she asked.

"You girls ain't going to get anywhere that way," Cook said.

"Sound like a ruddy pair of howls," Bentley observed.

"Owls," Cook corrected him. "Not howls."

"Knot howls?" It was Bentley's turn to look puzzled. "Never heard of 'em. Night howls, maybe. Night howls 'owl.'"

"Why?" asked Cook.

"They say 'oo, 'oo, 'oo. Hasking a question like. 'Oo, 'oo." Momentarily losing himself in this impersonation, he suddenly recovered and asked angrily: " 'Ow would I know? And anyway," plaintively, "I didn't mean my hunderdrawers; I never mentioned hunderdrawers till you brought the matter hup."

"Better up than down," interjected Hortense.

"I mean the drawers in my chest of drawers where I kept my Irish whisky. 'Oo peached? 'Ow did 'e know I 'ad it? That's what I am hendeavoring to hascertain!"

"Don't look at me," Hortense said. "I'd have taken it myself if I'd known."

"Me too," Cook declared succinctly.

Bella smiled her superior, though somewhat vacant smile. "He read your mind," she said.

"Rats!" said Bentley.

"He read mine," Bella persisted and at the memory turned red. "It wasn't nothing, but it was what I was thinking, all right. And I hadn't opened my mouth."

"This here house," Cook said, "is going stark loony."

"Oh, he's a different man now," Bella went on dreamily. "He's changed. She was so queer he won't ever be the same, being the widder of that one. She used to crawl up and down the vine outside the house. I seen her." Bella's voice sank to a whisper. "And she rode the goat through the apple orchard when the moon was shining, I tell you. She used to meet a man down there at midnight."

In spite of themselves the nitwit had them spellbound now.

Cook did her best to assert herself, to bring them all back to earth. "That Connolly," she sneered. "What a beat that man has! And he ain't got even a scooter. Does it all on his feet."

"Does 'e!" wondered Bentley. "Well, well, live and learn."

Hortense grasped the bread knife; she half rose. "Nah, nah," said old Bentley.

"It wasn't Mr Connolly," Bella whispered. "It was a man I never seen before. He was lame."

"Mallarkey," Cook said in feeble defiance. "You're so stuperstitious, my girl."

"Fiddle ends!" said Bentley, but his scorn was no more vigorous than Cook's. They'd all seen enough, too much, of recent days in this house, and while they did not want to believe that which might make them uncomfortable, not to say terrified, they had held belief at arm's length only with great effort. The whole house had lost its old-time isolated, tasteless, antiseptic status; now the very air of the big rooms had aged, was portentous, and no shadowed corner was empty.

"He can read your mind," Bella said and slowly nodded her head. "I know," she said.

It was Hortense who gave way first. Both Bentley and Cook turned to her. The latter demanded what she had learned during that outrageous morning party. "He can read your mind," Hortense said. "It's a curse she put on him. Maybe," she said to Cook, "you know more than Doctor Mannix. But maybe you don't. *He's* scared of Mr Wooly, scared to death of him."

"Why?" asked Bentley.

"Because he can read his mind."

"I don't want anybody reading my mind," Cook said.

"Not that I ever had an indecent thought, but I just don't like it."

"Think *I* like it?" groaned Bentley. "You don't have to go hup to the man morning noon and night and stand there, waiting, while 'e listens hin. 'Ow did I know 'e was listening hin when I was thinking 'ow I'd pop down directly and take a nip of that fine Irish whisky I 'ad 'id in my dresser?" He shuddered. "I'll give notice, that's what."

Cook thought of something: "How could a girl like you stand it?" she asked Hortense. "If I had a mind like yours I'd keep it well covered. How *could* you stand it, romping around up there, singing, and et cetera, and et cetera?"

"What do you mean, et cetera?"

Cook wasn't taking anything from Hortense. Not this morning. "When you wobbled down here, my girl, I decided right off it must have been something you et cetera."

"Ho, I say," cried Bentley, "that's very good, you know, very good." He turned to Bella. "Did you grasp that one?" he asked. "You see, the popular saying, the hidiom, is to say that it must have been something you et, particularly when you 'aven't been heating but himbibing. You see?" But here Bella turned her face toward him. One look told him he was getting nowhere. "Never mind," he said, "never mind."

"Didn't it give you the goose pimples?" Cook persisted. "Didn't it make you feel like he was stripping you stark-staring naked?"

"No," Hortense said. "When I'm naked I'm not stark or staring, anyway. I'm just, you know . . ." She seemed to be seeing herself that way, and the sight evidently did not give her goose pimples. She smiled a curious warm, dissolving sort of smile, like the faintest breeze momentarily touching the smoothest lake. . . . She looked up. "When he's tight," she said, "he's tuned out. Can't hear a thought, not the loudest sort of thought. Can only hear his own then."

They were silent, considering this. They gazed into this situation, which seemed not nearly so threatening now. They gazed into their several futures. Bentley heaved a sigh of great relief, for he did not want to leave this berth, not he. He never wanted to leave it. The phone was within reach. He reached for it, began to dial a number.

"Scheinfeld?" he said into the receiver. "This Scheinfeld's Superior Liquor Stores? Send up at once a case of brandy," he said. "Wait, make it two cases; make it six, I mean . . . Now, the whiskies, let's see. . . ."

The order was a long one. Bentley used his imagination, all his learning and the practically inexhaustible Wooly credit. . . .

CHAPTER XVII

Love's Ambassador

WHILE belowstairs was making preparations of its own to meet the new Wooly situation, upstairs in the master's bedroom something much more complicated was going on.

Dr Mannix had explained that it was his thought to bring Betty Jackson into the house as Mr Wooly's nurse. He had explained to the girl that Mr Wooly was perishing with loneliness for her; that he was sick and, moreover, injured; that if she called she could only call briefly, lest tongues wag, but if she came as a nurse she could not only remain but be in constant attendance of the man she loved. It had been Dr Mannix' little conceit to conceal this plan from Mr Wooly so that Betty's arrival would be a wonderful surprise. Alas, how badly it had all turned out! Dr Mannix felt blue about it. Although Mr Wooly accepted his explanation—indeed, they had wept tears together over it—still he remained terribly upset and anxious to repair the damage done—in other words, to win back Betty as soon as possible, lest the breach between them, the ghastly misunderstanding, prove permanent.

"What shall I do?" moaned Mr Wooly.

"Let me fix you a little more of this," Dr Mannix said.

"Want to keep your mind clear, you know; no time for the intrusion of other's thoughts."

" 'S true," said Mr Wooly. " 'S absolutely true. Thank you. Here she is; there she goes. Tastes like soda pop," Mr Wooly said dismally. "Tastes like tears and misery."

"You look like hell," Dr Mannix said. "How do you feel?"

Mr Wooly closed his eyes. "Dante," he said, " 'S novice."

"I see what's got to be done, but how are we going to do it?"

"We could eat a couple electric-light globes or order one exhaust pipe and two straws or dive into the empty fountain from here."

Dr Mannix shook his head. "Let's live. What we must do is go call on Betty. Explain everything, fix everything. 'Tout comprendre c'est tout pardonner.' "

"Name's Betty," Mr Wooly said. "Don't go calling her toots, you old doctor, you."

"That was French."

"Makes it that much worse. Anyway, she wouldn't receive me, not after this morning," sighed Mr Wooly in full defeat. "I couldn't even get to her door."

Dr Mannix thought: "Pretend you are somebody else."

"Everybody knows me," groaned Mr Wooly.

"Wear a disguise."

Mr Wooly was now drearily looking out the window with unseeing, woebegone eyes.

"Turn sideways," suggested Dr Mannix.

Slowly Mr Wooly turned. He slanted forward from his waist, grotesquely misshapen by the bandages.

"If you leaned a little more," Dr Mannix said reflectively, "and put your hands up you could go as a kangaroo—an old, ragged sort of kangaroo."

"What I know of that hotel doesn't make me feel they'd be pleased to meet a kangaroo. Anyway, I don't *feel* like a kangaroo, and I don't want to be one."

"Don't be so unreasonable," complained Dr Mannix. "I'm doing my best. I'm studying here, concentrating, and what do you do? You just say you don't want to. Do you call that co-operation? After all, you have got that enormous bustle on you. Let me see; if it was Christmas you could go as Santa Claus. A Santa Claus who carried his toys in the seat of his pants."

"It isn't Christmas," Mr Wooly said drearily. "It isn't, and so it isn't."

"Did I say it was? Up to now we've been getting along all right, haven't we? Let me think. That bustle." He snapped his fingers. "I've got it, Wooly; I've got it! Go as her aunt from Perth Amboy."

"I'm not her aunt from Perth Amboy."

"You could dress up to look like her."

"What does she look like?"

"I don't know," Dr Mannix said. "But I know she's got an aunt in Perth Amboy, because she told me so. She has gallstones. But you don't have to have gallstones. They don't show."

"That makes it simple, doesn't it?" said Mr Wooly with a slight stir of interest. "What else has she got?"

"I don't know but my God," cried the champagne-soaked doctor, "it's foolproof! The clerk phones up that her aunt from Perth Amboy is here, so up you go, and in you go, and once in there you tear off your wig and you say: 'It's only Mr Wooly!' "

"Why?" asked Mr Wooly. "I don't care for that 'only.' If I was going to use that word at all, Doctor, I'd say, 'The one and only Mr Wooly.' Notice the difference?" He was silent a moment while he considered the plan. His face became enlivened; color returned to his cheeks. He smiled. At sight of this the doctor let go a slight cheer. "Good boy!" he said. "Where do you keep the wigs?"

Mr Wooly said he didn't have any wigs but then bethought himself, and they went together into the next bedroom and rummaged. They found a blonde one, very thick and wavy, something the first Mrs Wooly had worn with a Brunhild costume at a church recital twenty years before. They found a closetful of dresses left by Jennifer. These did not fit. They simply did not fit. Dr Mannix did not at once despair. Again he took recourse in deep meditation. He submerged, so to speak, but at last said: "Soapless! Unless you are somebody else you can't see her, but you can't be somebody else, so you can't see her: that's logic. You can't beat logic."

His despair served only to arouse a fighting spirit in the hitherto despairing Mr Wooly. He resorted to logic himself. "Not the only woman in the world," he said. "By no means. Right?"

"When you put it that way," Dr Mannix said carefully, "it's right."

"How else would you put it?" Mr Wooly asked him.

"What difference would it make?" countered the doctor.

"Well, that's another question," admitted Mr Wooly. "Very hard to say what difference it would make; I admit as much. Might not make any difference."

"Between what?" asked Dr Mannix.

"Between?"

"The difference," said Dr Mannix. "You can't have a difference between one thing. It's got to be at least two. Or then split the one thing, which amounts to the same thing. See what I mean?"

"Perfectly," Mr Wooly declared with enthusiasm. "Perfectly. That's how it is with you and me, Doctor, an easy, thorough understanding on the most obtruse subbics."

The word stopped the doctor, anxious as he was to share Mr Wooly's warm, intimate mood.

"Subbics?" he wondered.

"One or the other," Mr Wooly explained. "Take your Joyce. Sub or top."

"Sub or top?"

"Icks," said Mr Wooly with a very winning smile.

"You got hiccups," Dr Mannix said.

"And jects too!"

"Jects?" It missed the doctor.

Mr Wooly, too, was troubled. He sighed and frowned, gazed with a wide-eyed, joyless gaze upon his comrade, who, having just opened another one with a fine "pop" and losing some of it on the rug, exclaimed: "Whatsa madder?"

" 'S mystery," sighed Mr Wooly.

"What is?"

"The subbic. What are we talking about?"

"Don't know."

"Ought to."

"That's true," agreed the doctor. "I was going along fortified by the thought you knew. The subbic, I mean. You *ought* to know. You brought it up."

"I did not."

"You did."

"When?"

"Long ago," said Dr Mannix.

"How long ago? Muntz?"

Dr Mannix shook his head. "You aren't going to pin me down," he said. "Stick a pin through me and put me on exhibition! Nos sir!"

"Years?"

"Go on, threaten me; I won't budge."

Mr Wooly fell into a brown study. After a time: "Nightgowns!" Mr Wooly said, the word coming up like a sudden geyser from his subconscious, which had been, no doubt, busy all through this odd estrangement.

"Nightgowns?"

"No hard and fast frontiers," Mr Wooly explained.

"That's countries," objected Dr Mannix.

"Equatorially," Mr Wooly elaborated.

"Here?" asked the doctor, showing with his hands on his own meager person. "Why, of course. Absolutely right. Her fur coat! Chinchilla coat on rye."

"Brandy," objected Mr Wooly.

"Brandy," the doctor agreed. "You hear of bandy legs. You got brandy ones."

The doctor and Mr Wooly had now arrived at where

what they decided to do was the right thing to do, a wonderful realm wherein what they wanted to believe was ipso facto the truth itself. Before becoming completely stinko Dr Mannix and Mr Wooly had decided that Mr Wooly was to go find Betty Jackson and win from her a reconciliation, decorated with forgiveness, understanding and kisses. Now that they *were* completely stinko they were by themselves in their own world, wherein instead of a law of gravity there ruled this decision about Betty Jackson. That Mr Wooly should go disguised as Betty's aunt from Perth Amboy, the one with the gallstones, seemed not only sensible but inevitable. There was, however, this obstacle in the form of Mr Wooly's reluctance to wear skirts, particularly skirts that refused to come together at the waist. (He tried on a nightgown and said: "No!") It was such an enormous obstacle that for a time they couldn't see anything else, and then Dr Mannix had a revelation. Very simple, simple as that world-shaking simplicity, the placement of the eraser on the end of the pencil, or that other one, the placing of the eye of the sewing-machine needle in its point. "But we're overlooking something," yelped Dr Mannix. "Women themselves don't wear skirts, not very often. You want to wear pants? So do they! Wear 'em! That's the answer!"

Wooly was overwhelmed. "You are a genius," he said earnestly.

Dr Mannix looked into the last bottle. It was empty. He rang for Bentley and went into Mr Wooly's chamber when he heard Bentley's entrance. It had been Dr

Mannix' intention to order some more of the same. That thought Bentley, apparently, had caught with the ting of the bell that summoned him. Bentley brought a tray with bottles and bottles with everything, enough to drown Mr Wooly's terrifying new faculty for a week.

"The very thing, Bentley," Dr Mannix said. Bentley looked around, seeking his master.

"Mr Wooly went away," Dr Mannix said.

Here a figure entered from the door of the other bedroom. It was not a figure that seemed to please the fat-faced butler. He stared and began to shake all over. He made no other comment. The figure approached slowly. Even Dr Mannix, when he turned around to see what was scaring Bentley to death, gasped. Here was a woman in an old straw hat with curving green feathers moored firmly to her head by a black veil that was so thick it made a horrid mystery of all her face. She wore a chin-chilla coat (worth five thousand dollars) that reached to her knees, and below the coat appeared a pair of old flannel pants from which, in turn, peeped high-heeled patent-leather pumps. This female figure had an enormous southerly exposure, a figure which, associated with that hat, that veil, suggested she had wandered here from another age—when females had figures like that. She moved not only slowly but with a sort of billowy motion, like something seen in desert heat or under water. . . .

"Why, Mrs Wigglesworth!" exclaimed Dr Mannix, for that indeed was the name of Betty's aunt. "Bentley," he said sternly. "Open a bottle for Mrs Wigglesworth!"

With a courageous effort Bentley obeyed; then he

backed out of there. And the two madmen, grabbing for the icy glasses, heard how his feet scampered down the broad stairs in the incontinent pace of sheer, superstitious terror. They laughed the boisterous, carefree laugh of

men who are bereft of conscience, of all sense of decency. They laughed till tears poured down their cheeks. They congratulated each other; they emptied their glasses.

"You," Dr Mannix said with utter appreciation, "look horrible. Your veil slants down from the brim of your hat to the point of your chin and behind it. What did you do to your face? One can see it and one can't at the same time. Your eyes are like dark, shadowy pools."

"I fixed 'em up," Mr Wooly admitted. "With pencil."

"And your nose?" Dr Mannix said. "It is a dark, shadowy pool also."

"Musta smudged it."

"And your mouth is red as a rose! Look," warned Dr Mannix, "don't try to drink through that veil; raise it a bit, just above your mouth; that's perfect. You Jezebel! You look like the Apocalypse!"

Swanson seemed to think something like that too. And Cook and Bentley. They all, even Bella, contrived to get a glimpse of Mr Wooly's descent. He came slowly, carefully, not only because he was too full to tip but because his bandaged rear end was opposed to movement, because movement hurt it. One gloved hand on the marble balustrade, slowly, down he came, while from this door and that glinted eyes bright with a horrid fascination. How Mrs Wigglesworth had got in not one of them could guess. Bella morbidly suggested that she had been living in the attic for years. They were agreed about one thing and one thing only—that this mysterious appearance was of a piece with other recent events, irregular, indescribable—events that had no business in a respectable household. But what could they do? Uneasily, after the front door had closed behind Dr Mannix ("drunk as a coot," according to Cook) and Mrs Wigglesworth, the Wooly servants returned to their several tasks as best they could. But poor Swanson, he had to sit there in the driver's seat, a yard only from that creature in the veil, misshapen with holes for eyes and a hole for a nose behind that dreary veil and a mouth that was a smear of crimson. Swanson glanced into the rear-vision mirror and met that veiled, female death's-head and almost swooned right there. After the one glimpse Swanson didn't look again; he drove where he had been told to drive—to the door of the Hotel Dearborn; he heard the unregenerate, the scoun-drelly Dr Mannix boozily smack his lips (as he kissed his own hand, a fact Swanson did not note) and say: "Well, goo'-by, sweedheart, horribly nice to see you go, you frightful old squirt, you. Give my love to Hannibal; he's the clerk in there, baby doll. Don't do anything I wouldn't do."

The fraudulent Mrs Wigglesworth of Perth Amboy wobbled up the white stairs of the Hotel Dearborn, and Swanson drove Dr Mannix away toward the Mannix of-fice. As the doctor got out there he fell down but did not stay down. He was up at once, albeit leaning a bit heav-ily on the shocked Swanson, who had leaped to the rescue. "I was pushed," Dr Mannix declared, "and I can prove it."

Since there was no one in sight, the chauffeur had his doubts. "You were pushed," he said soothingly, however. "Tell me," he said, "who is Mrs Wigglesworth, if I may ask?"

"Who?"

"The—ah—lady we yust left at the hotel."

"What lady?" asked the doctor wonderingly. He closely inspected the chauffeur's unhappy face. "You been dring," Dr Mannix said, slowly wagging his head. "You been dring, my man." And with that he slanted across the walk and so into the door of his office, which was fortunately at street level and unlocked. He disappeared within.

Swanson took off his cap, scratched his wild hair. "Yumping Yeesus!" he said distinctly.

CHAPTER XVIII

The Old Adam in Madam

THERE WERE many disadvantages to the state our Mr
Wooly was in; there can be no denying. He did not walk
as well as he did normally, not as surely, accurately. His
optical faculty was not at its keenest. He was very hot.
His veins seemed filled with live steam; also, the hiccups
had returned to heckle him, exploding from time to time
like depth charges within him, making him too suddenly
stretch his neck straight upward, wobbling that green-
feathered hat. On the other hand, there were advantages
that more than offset these disadvantages. First of all, he
couldn't hear the thoughts of others. He didn't, indeed,
even have to notice the expressions on their blurry old
faces. Secondly, he hadn't a worry in the world. Not one.
Nor any shyness. Thirdly, he was brave as a lion. Two
lions. Hungry. Had Mr Wooly been sober and found
himself in that costume, there in the long pillared lobby
of the Dearborn Hotel, he would have dropped in a faint.
Or he would have fled headlong out into the street and
along the street, anywhere, nowhere, and so under some
strange porch like a frantic pup; as it was, he tacked
that way and then this, absorbed by the columns which
seemed to be ganging up on him. They parted as he headed
into them, only to gather their forces behind. A mile
away, or so it seemed, Hannibal, the clerk, a black-haired,

thin-headed gigolo, watched him sailing up. It was Mr
Wooly's impression that he watched through a telescope.
However, that was a mere notion. All of a sudden Mr
Wooly was there at the desk, practically nose to nose with
Hannibal.

"Good morning!" said Mr Wooly.

"Good afternoon," smirked the fellow.

Mr Wooly, motionless, stared at him. Nobody could
stand that veil, the dark holes of his grease-penciled eyes,
the curious fact that his nose, too, seemed more of a
depression than an obtrusion. Hannibal quailed.

"Don't contradict me, young man," said Mr Wooly.

"No, madam."

"And don't call me . . ." Mr Wooly remembered that
he was, in appearance, a woman and checked himself in
time. "Is Miss Betty Jackson in?" he asked.

"You are her aunt from Perth Amboy?" (It had been
agreed that Dr Mannix telephone the hotel from his office. He had.)

"Am, boy," answered Mr Wooly with a sudden giggle.
He slapped the fellow's hand to make sure that he got it.

"She is expecting you," said Hannibal, removing his
hand, keeping a watchful eye on the horror before him.
"She left word that she had gone into the Turkish bath
and you were to join her there. It is on the seventh floor."
He struck his desk bell: "Boy! Show Madam to the Turkish baths."

When events happen one after another under the direction of a personality that finds them reasonable—indeed,
inevitable—they are likely to go right on happening in the
expected order. . . . There was plenty of time for Mr

Wooly to back out. He was free; there was no law about
his going to the baths. He might have said that he was
allergic to everything and anything Turkish—towels, to-
bacco, carpets, harems, baths—and told that Hannibal
that he would wait in the waiting room. He might merely
have shoved the pasty-faced bellboy into the elevator
shaft where workmen were greasing something or other
and had left the doors half open. Or he could have
beaned him with a fire ax from that glass case. But Mr
Wooly merely followed the boy, rode with him to the
seventh floor.

"Get a load of this," the boy said to the elevator operator, and then as they shot upward, "Where 'd you get it,
sister?"

"What?" asked Mr Wooly.

"Oh, why don't you stop?" asked the boy.

It was beyond Mr Wooly. He decided to stare at the
horrid person before him, and that's what he did, moving
his mysteriously veiled face a few inches nearer, but
slowly, imperceptibly. "Who?" asked Mr Wooly in a deep
voice. "Who?"

"Heh, heh." The boy tried a polite laugh. It was a
ghastly imitation. Beads of sweat stood on his brow.

"Seventh floor," said the operator.

They got out. As best he could with the handicaps of
those high heels, that low bottom, Mr Wooly followed
after the fear-quickened bellboy. The door was opened.
Mr Wooly went in.

If he were thinking at all, which seems improbable, he
must have felt some relief at finding that in this outer
lobby all the females were dressed, attendants, clients

coming and going. A white-haired woman at a desk behind a grill called: "Right here, modom." Mr Wooly, who
had been standing, lost in the middle of the floor, went
toward this pleasant voice but, achieving the grill, merely
stood there slightly swaying. The silence between him and
the white-haired woman grew heavier as it lengthened.
Mr Wooly was not, however, idle. He was searching for
words, almost any sort of words, just so they would make
a sound and end this ordeal, but his words had flown; he
had been stripped of them as the maple of its leaves in
November. Mr Wooly, now in full realization of where he
had put himself, could only vainly wish that he were
somewhere else, anywhere else.

The eyes of the white-haired woman were not cen-
sorious, however, or even curious. She had not been born
yesterday. By no means. She had few illusions about the
superiority of her sex—at least in the matter of getting
stinko. She had seen all kinds and classes of females in all
kinds and classes of stinkodom. It did not surprise her
at all that the only salutation, comment, communication,
the heavily veiled, large-bottomed old horror before her
could make was: "Hic . . ."

This hiccup of Mr Wooly's was loud and curiously vio-
lent. His head rose on a momentarily lengthened neck. He
adjusted his green-feathered hat as best he could. He
saw that with an all-out effort he might be able to say
something like " 'Scuse me," but he was tired now. He let
it go and continued to stand there, blinking.

"You'll be right as rain by morning," said the white-
haired woman briskly, and she called "Alice" to a youngish female in starchy white. "Modom," said the white-

haired lady to Alice, "wants a private room, a bed; first she will have an electric cabinet, then a colonic."

"Certainly," said Alice briskly. "If you will follow me, modom."

"Better give Modom a hand, Alice," said the white-haired lady. "Modom seems very tired."

"Modom certainly is very—tired," Alice agreed, taking Mr Wooly's arm. "Never saw anybody tireder. If you will come this way, modom?"

As Mr Wooly was to remember this later, Alice now opened swinging doors, gently shoved Mr Wooly ahead of her into Dante's inferno, an unlimited room, filled with fogs and clouds, through which glided, soared, swam, women of various heights and shapes and ages, some with towels around their middles, some with towels over shoulders. Women were seated on benches, in chairs; through and beyond an arched doorway was another great room with more women. There was a babble of talk. Mr Wooly paused in his tracks to ponder a question he had put to himself: which were the most modest, those women who covered their breasts or those who covered their hips? It was a difficult question, for now he observed a further fact. Some who wore their upper figures with all their natural frank obtrusiveness had far more to conceal than those who concealed them. Before he could meditate further on this interesting matter Alice gave him a gentle but firm shove, saying, "This way, modom." They turned into some sort of passageway or cave (we are still seeing this as Mr Wooly remembered it), and presently Alice was opening one of a bank of narrow doors. In the cubicle beyond was a single bed, a stool, a

smell of antiseptic. "First," said Alice, "we will have the electric cabinet, then the colonic, then a shower; then we will sleep, and tomorrow Modom will feel rested and refreshed. Shall I help Modom to undress?"

Mr Wooly here found voice at last. "No," he said distinctly.

"I will go arrange the cabinet," Alice said. She went.

The cabinet was one of several, located down the passageway a few steps from Mr Wooly's door. What he thought while he undressed himself we do not know. We know from later happenings that he stripped to his shorts, clinging to this minimum of modest protection, and then, swathed in the terry-cloth wrapper he had been given, he scampered to the cabinet, which stood open, and popped into it, half closing it around himself. Centering the top surface of this box was a round hole for his neck. Within the box electric globes and a cushioned stool on which he sat. To sit was not pleasant, thanks to his wounds, but he sat. He was grateful for the concealment of the box, grateful that apparently no one had yet guessed his identity or his sex.

Alice came out of the mists and closed the box around him, adjusted the thermostat. Then she did a strange thing. She jumped backward several feet and exclaimed: "But, modom!"

Through his dark veil poor Mr Wooly gazed at her. Only his head was there. On the flat plate of the cabinet's topside—like a gift for Salome. But Mr Wooly's head was not so naked. In fact, upon it rested the blonde wig and upon the wig the hat with green curving feathers, and over all this the veil. It was a strange, a hideous, sight, the head all by itself, thus decorated. "But, modom!"

Mr Wooly, who for ten minutes now had been sliding earthward, said, "What?" though he well knew what was up.

"Your hat, your veil! Here, let me help you remove them."

"Thank you," Mr Wooly said. "But no."

"No!!"

"No! I always wear my hat and veil. Even in bed I wear them."

Alice looked about as if seeking reinforcement, as if determined to strip this head of all its covering. Mr Wooly was in utter panic. He did not know what to do.

He could not even pray. But God, Who is so partial to children, fools and drunks, must have struck into poor Mr Wooly's brain with His lightning. Inspiration came to Mr Wooly. He whispered: "Alice, please," and then as she bent her pink ear toward his veiled mouth, he whispered further: "I cannot remove my veil."

"Why not?"

"It is very difficult to say, you know."

"Yes, yes?"

"I haven't any nose," whispered Mr Wooly. "I blew my nose—off. There's only a hole where my nose is. I have a celluloid nose, but I lost it in a bar. I ought to be ashamed of myself!"

It worked like magic. Alice moved away from there at once, and from a distance of about two yards she signaled the imprisoned Mr Wooly—or rather his fantastic head—nodding, spanking the heated air with horizontal palms. "I . . . I," she exclaimed, "I quite understand." She fled. In her first frightened jump she had set the thermostat too high. She did not know this.

Mr Wooly grew hotter. Perspiration streamed from him. And now that happened which is difficult to relate because of one's natural sympathy for Mr Wooly. Had ever, in all the histories of this calvary we call life, anything so hideous, so torturing, ever happened to an innocent man—a more or less innocent man? There was Mr Wooly, imprisoned, only his hatted, bewigged and heavily veiled head visible to his fellow man—or fellow woman, rather—he had to stay there perforce, and yet, and yet, what with the heat, the curative effects of such copious perspiring, Mr Wooly was beginning the long descent

toward sobriety, utter sobriety. With sinking heart he
saw it coming and could do nothing to fend it off. How
hold onto a binge, by what handles? He tried to do it by
mental power alone, but the more he thought the more
sober he became. He told himself that this growing sobriety was itself a drunken illusion, but then proof stirred
in that inner ear of his. Thoughts not his own came into
his mind, interlopers against which he was helpless.

These thoughts came from a blonde woman who had
sat herself, back to Mr Wooly, on a bench near by. She
was one whose ideas about modesty were not hemispheri-
cal, so to speak, but equatorial. Her thought was quick
and singularly direct, having a tone of appalling, heartless
cynicism. "Good lord, look at that one. She ought to stay
in hiding; if mine hung like that I'd have them tied in
simple, tasteful knots." Apparently she was thinking
about some passing woman who, because of the jutting
wall there, was invisible to Mr Wooly. "Knock-kneed,
too," went on the blonde's thinking, "but she got a man.
. . . Wedding ring on her. A man will marry anything.
Crocodile, kangaroo. God I'm hot . . . and clean. I feel
. . . If I called Bert . . . but wouldn't Henry just put
it that way? Maybe he'll come home today, maybe tomorrow, so a lady don't know from minute to minute what
she can do. Of course I could go to Bert's apartment . . .
but that doorman and people going by, too risky. . . .
But I wish I could. I'll give Henry leg of lamb, mashed
potatoes and some kind of pink jello; he hates lamb, but
that's unreasonable. . . . You aren't supposed to hate
lamb; nobody is. Better than no husband though. I didn't
do badly, hundred and twenty-five a week he makes—I

wouldn't know how. What's the matter with businessmen? They hire a moron like him and pay him real money;
I never could get it, so it 'll be lamb and you'll like it,
Henry. . . . If he only wouldn't talk so much and if
he only would sleep in his own bed. . . . God, his idea
of love! Sometimes I can hardly stop myself from telling
him about Bert, and I used to think if it was a man it
was a man, as if they weren't as different as day from
night. Six of one? My eye. Dozen of another, and it's personality too. I wonder what Henry would think if he
knew Judge Bert Gilead was my boy friend, and for
Henry being so unappreciative as to leave such a wife all
alone by her lonesome he ought to have six months in
jail, and Bert is going to give him a month for speeding,
anyway. What we can't do in a month! Calling me 'Honey
Pot,' and with his beard more like the Supreme Court or
a general or I wouldn't say what, so crinkly. That goat
we saw driving reminded me of Bert. After knowing Bert
I'll always have tender feelings for goats, I suppose. . . .
There's Betty Jackson. Who is she looking for, I wonder,
her boss or somebody? He isn't likely to be here, Betty
old girl."

Now she spoke aloud. Dimly Mr Wooly saw his ex-
secretary. She was dressed and apparently taking a last
look round before leaving. "No," said the blonde, "I
didn't see your aunt, and I wouldn't know her if I saw
her, darling."

"She's a little thing with red hair, and she wears
glasses," Betty said.

Mr Wooly heard the clashing, indistinct confusion of
their thoughts against a background of the wider murmur

of more distant thinking. He was now sober. His mind was open to everybody's. He had never in his life been so troubled in mind and in body. The latter was being slowly cooked. He felt his very life streaming from his open pores. He wanted to get out of there, but what could he do?

Betty looked toward him, appearing momentarily around the jutting wall by the bench where "Honey Pot" lounged. Betty stared and, seeing for the first time the horrendous sight of the veiled head of Mr Wooly, one fair hand flew to her mouth but too late to stifle a piercing scream. This scream brought the attention not only of "Honey Pot" but of a dozen or so other clients out of the baths. From a good distance they stared at the weird sight provided by Mr Wooly. He heard their murmured comments, the blurred sound (as of the voices of a mob at a public hanging) rising and falling.

Mr Wooly heard a voice say: "I don't believe it," and another: "Has it got green feathers and a veil? Then you do, too, believe it, because I see it, and it's there."

"Where 'd it come from?"

"Who is it?"

"God have mercy on us."

"I come here for my nerves because I'm so nervous. Well, I don't intend to come back. I'll sue 'em. I been set back months. Call the manager! Call the police! Call somebody!" The voices mounted to a single soprano hullabaloo, and all Wooly could do was stare back at them, wrestling with his horrible state. He was being roasted alive—that is to say, steamed alive, like a pot of spinach, like a lobster. He felt like a lobster, like a lobster in a golden wig, a hat with curling green feathers and a blinding black veil. He could no longer communicate with that Mr Wooly who had considered this little excursion of great importance and devastating wit. He thought of his friend—Dr Mannix, that decayed old souse—and for the first time since that Saturday way back at prep school in the fall of 1915 when he had said, "Damn it all," Mr Wooly swore, damning the covey of females there at the end of the narrow room, squawking like so many hens. . . . He cursed them as swearword-swearwords, these terms bubbling up promptly to his service, proving that he had sometime, somewhere, actually heard them, had noted them down on the imperishable tablets of his subconscious. He said them aloud courageously, but they were not heard since the swearword-swearwords themselves were too busy cackling and squeaking and yelping to listen. Enraged, forgetting the presence among them of his lovely and sensitive darling, Betty Jackson, Mr Wooly got the veil off his chin by the simple device of scraping said chin on the top of his box, and so, his mouth free and naked, he extended from it as much of his tongue as he could manage. He waggled it at them. Under different circumstances it might have seemed more absurd than anything else; had they all been under ten years of age it might have seemed supportable and even natural, but as it was it was a sight of such meaningless, psychopathological, eccentric—nay, supernatural—horror, all the girls fell back as before a blast from a bomb and together said "Ohhh" and "Ooooo," forgetting their absurd towels, standing shamelessly naked, fat-limbed, thin-limbed, raising their ineffectual paws, dying of shock, the sensitive innocents, but not going away from there—not one, certainly not! Mr Wooly withdrew his tongue. "Bla-a-a-a," he said, thus in one word summing up his whole opinion of their figures, their sex, their present foolish actions.

Silence descended.

A fat black-haired one declared in a tone of voice infuriatingly angelic: "You should be ashamed of yourself, madam, to come here disgracefully, lewdly intoxicated, shocking young girls!"

"Young girls!" shouted Mr Wooly, beside himself. "Ha! Ha! You, you"—he sought for the name of something he despised thoroughly and found it—"you fat old bowl of custard," he shouted. "And don't show your teeth at me." He had noticed that she had very white, large teeth —teeth she was proud of—so with the worst of his suppressed nature again rising to complete expression, he sneered: "Yellow teeth! Corncob teeth!"

You can tell a woman her virtue is imaginary, that her brains are soup, that the location of her hips is too near the ground, that her eyes are crossed or wall, that the gray is showing in her hair or even that she is in danger of growing bald, and all you may get is a superior, tolerant smile; but tell her that her teeth are yellow and you invite your own destruction; they cannot take it. Only dimly had Mr Wooly's intuition seen this; he was surprised at the success of his terrible jibe; so was everybody else, including Alice, that attendant, who now came on the scene at a fast dogtrot. But Alice arrived only in time to see the fat black-haired woman charge the head of Mr Wooly. There was no battle, of course, not any more battle than there could have been between a nervous cabbage striving to keep its roots in the ground and a famished cow. She peeled Mr Wooly's head with amazing speed. It was easier than pulling the outer leaves off the cabbage. One yank at the hat and it, the yellow wig, the black veil, all together, came instantly off, and there he was, Mr Wooly, or the pathetic, wild-eyed head of him, smudged with rouge and mascara, defenseless, foolish.

"A man!" howled some female ass.

"Mr Wooly," screamed Betty.

The box had been opened, and from thence he was dragged, slapped, pushed, sent headlong toward his bedroom in his pathetic shorts, his fish-belly legs with their wiry *décor* of black hairs. What a sight! As if they were the myrmidons of the Ogpu and he the last of the Romanoffs caught adding arsenic to a commissar's caviar, they flung him into his dungeon so that he fell upon the stone floor. Crash! His door closed behind him.

CHAPTER XIX

The Trial before Judge Bert Gilead

JUDGE BERT GILEAD knew, of course, before he left his residence that his first case this Tuesday morning would be that of Mr T. Wallace Wooly. He knew it but—and here he was in agreement with most of the population of Warburton—he found it difficult to believe that Mr T. Wallace Wooly had actually been arrested disguised as a woman in the Turkish bath of the Hotel Dearborn. Giving his iron-gray bifurcated beard a last combing before the mirror in the hall, Judge Gilead said as much to his wife. "Bertha," he said, "Chief Williams says they say he did, but I don't believe it. In the first place, our ideal citizen, our number-one civic inspiration, never even thought of an improper thing in his life and, in the second place, if he did he wouldn't have the enterprise to put it into effect."

His wife, who was in the living room, replied: "One might think from your tone of voice that not having indecent thoughts is something to be ashamed of. Enterprise, is it? It takes no enterprise to be bad, Bertie; the path of iniquity is broad and smooth: you just let go and slide."

Judge Gilead let his thought briefly review his most recent iniquity—the good book, the flowers, the long, boring conversations on elevated topics, the fifty-mile

drives to see double features that bored him until all the
hairs on his head and chin seemed to be growing inward,
the cautious hand holding, the kiss that had to be under-
taken as if it were something else, the dinner with wine
in Manhattan, the bracelet. And so to bed. Judge Gilead
thought all this much more like climbing an Alp than
descending a chute the chutes. It was on the tip of his
tongue to say that she didn't know what she was talking
about, that successful sin, also, alas, took character, perseverance, strategy, but another thought crossed this one,
and he said to his invisible wife: "How true, my dear!
How well you put it!"

"And as for Mr Wooly," she said, "how do we know
he hasn't been leading a double life for years? Instead
of mourning his poor wife, what does he do? Carouses in
public bars; that's what he does. And look at that secretary of his, Betty What's-her-name."

"What's the matter with her?"

"She's too pretty to be just a secretary. Besides that,
he's just coming into the age."

"What age?"

"Of peek, pinch and leer," said his wife. "But the fifties
are nastier."

"Good God!" The judge was genuinely shocked. "Where
do you get such ideas?"

"You're such an innocent, Bertie," she said softly.
"You're *so* naïve." She came to the door now, a medium-
sized, middle-aged female in a gray tweed suit, brown hair
braided and wreathed round her head, her thin face chilled
by an expression of sardonic intellectuality. She directed
shows at the Warburton Little Movement Theater, was

secretary of the Dramatic Revolters, Inc., or, as the judge in secret called them, the revolting dramatists. She was (unknowingly) in this moment playing a role that is usually a forbidden expression in our American civilization—the role, that is, of a female pighead, an opinionated ass in petticoats, though God knows there are enough of her. The unwritten law, woven so pervasively in the fabric of our *mœurs* that we hardly realize it is there, is not that fair woman is good or pure or anything of the sort. You may impugn her character, even her appearance (except her teeth)—and that is passed by the invisible censor who holds final and absolute veto power in all publications, all theaters, all radio and picture studios—but you may not ever impugn her "intuition," that is to say, her instinctive, natural, inalienable right to intellectual superiority. The American woman in American literature *always* knows more, is more cunning, more sophisticated, more subtle, than her husband—never mind who he is, what he does. . . .

Why Judge Gilead married Bertha, his wife, I do not know. I have not the least idea. To begin with, she had no bosom, and if I were given the choice of marrying either a—let me see—say a Peking duck or a woman without a bosom, I would plump for the duck, so to speak. Perhaps Judge Gilead himself did not know why he married his wife, that flat and bony creature with the slightly inflamed nostrils, the nervous brain. But then who, of observers, of participants, knows anything about matrimony's motivations? For all we know marriage is indeed ordained in heaven—by a deity with one of those private, dead-pan senses of humor. . . .

It was Mrs Gilead's fond illusion that her husband's temperature reading hovered around that of a normal, medium-sized fish's because of his attitude toward her. This, of course, is a perfect example of the working of female intuition. "He lusts not for me; therefore, he is indifferent to feminine charms, the worm," as the Finnish folk poet has it.

Judge Gilead, as a matter of historic fact, used his position, his really fine mind, his money, whatever strength he could muster, in a constant hunt for young and bosomy companions. He got in beard and all where better-looking, wittier, more charming but less earnestly persevering and responsible hunters failed. It was not only that his approach was gradual and on an exalted plane—that he could, for instance, test the silkiness of silk and make this seem like a profound comment on the infinite, rather than a mere animal scrabbling about for an animal objective— no, it was that he took all responsibility. The absurdity, the humiliation, the moral guilt, was not merely shared by our Judge Gilead in his many peccadilloes; it was all his. *All.* His newest, youngest darling, abandoned to her reminiscent and solitary couch, was left not only content, so that her veins coursed gentle music, but was left also— a guiltless victim. What could be sweeter in this vale of cause and effect and inexorable time? Echoes answer what?

So Mrs Gilead, his wife of these twelve years, came out into the hall and smiled her superior, sardonic smile on the innocent, bearded child. There were times that she found it within herself to wish that he were more ardent, less a cool-blooded child, but after all, who had perfection in matrimony, anyway? She had, like Honey Pot, done, she admitted to herself, fairly well.

"You are so learned," she said to her husband now. "And you know so little of the world: how charming."

He brushed her brow lightly with his two-pointed beard, and now belatedly he noticed that she wore her hat—or rather her cap—a blue beret. Very aesthetic and intellectual. "Where are you going?" he asked.

"To court," she said.

He looked his surprise.

"Do you think I would miss Mr Wooly's hearing? How little you know of women!"

As has been said, Bertha Gilead was no heroine for a woman's magazine or radio serial, either. She was a pighead. She knew all. She knew she did. Thus her face, her walk, her tone of voice and choice of words.

"Very well," said Judge Gilead, little knowing what that hearing held in store for him.

The court was at the back on the first floor of City Hall, the new brick colonial-style building in the Civic Center. It was new, but it was old, for all courtrooms are old. The grinning, crippled dwarf hobbles through them the first day and they are, presto chango, old. She, the dwarf, is man's justice. She carries with her a hand mirror so that she may gaze upon her own hideous features from time to time but never with understanding, only with self-satisfied smirks. Justice! But thou shalt not judge! The prohibition is laid down flatly, without equivocation. Thou shalt *not*. Yet here sits man judging between—between what? Between that which is not comparable. Comparing ostriches with minnows, blaming both for the lack of what the other has! "Thou, croco-dile, why singest thou not? Observe the canary, with a mouth, so much smaller than thine, hear how he sings, how sweetly! And thou! Ten years in prison, crocodile!"

The courtroom had a municipal smell. This is also the smell of government in all parts of this planet, a smell commingled of the smells of cement, of chloride of lime, of human sweat, of dusty books, of an impersonal lassi-tude—the smell of life that has momentarily stopped. Twenty thousand learned volumes may be written to prove that to live governmentally, to give all choice and, in the name of its preservation, dear liberty herself, to government is the best, not to say the only way; and yet one good normal set of nostrils applied to the task of judg-ing the municipal smell can report: "Rotten" and "Evil."

To Judge Gilead his job was his job. Had he believed in justice he would long since have left his bench. But he was not a bad man. He did not hate his fellows. On the contrary. So he equated his own security with his instinc-tive, cynical desire to free every culprit brought before him, save only those caught in cruelties to children and animals—crimes which made him frantic. For the rest he only saw himself out of luck.

His desk was on a platform at one end of the court-room. He came to it through his own door. His wife, he noted, was seated already in the middle of the front row. The people were already in place.

A policeman shouted something or other, and every-body stood up, then sat down again as Judge Gilead sat down. The judge read a paper laying before him. He looked at Chief Williams and said, "Well?"

"Charley White," said Williams. Charley White, a dreary, lonesome drunk stood up and gazed at the judge, who mumbled something about vagrancy, resisting an officer, and so on. Guilty? "Guilty," Charley White said. "Thirty days," said Judge Gilead. "Suspended. Go on home, Charley. Your faithful wife awaits you."

"That's what I'm afraid of, Judge," Charley said. Charley was not new to this court. "Thanks, Judge," he said.

"Go away," Judge Gilead told him. "Next?"

There were some traffic cases; a couple of skinny boys, dazed from a night in the lockup, which was in the cellar of this building, contended that in borrowing the car of their neighbor they had meant no harm and were returning it when arrested.

They were lectured and released. Judge Gilead, so the clerk, the police, the hangers-on noticed, was not at his humorous best this morning. Maybe because Mrs Gilead was sitting there smack in front of him, keeping her eye peeled; maybe because in contrast with the Wooly case all else was small potatoes.

Mr Wooly sat in the front row, too, next to a policeman. From time to time Judge Gilead glanced at Mr Wooly with the expression of a man who is trying to believe his eyes. They had known each other for years. They belonged to the same organizations, including the fire department, but nothing the judge had known about Mr Wooly had prepared him for the scandal of the Turkish baths. Of course there was that rescue of the second Mrs Wooly, before she was the second Mrs Wooly, from the Hotel Monroe, and there was the now-current story of how tight Mr Wooly had got himself at the

Marlborough, but as had so many others, the judge had thought Mr Wooly's lifelong sobriety had cracked under the strain of sudden grief, and he had defended Mr Wooly against the sneers of his wife and other intolerant critics.

"Henry Tiddle," said Judge Gilead, getting on with it. (Mr Wooly's case would be next.)

Henry Tiddle stood up. He straightened out his various joints carefully, as if fearful that a more abrupt adjustment would result in serious dislocations. He started talking at once: "Judge," he said, "I wasn't doing more than forty miles an hour, and all at once this snot nose Ferdy Lyons——"

"You mean Officer Lyons?" asked Judge Gilead.

"Now you know who I mean, Judge; we were all boys together," Henry Tiddle said. "Ferdy Lyons. O.K., he comes up and says I am driving too fast. . . ."

"What's the matter with your car?" Judge Gilead asked him mildly.

"Nothing," Henry Tiddle said. "It's practically brand new."

"And you were doing seventy."

"Well, I was doing maybe fifty-five."

"Where were you going when Officer Lyons stopped you?"

"Straight home," Henry said virtuously. "Like an arrow."

Judge Gilead looked over at Officer Lyons. "What's your version?" he asked confidently.

"He was tearing along at better than seventy-five miles an hour, your honor, and lit up like a sign. I ast him what the so-and-so was up; do you see? He answered fresh as paint that's what he was going to find out. So when I ast him to esplain himself he wouldn't. So I ast him was he going to a fire? He said that's where he was going—to a fire. And she's six feet tall," he says.

Judge Gilead looked concerned. His eye ran along the front row, skimmed over the intent intellectual face of his wife, paused a moment when they met the large brown eyes belonging to Mr Wooly. Mr Wooly looked dazed. He was. His own thoughts would have been sufficient to fill his mind this morning, but he had also the thoughts of everyone within thought-shot of him all mixed up. He was mentally deafened, as one might auricularly be deafened in a boiler shop going full blast. His head felt like a telephone exchange with all messages mixed together into one set of earphones. . . . Nevertheless, his mind picked up and understood one thought, apparently originating in the mind of the judge himself, and this thought was: "Honey Pot is not six feet tall, not more than five ten. . . . Wonder where she is this minute. Probably in bed, thinking. . . . Imagine this odd specimen, this damp scarecrow, being her husband, sharing her. . . ." It faded out of Mr Wooly's mind, and for a time there was only confusion there; then, glancing along that front row, meeting the eyes of Mrs Gilead, he received another fragment—hers: "Just like Bert's innocence to let the man go with a mere reprimand. . . . Oh, Bert, be a man, be stern, be just. . . ."

Mr Wooly's troubles were so many, so complicated, that for once in his timid spirit a low craftiness stirred. He remembered Honey Pot, that tall blonde, remembered her lewd and nefarious meditations as he had received them in his own mind while being cooked in that electric cabinet. He realized that Judge Gilead, this honored fellow citizen of his, was about to sentence the husband he'd outwitted and dishonored to a month in the jail so that he, the judge, might more conveniently continue his intrigue with the man's wife. It came to Mr Wooly that Judge Gilead would want no part of this low conspiracy to be brought to the attention of the community, not to mention his wife and Honey Pot's Henry. But what good would any of this do Mr Wooly himself unless Judge Gilead knew Mr Wooly knew all?

"Tiddle," said Judge Gilead, leaning forward a little, using a solemn tone of voice, "Warburton has suffered too much of late from reckless drivers. You say you were speeding home—and at nine o'clock in the evening. If you had told me, Tiddle, that you were speeding away from home, say to some night spot to go on carousing, I would have been inclined to credit your story in this and all its other details, but as you have related it your story lacks credible motivation, Tiddle. First place, you were somewhat stimulated, to say the least. In the second place, it was early in the evening; in the third place, you were speeding homeward. Why? To exhibit your deplorable condition to your wife as something of which to be proud, like an increase in salary or a wreath of laurel just awarded your laudable head by the sales manager? Come, Tiddle, why were you rushing homeward?"

Tiddle stood there silent, uncertain, burning up. Mr Wooly heard the busy Tiddle thought. "Why was I racing home like an arrow? Because I was two days ahead of time, and I meant to find out once and for all how she spends her evenings while I'm on the road working myself to death. . . . I was rushing to find out who in hell is this here Bertie she talks about in her sleep, but how can I say that out in court about my own wife?"

Meanwhile Judge Gilead, reflectively stroking that divided beard of his, thoughtfully shook his head. His eyes wandered from contemplation of his victim, met Mr Wooly's, and the latter heard the judicial train of thought clearly for a minute or two: "Tiddle, my friend, it's a shame to do it, but somehow in this world the only way to treat Tiddles is the way I'm going to treat you. . . . Because I'm the malefactor here I have less than no sympathy for you, Tiddle, much less. What a face, to be sure, what a face; like the south end of a picked chicken, Tiddle, except that hasn't snaggleteeth. Out of my sight, thou cuckold. . . ." As he thought these criminal and heartless thoughts Judge Gilead looked the picture of virtue.

Judge Gilead opened his mouth. He spoke: "Thirty days," said the beamish monster.

Tiddle staggered under that blow. He exclaimed: "You can't do that to me, Judge."

"Oh yes, I can, Mr Tiddle," said Judge Gilead. "And what's more," with a smile, "I get paid for it." There was a murmur of wolfish laughter from the craven spectators, delighted to see a meek and uxorious sucker get what was coming to him.

"But my wife!" cried Mr Tiddle. "What will she do?"

Again a wave of unkind, fang-bared laughter from Tiddle's fellow citizens.

"Order, order," said Judge Gilead. "Next case. Ah, Mr Wooly," he said, pretending to read this from the printed docket on his desk before him. Apparently he had forgotten Mr Tiddle, who with unconcealed reluctance was being escorted toward a side door and his long incarceration.

"Well, well, Mr Wooly," sighed Judge Gilead. His fans licked their lips. The judge pointed his beard at the tall scholarly figure of Chief Williams. "Arresting officer? No notation here, chief."

"The entire force, your honor," Chief Williams said dryly. "All six of us."

"H'm twelve counts," murmured the judge, reading them over. "Appearing in public disguised as a woman. . . ." He shook his head. "Very serious."

"On the contrary," said Mr Wooly, "very funny." His tone was sharp and indicated that woebegone as he might look Mr Wooly's appalling adventure had not brought him the boon of true repentance. Judge Gilead, surprised and wounded, gazed down upon Mr Wooly. "You will stand," he said, "and you will not address this court unless you are directed so to do."

Mr Wooly stood. It had come to him that the countersign, the key word, the open sesame, was in his possession. All he need do, as with the old magics, was say the potent word, then locked doors would swing wide, the great and powerful bow low before him. The word, of course, was Honey Pot. Had ever a mature man, a bearded man, hit upon a sillier word than that with which to crown his ladylove? Oh yes, many and oft, Mr Wooly said to himself. He was in a sardonic mood. His opinion of mankind and the world was not high. He looked down on both in unsmiling derision. Moreover, he had a hang-over again.

It was not a nice hang-over. But it was a different hang-over than that first one—yesterday's. That one was a wolf; today's seemed somehow more familiar. Like a detested relative who'd come to visit, rather than an alien and hostile invader. It was hard to keep his own thoughts disentangled from the mental hullabaloo that flowed into his mind from judge, policemen and spectators. He felt bitterly about this, about everything.

Judge Gilead gazed at him with moody dignity for a long moment, then returned to the list of Mr Wooly's crimes. "Drunk and disorderly, resisting officer," he murmured, "lewd and lascivious . . . assault and battery . . ." and so on. As he concluded he returned his gaze to Mr Wooly.

"Jack the Ripper," said Mr Wooly with bitter scorn. "Peeping Tom, Bluebeard."

Judge Gilead seemed to ponder. "Your defiant attitude, Mr Wooly, will not help your case, I'm afraid. Have you counsel?"

"I'll need no counsel."

Judge Gilead looked away from him with obvious distaste. "How does the prisoner plead?" he asked Williams.

The chief raised his shoulders and looked at Mr Wooly.

"Guilty?" Judge Gilead asked.

"Not," Mr Wooly said, "by the hairs on your chinny chin-chin."

"I don't think that is necessary."

"Neither do I! I'd have 'em all shaved off if I were you. For years I've wondered what you were hiding."

Judge Gilead raised his eyebrows and his voice: "Mr Wooly!"

"And tell me when and how a man decides to part his beard in the middle, for heaven's sake!"

"It grew that way," Judge Gilead said, a look of anxiety stealing into his eyes.

"I doubt that," Mr Wooly said with studied malice. "I think you did it on purpose."

"I can prove it. My wife, who is sitting right there, will testify that it grew that way, and all I did was give it only the slightest brush this way and that to confirm a natural tendency."

"Your wife," sneered Mr Wooly.

"What's the matter with my wife?"

"How do I know? As a wife I suppose you'll contend she has all sorts of things the matter with her, but I don't want to hear about them. Understand? Not a word."

The judge tried to speak, but Mr Wooly plunged onward. "You, a judge! Great Scott, not even knowing that you cannot call a man's wife to testify against him."

Judge Gilead was silenced. He looked pleadingly at Chief Williams. He beckoned to him, and that tall man stepped up to the judge's high desk and for a minute they were in whispered tête-à-tête.

"When you two are through muttering in Judge Gilead's beard," Mr Wooly said, "perhaps we can resume the trial of this case."

"There is something you forget, Mr Wooly," Judge Gilead said as Chief Williams returned to his previous stance by the window, "and that is . . ."

"Yes?"

"That I am not on trial here, but you *are!* See the difference?"

That silenced Mr Wooly.

Judge Gilead smiled. He said: "I think you do not realize the seriousness of your situation here, Mr Wooly. It seems to me to be a case for the higher court."

He gazed at Mr Wooly. Mr Wooly gazed at him. Mr Wooly had the advantage of his unnatural talent. He could hear what the judge was thinking. It jumped all over the place, Judge Gilead's train of thought; scenting triumph, it had a scornful word or two for the always deluded intuition of his wife sitting there before him, knowing nothing of Honey Pot; it ran panting to Honey Pot, imagining her again reclining—ah, she was a woman that should never waste her strength, her talents, in mere aimless trudging about. Let her remain there, on her back. Ah yes. . . . And the judge's thought considered Wooly, naming him mad as a hatter. Better hold him for the Superior Court. The little man seemed to have blown up. Gone right off his chump after all these purposeful, exemplary years. . . .

"Mr Wooly," said Judge Gilead softly.

"Yes, Honey Pot?" said Mr Wooly, just as softly.

The most inward inwardness of this terrible event was expressed by the eyeballs of Judge Gilead. He peeled both of them as thoroughly as he could. He used them to give the anterior brain as clear an image as possible of Mr Wooly. After a time his vocal cords got into play. "What?"

"Honey Pot," repeated Mr Wooly heedlessly, shamelessly. But after all, he was fighting for his freedom. He did not smile at his adversary.

Chief Williams, completely in the dark, looked from

judge to defendant. He approached Mr Wooly, whispered: "Don't you want counsel?"

"No," said Mr Wooly. "I would like to speak to the judge. Privately."

"Go up to his desk," said the chief.

Mr Wooly did so.

"Yes?" said Judge Gilead in a low—nay, a pleading-– voice. "Yes?"

"Judge," said Mr Wooly, "I read minds. Never mind how or why, but I do. Never mind even believing this. But just consider the fact that I know Honey Pot well; indeed, I have bathed with her. She is the wife of Mr Tiddle, the little man you have just sentenced to thirty days so that you may spend thirty nights with his wife, your Honey Pot. You dirty dog."

Judge Gilead slewed around his crafty, greenish eyeballs to check on Mr Wooly's facial expression. What he caught was not reassuring, it seemed. He sighed.

Mr Wooly continued: "Your wife thinks you are an innocent child, bearded withal, but a child. It is not Mr Tiddle's plight that most wrings my heart, Judge Gilead, though I do feel for him, you understand, and will certainly contrive to express my sympathy and my confidence in his complete innocence, explaining why I feel this way, of course; no, it is the plight of Mrs Gilead that most attracts the pulsations of my pitying heart."

"Yes, yes?" sighed Judge Gilead.

"Your life, I think, would be quite changed, would it not, once Mrs Gilead knew what I know about Honey Pot?"

The question, sheer rhetoric at best, and no more sin-

cere than the evilest efforts of the blackmailer, the extor-
tionist, expressed very well the depth to which Mr Wooly
had fallen, thanks to his mistaken marriage, his sinful device for avoiding the rigors of that curse his wife had
placed upon him.

He put the question to Judge Gilead, painful as it must
have been to him, without a qualm, without a thought
of sympathy for the poor bearded fellow before him.

"I can read you like a book," he went on, whispering,
grinning. "A filthy book. With pictures. Shall I tell you
what you thought about Honey Pot just before you sentenced her husband?"

"No," whispered Judge Gilead. He raised his head,
spoke to the courtroom: "Certain matters of importance
have just been brought to my attention," he said. "Court
will recess for thirty minutes." There was a murmur, the
sound of scraping chair legs, the pound of swinging doors,
as the citizens straggled out into the hallway.

"Come into my chambers," Judge Gilead said. "And
you, also, chief," looking at Chief Williams.

"Better send him home," Mr Wooly said, and he added
without waiting for any corroboration from the judge,
"Good-by, George."

The chief accepted this dismissal. It was plain now that
the situation was in the hands of Mr Wooly.

There was a desk, couch, cupboard, in the judge's chamber. Mr Wooly stretched himself out on the couch. He
did his best to enter a serious and fruitful conversation
with the judge, but the judge's confused thoughts confused everything. The judge was thinking about his wife,
his bank account, his Honey Pot and other things, all

more or less at once. Mr Wooly found this wearisome. He said: "Judge Gilead, when I am sober as I am now, and particularly when I am suffering from the effects of a previous night, as I am now, I am open to the thoughts of others. I hear everything you are thinking as I heard the thoughts of Honey Pot. You may say all the words of incredulity that you can think up, but you might better save your breath to cool your soup, for I will in the end prove to you that I can, indeed, hear the thoughts of others. At this moment, for instance, you are thinking— I do not enjoy sharing this with you, I must say, but I cannot help it—of the peach-pink scanties, I believe they are called, that you bought for Honey Pot; really, Judge, what an expression of endearment, what an absurd, un- dignified locution it is, to be sure. Honey Pot! As I was saying, you were thinking about these peach bloom————"

"Spare me," Judge Gilead said. "I am quite ready to grant that you can read my mind. Can you read it when you are not sober?"

"Not at all," said Mr Wooly.

The judge favored him with a beseeching look. "I beg your pardon?" he said. "I thought you said, 'Not at all.'"

"And so I did," Mr Wooly assured him impatiently.

"I have some Scotch," Judge Gilead said.

"Are you?" asked Mr Wooly politely.

Was Mr Wooly merely trying to be difficult? That was the question Judge Gilead asked himself. He peered at the man. He said, holding his temper in leash as best he could: "I mean whisky."

"Oh!" cried Mr Wooly. "Why did you not say so at first?"

So it was brought forth. This has become a straight-out immoral tale, alas, but then the plight Mr Wooly was in was immoral. It was unnatural. It was undermining. His life had come to be that of some crazy tightrope walker, on that side hang-over, on this side the horror of having to listen in to the thoughts of his fellows. Here, wisdom —there, wild nonsense and obfuscation. What a choice!

"Smells," Mr Wooly said as Judge Gilead squirted soda into the whisky, "like disinfectant. What do you do with it—rub it on?"

"You drink it," Judge Gilead said.

Mr Wooly raised his glass, applied his lips, drank. "It tastes like it smells," he observed. "I suppose one gets used to that?"

"One does."

"Prefer bourbon," Mr Wooly said ungraciously. "Or a good brandy. Have you any champagne?"

"Sorry." The judge looked contrite. His eyes wandered.

"Stop thinking about Honey Pot."

The judge started. The unhaired portions of his cheeks grew pink; his blush rose out of the bush as a sunrise in Africa.

"While you were sentencing poor Tiddle," Wooly went on, "it was disgusting to hear your thoughts about Honey Pot in bed—stretching her legs. By the way, the woman has the normal complement of other limbs and features. Why always think of her fair ankle, her dimpled knee?"

"Please, I beg of you," gasped Judge Gilead.

"I beg you to keep your lecherous, libidinous thoughts to yourself."

"God sakes!" cried Judge Gilead, tortured. "I am try-ing to. Won't you have another?"

Mr Wooly downed it. "One thing about this," he de-clared, "it certainly tastes like medicine. Brandy doesn't, you know. Brandy tastes as if it were designed for drink-ing rather than taking." He winced at another mental invasion from Judge Gilead's seething mind. "Why don't you get off Honey Pot?"

"I beg your pardon," said Judge Gilead. "I'm doing my best."

"Let's sing something. When I sing loudly enough noth-ing comes through, and if you'd join me . . ."

The judge looked unenthusiastic about this. He said he couldn't sing in key and didn't like to sing, anyway.

"But there you go thinking about her again! So you bought and presented to her the peach-blow scanties. Why linger over them? Please remember," Mr Wooly said, "that I can hear every thought you think; they are formed; they make their vibrations, and these vibrations ringing outward through the protons, the ether, or what have you, pour into my mind, and I wish they wouldn't. You might try to remember that while you think of Honey Pot you have this advantage over me—you're not able to see your own bearded, leering face, while I have to look at it! It is"—he sought for a word—"too much."

"I'll sing," cried Judge Gilead wildly. "I'll sing!"

"Generally I sing 'The Star-Spangled Banner,' but that may be too high for you. How about 'Santa Lucia'?"

Judge Gilead nodded miserably. He looked very un-happy, very unlyrical. They sang.

"La, la, la, lalala, in something sleeping . . .
Bright is the summer sea, summer sea silver bright,
Santa Lucia, San . . . ta . . . Lu . . . cheee . . . yah. . . ."

Mr Wooly shook his head. "Louder," he urged. "Louder!"

So they sang louder and filled the judge's chambers with their voices.

The public lingering in the hallways submissively heard the weird sounds emanating from the judge's chambers. Mrs Gilead heard them. They and she wondered.

Betty Jackson in navy taffeta with a serge bolero effect and a small round hat at a slant heard it and also wondered, but with a greater anxiety than the others. Her heart ached for Mr Wooly. His behavior had been outrageous. She did not condemn him for that, though she, no more than any other decent woman, approved of a man effecting an entrance into a woman's bath by the methods he had used. Betty had merely decided that he had "not been himself," a formula, incidentally, by which all criminal law could be subverted; more than that, she had judged that his condition was of dual composition: the half alcoholic, the other some sort of mental collapse brought on by worry arising from the demands and machinations of that terrible woman he had married. Betty Jackson had come to Mr Wooly's arraignment not to condemn but to defend, by whatever means might offer. It had not been easy to come, for all there knew it was because of her that Mr Wooly had invaded the baths in his ridiculous attire, his horrible condition, and it was supposed—accurately, as it happened—that, having arrived drunk, the idea of arriving must have culminated a soberer, clearer state; in other words, that the pursuit, though a frightful caricature of a wooing, nevertheless such was its nature; and they wondered, gazing at the long-legged, slender Betty, with her thick and golden hair, her lovely figure, not to mention her languorous eye (it was a lover's orb even when, as now, it was quick with apprehension), just what had been going on between the rich Mr Wooly and this one, what and for how long and how often and what was that about Mrs Wooly's death. *Was* it, after all, an *accident?* Their minds considered the worst and were thus pleasantly occupied while they waited for Mr Wooly's inquisition to be resumed.

And Betty, moving slowly along the hall and back again with her graceful step, considered the plan she had made for helping Mr Wooly. It was daring; it was not honest. She deemed it but a small service, however, for the man she loved.

In the meantime Mr Wooly in no uncertain terms was putting it up to Judge Gilead. Either he, Mr Wooly, went scot free, or both he and Judge Gilead fell into the toils of the law, for, said Mr Wooly, if he were to be tossed into the lockup, then assuredly would every resident in Warburton learn at once all there was to know about Honey Pot and her betrayed and persecuted husband, Mr Tiddle. His program, he explained to Judge Gilead, had two parts: the first, free Scotch; the second, scot free. No great shakes as a jest under any circumstances, this one in these, briefly sizzling like a damp squib before the harassed countenance of Judge Gilead, did not cheer him up at all. He said feebly that complete clearance of Mr Wooly was simply an impossibility. Look at all those witnesses, scores of them. What could his defense be? At the very least, Judge Gilead explained, Mr Wooly must plead guilty and be fined and, for the sake of appearances, lectured for his inebriation, and even that would cause a scandal as seeming to be too lenient.

"Leave it to me," said Mr Wooly. "Come, your honor, the bottle's empty and my mind is closed, at peace. Our public awaits us."

Mr Wooly came back into the courtroom first. He resumed his seat in the front row. Chief Williams had been joined by the district attorney, a short, stout man who habitually stood on his toes, hands clasped behind him. They looked gravely at Mr Wooly. He winked. They were surprised by this and not pleased. Judge Gilead now took his chair behind the judicial desk. He saw the district attorney and turned green.

"The prisoner Wooly," said Judge Gilead, avoiding all eyes, "having pleaded guilty to all charges, I hereby——"

"Wait a moment," said Mr Wooly, arising. "I plead neither guilty nor not guilty. I simply do not understand why any of those charges should have been leveled at me, since I have never been in the Turkish baths of the Hotel Dearborn nor ever want to be. Why should I? I have six bathrooms in my own residence, and I dislike the Turkish variety. As for bathing with a lot of women trying in their vain, pusillanimous way to sweat off the fat a wise Providence inflicts upon them as punishment for their laziness and other porcine transgressions—that is beneath denial, your honor!"

There rose up a confused angry sound.

The judge, at a loss, only said, "Order, order!"

Mr Wooly went on: "We have here an obvious example of group hysteria and delusion. An overt expression of some deep-seated desire, too long suppressed. Yearning to see me there, the poor addled creatures *saw* me there."

He sat down.

"Stand up!" yelled the district attorney, furious. Mr Wooly had, however, discovered that he was seated next to Mrs Gilead. He leaned toward her and she, smelling the Scotch on him, leaned as far as possible in the other direction. He leaned still further. He whispered with a leer: "Afraid your husband's intoxicated, the old goat!"

"Stand up!" repeated the district attorney. Mr Wooly, hearing this time, stood up with an agreeable smile. "I'd like to examine the prisoner," said the district attorney.

"Take the stand," Judge Gilead told Mr Wooly, who stepped up, was sworn, sat down in the raised chair.

"So you deny everything," the district attorney sneered.

"Oh no."

"What don't you deny, may I ask?"

"Lots of things."

"Well, for instance?"

Mr Wooly thought. "The second law of thermodynamics, for instance," Mr Wooly said.

"Oh, you don't?" The district attorney seemed, in spite of himself, somewhat impressed. "Do you believe in free will?"

"Come, come," said Mr Wooly, "this is no time for metaphysical discussion. And besides, are my fundamental beliefs any business of yours? Has it come to this in the state of New York that a man may be had up for his philosophy? Are you the Spanish Inquisition?"

"I'm Irish myself," said the D.A., "and proud of it!"

"Never in my whole life have I criticized the Irish; as a matter of cold fact, I wouldn't say I was proud of them. I'd put it simpler than that. I'd merely say, 'There they are—the Irish! Always have been! Oh, the Irish!'" he said reflectively, as if remembering thousands of merry, bighearted fellows smoking clay pipes, swinging picks, halting traffic here and there, everywhere. "Kilkenny, Balmoral, Dublin, dear old River Swilly and the Shannon, County Cork." Here he paused in his dreamily poetic list. "Cork," he repeated with a touch of longing in his voice, and he glanced sideways at Judge Gilead, but Judge Gilead was staring straight at the ceiling, avoiding the eye of his wife. Mrs Gilead was staring at her husband, piercing him with her eyes, a terrible suspicion, planted by Mr Wooly, expanding in her mind; the "bearded child" didn't always tell her the whole truth— could that be it? No wonder the judge gazed at the ceiling!

The courtroom was noisy. People were disappointed in the examination of the prisoner, because they found it difficult to follow. Chief Williams, however, managed to keep his head. He stooped low and whispered in the district attorney's ear.

"That isn't fair!" complained Mr Wooly. "Whispering!"

But they paid no attention to this.

The district attorney nodded. He again faced Mr

Wooly. He freed one of his hands and pointed at Mr Wooly.

"Do you know Miss Betty Jackson?"

"You know I do."

"Are you her aunty from Perth Amboy?"

"No."

"Have you ever been?"

"I was never anybody's aunt," Mr Wooly said.

The district attorney spoke to Judge Gilead: "I should like to call Miss Betty Jackson."

The judge raised his hands. He seemed to say that they could do as they pleased; it had got beyond him. His wife had now taken to slowly nodding her head. It was indescribably threatening; it was gruesome.

"Miss Betty Jackson?" called Chief Williams.

But now Mr Wooly collapsed. He looked half the size he had been. He had not known that Betty was there.

"Step down," said the district attorney. He stepped down and gazed in miserable fascination as Betty took his place in the witness chair. She was sworn. She did not look at Mr Wooly. He feared the worst. He was in a state with visions of prison, of bread-and-water diets; he even felt exhausted, by anticipation, from working on a rock pile. The first portions of Betty's testimony he missed entirely. When he could listen she was saying: ". . . yes, I was there in the baths. I was there with my aunt, Mrs Wigglesworth of Perth Amboy."

That seemed to stop proceedings. She said it so sweetly, with such utter candor, that even Mr Wooly himself found himself almost believing her.

"When did you first see the prisoner?"

"Where?"

"In the aforesaid baths?"

"But they are for women only," said the beautiful Betty, widening her eyes.

"Please answer the question. When did you see him?"

"I didn't see him."

"Why not?"

"Oh, come," said Judge Gilead, "that is hardly a proper way to put your question."

But already Betty was answering it. "Why not?" she echoed. "Because he wasn't there. Oh, I heard some silly screams. You see, an attendant had left a large bath sponge on top of an electric cabinet, and some woman, far gone in delirium tremens anyway, I suppose, saw it and, recognizing in its enlarged pores a superficial resemblance to her own complexion, thought it was a face."

There was more of this sort of testimony, but it was heard with great difficulty because of the exclamations, the muttering, the groans, the hissing sounds, that came from the women spectators, and yet into all these sounds crept gradually a note of unreality, as if the sounds were being forced against a growing inner doubt; and it is true that while a woman may have deathless memory of what has happened to herself and within herself, her memory is not nearly so retentive or as assured when it comes to objective events, which she watches always with a certain agnosticism, doubting them a priori simply because they aren't actually happening to herself. One need but speak with full authority and confidence to make a woman doubt the evidence of her own eyes, ears; thus, for example, if you should come to the bedside of a woman who had the day before fallen from an elephant, and if you should tell her that she must never again, all by herself, try to shingle the roof of the garage, *because*, after all, the garage does not need shingling, she will at once begin to doubt the elephant, and in about a week begin to think she must have fallen off a garage! To this day Mr Wooly's invasion of the women's Turkish bath lingers in the memories of Warburton women as something between fact and fancy; it is generally believed that the witnesses against Mr Wooly were all disgustingly drunk, while Mr Wooly himself, having that afternoon chanced to walk along the hallway of the seventh floor and so past the Turkish-bath door, was the victim of a whole series of errors arising from "crowd psychology." This was a phrase used by Judge Gilead. It put the seal of science and wisdom upon his truly outrageous complacence about the whole affair.

"Case dismissed," said Judge Gilead at last. And got away with it. But then he had to go face Mrs Gilead!

Betty Jackson, having favored Mr Wooly, whom she had just saved, with not even a glance went away by herself. Our Mr Wooly covered his stricken features with his hands, seeing amid the fumes of Scotch in his poor head that Betty had saved him, only to cast him aside.

That was what he thought. Alone he wandered from the courtroom, down the stair and out between the Jeffersonian white columns of the entrance. The trees in the small park were tall and gave a gracious shade. He did not notice. He looked ahead but once and then to check the

location of the curb where he would pause and hail a
taxi; then he lowered his head again, meditated the slow
alternate motion of his shoes. Once or twice the cement
beneath him wavered, but each time he kept his balance
with not more than a quick sideways step. Thus gloomily
isolated, he felt another's arm under his, smelled a pleasant perfume.

"Mr Wooly," said a low, yearning voice. It was Betty,
and before he knew it they were together in the dusk of
a speeding taxicab.

She took his gray hat from his head, brushed it lightly
and put it back. She fixed his tie. While she did these
homely tasks she said, "Oh dear" and "My" and clicked
her tongue, "Ts, ts, ts, ts." Mr Wooly kept his eyes closed.
He was plastered and he knew it quite well.

Betty took the folded handkerchief from his breast
pocket, unfolded it, put it back in so that the points
showed modishly. She then looked at her handiwork and
gave her sign of approval. She kissed him lightly on
the lips.

Mr Wooly opened his eyes. "After all I've done," he
murmured, "why do you not hate me?"

"Why should I?"

Mr Wooly thought of all the reasons why she should
but mentioned none of them.

"Because you came into the baths in that? . . ."

"Don't mention it," groaned Mr Wooly. "I am dis-
graced for life."

"Oh, fudge, you will come to boast of it," Betty said
cheerfully.

He sighed. "I love you, but what do I bring you? Humiliation, perjury."

"But after all," she said, "you came to the hotel; you went to all the trouble of that crazy disguise, just to see me, didn't you?" She cuddled closer to him. "It is romantic."

He could hardly believe his ears.

"What time is it?" she asked.

He didn't know.

"Not yet noon," she said, showing she knew all along. "And you are tight as a tick."

"What kind of a tick?" Mr Wooly asked, an idle question; he really did not care.

"You are soaked," she said. "Oh, Mr Wooly, poor darling, you are drunk."

"Guess I am."

"Why do you *do* it?"

It was on his tongue to tell her why. But something whispered: "Careful. Now you have her again, don't frighten her away." He remained silent.

She went on: "It isn't good for you, dear. Oh, it is understandable, after all—considering what you've gone through. But, Mr Wooly, don't you realize that if you go on like this you will wake up some morning feeling all out of sorts? The stimulation is only temporary."

"After all," he said, "what does last forever?"

"Now you are being contrary." Betty hugged his arm very pleasantly. "But, darling, I want you to stop this new vice. You mustn't misunderstand, my darling." Here she kissed his cheek. "It is not that I don't understand. I don't object to drinking. I drink. My friends drink. But

you are not the type. When you came out of City Hall a
minute ago you were *staggering*. And everybody in Warburton saw you."

"Who cares?"

"I do, and you should, dear. Do you want to be the
town drunk?"

"Do you want me to be?" he asked her hopefully.

"No," she said. "Oh, Mr Wooly, it's only for your own
good, but you must stop drinking."

He thought, "Little you know what I'm like these days
when I'm sober." And he thought: "I'd listen in to whatever you were thinking, my girl. How would you like
that?" But here a strange feeling came to him: that he
would not want to listen in to Betty's thoughts; indeed,
that he must not.

She had been talking while he thought.

She said: "Will you promise?"

"What?"

"Oh, dear, aren't you even listening? Will you promise
not to drink anything at all for a while? Oh, Mr Wooly,
we can be so happy, you and I. It will not be necessary
for you to drown your troubles with drinks. I will love
you enough to drown them. Promise."

What could he say? Nothing.

"Dear?"

"I'm sorry," he said.

"But why?"

"You would not understand."

She it was who now became silent. It was a hurt silence.
It hurt him too. It began to sober him. Ahead he saw a
sign that read BAR. And the bars to his mind were going

down as he grew sober. In a few minutes now he would be as close to Betty's mind as she was. He no more wanted this to happen than a true lover would want to peek through a keyhole at his love. It became suddenly of the utmost importance that he maintain his mental isolation.

"Pull up here," he said to the driver.

"Where?"

"In front of that bar."

"Oh, Mr Wooly," said the distressed Betty.

"Listen, my dear," he said as the car drew to a stop. "It is quite different with me. . . ."

"That is what they all say," sighed Betty.

"But with me it is: I can take it or leave it alone, but I do not leave it alone. Why?"

"Why?"

"Because it is not mere indulgence with me, you understand. It helps me; it stimulates. . . ."

But she was slowly shaking her head. "How you fool yourself," she said.

"But listen . . ."

"My uncle Jim was like this," Betty said sadly. "His wife spent all her married life looking for parking lots she didn't know the name of. It was in Cleveland."

He was almost irritated. "But, Betty . . ."

"When Uncle Jim," she continued, "felt the impulse to get drunk he would park his car in a parking lot, and then when he woke up the following Tuesday in Manitowoc, Wisconsin . . ."

Unwillingly Mr Wooly found himself getting interested: "Did he always wake up on Tuesday?"

tion in matrimony, anyway? She had, like Honey Pot,
done, she admitted to herself, fairly well.

"You are so learned," she said to her husband now.
"And you know so little of the world: how charming."

He brushed her brow lightly with his two-pointed
beard, and now belatedly he noticed that she wore her
hat—or rather her cap—a blue beret. Very aesthetic and
intellectual. "Where are you going?" he asked.

"To court," she said.

He looked his surprise.

"Do you think I would miss Mr Wooly's hearing? How
little you know of women!"

As has been said, Bertha Gilead was no heroine for a
woman's magazine or radio serial, either. She was a pighead. She knew all. She knew she did. Thus her face, her
walk, her tone of voice and choice of words.

"Very well," said Judge Gilead, little knowing what
that hearing held in store for him.

The court was at the back on the first floor of City
Hall, the new brick colonial-style building in the Civic
Center. It was new, but it was old, for all courtrooms
are old. The grinning, crippled dwarf hobbles through
them the first day and they are, presto chango, old. She,
the dwarf, is man's justice. She carries with her a hand
mirror so that she may gaze upon her own hideous features from time to time but never with understanding,
only with self-satisfied smirks. Justice! But thou shalt
not judge! The prohibition is laid down flatly, without
equivocation. Thou shalt *not*. Yet here sits man judging
between—between what? Between that which is not comparable. Comparing ostriches with minnows, blaming

both for the lack of what the other has! "Thou, crocodile, why singest thou not? Observe the canary, with a
mouth, so much smaller than thine, hear how he sings,
how sweetly! And thou! Ten years in prison, crocodile!"

The courtroom had a municipal smell. This is also the
smell of government in all parts of this planet, a smell
commingled of the smells of cement, of chloride of lime,
of human sweat, of dusty books, of an impersonal lassi-
tude—the smell of life that has momentarily stopped.
Twenty thousand learned volumes may be written to
prove that to live governmentally, to give all choice and,
in the name of its preservation, dear liberty herself, to
government is the best, not to say the only way; and yet
one good normal set of nostrils applied to the task of judg-
ing the municipal smell can report: "Rotten" and "Evil."

To Judge Gilead his job was his job. Had he believed
in justice he would long since have left his bench. But he
was not a bad man. He did not hate his fellows. On the
contrary. So he equated his own security with his instinc-
tive, cynical desire to free every culprit brought before
him, save only those caught in cruelties to children and
animals—crimes which made him frantic. For the rest he
only saw himself out of luck.

His desk was on a platform at one end of the courtroom. He came to it through his own door. His wife, he
noted, was seated already in the middle of the front row.
The people were already in place.

A policeman shouted something or other, and everybody stood up, then sat down again as Judge Gilead sat
down. The judge read a paper laying before him. He
looked at Chief Williams and said, "Well?"

"Oh, of course not. I meant that just for example."

"And always in Manitowoc?"

"Oh no, not necessarily; he'd wake up everywhere, anywhere, someplace far from Cleveland; why, then he wouldn't be able to remember where he had parked his car."

"Wouldn't he get some sort of receipt or parking ticket?"

"He always ate them," Betty said. "The only clues he'd ever get about where he might have been on his binges would be that from time to time some strange woman in a strange town would come running at him, pushing a baby buggy ahead of her. But when that happened to Uncle Jim he always ran with all his might."

Mr Wooly was beginning to sweat. In his mind he detected certain low-keyed disturbances that might be thoughts—her thoughts—stirring in his mind. It wasn't that he feared to hear her opinion of him, though at the moment he wasn't exactly keen to hear this, or that he suspected her mind might be not all that it should be—that might have its advantages—it was only that he did not want to peek, to eavesdrop. He said hurriedly: "But, you see, I would never go off to Manitowoc and seduce a strange female; it isn't in my nature."

"But look what you did the last time you were that way. . . ."

"Betty," he said in a low, earnest voice, "I have to have a drink."

"I'm coming with you."

So she did, and after he paid the cabby they entered the bar and Mr Wooly ordered four bourbons.

"Two," said Betty.

The barman looked concerned, hesitated.

"Make it five then," Mr Wooly said. "I want three for myself."

She only gazed sadly at him.

He downed them one after another, shaking and shuddering, then gave her his friendliest smile, saying, "Ah,

now that's better." (Hearing how that ominous rising murmur now subsided.) But she opened her blue leather purse and abstracted a bit of handkerchief. This she applied to the bridge of her nose and began to weep quietly.

He gazed sadly upon her.

When she could speak she said: "*Please*, for my sake."

He only signaled the waiter. "Two more," he said.

Suddenly she was on her feet; as suddenly she was

gone out the door. He did not move. He looked at the barman and he raised his shoulders in a shrug that was the most pathetic, helpless gesture of that sort the barman, who was no chicken, had seen in all his experience.

"She doesn't understand," Mr Wooly told him. "She will never understand."

The barman nodded at him. He thought up something to bring cheer to the dreary scene. "Life is short," he said. "A little while here, a drink or two, and then—all over."

And he, too, shrugged.

CHAPTER XX

Plea to a Horse

AWAKING in midmorning and ringing for Bentley, Mr Wooly was surprised by the entrance, not of the fat-cheeked butler, but his daughter Sara, home unannounced from camp the day previous. Mr Wooly, suffering his now-usual early-morning headache, remembered vaguely that Bentley the night before while tactfully assisting him upstairs had said something about Sara.

Sara, very pretty in gray slacks and a red-and-white pull-over, her brown hair cascading upon her shoulders, cheeks pink with a filial excitement, bore on her two hands a wide silver tray.

She said: "Good morning, Dad, I'm home! And here's a lot of special breakfast! Bentley said you didn't eat breakfast any more, but I told him that was silly." She put the tray down. "Aren't you glad to see me?"

Mr Wooly was not glad, as a matter of fact. He looked at his daughter with anxiety instead of joy. He was a disillusioned Wooly, a Wooly who knew what others thought of him, who had drunk to the dregs of wisdom distilled from the knowledge of egos not his own. He, of all men, he alone, really knew what others thought about him. He looked at his pretty fifteen-year-old and was despairingly frightened of hearing what her thought of him was. He did not want to learn that it was derogatory, contemptuous, hostile. He couldn't have stood that. He knew now that he was far from being the man he had thought himself; he had seen through his own dignities, his solid virtues. He no longer held illusions about what sort of a father he had been to this his only child, become so surprisingly a young woman already. A dime-a-dozen father, an irresponsible and heedless father, who by payment of a spot of cash here and there hired others to do his parental duties, the school, special teachers, camps. . . . She looked anxiously at him and her smile faded. She saw that he drew away from her, that he did not smile. As if, indeed, he feared or even loathed her. . . .

For a moment there was blank silence in poor Mr Wooly's mind, and then he heard the murmur of his daughter's thinking. A single word, one he recognized at once as not his because of its clear and youthful tone—if one may use such a word to describe so silent a thing as a thought—the word "ashamed." Receiving this word, his spirit quailed, but now by curious unliterary groupments of other words her whole thought came to him. Absurdly tears came into Mr Wooly's large brown eyes. Sara's whole thought was that she, Sara, should be ashamed for having taken such poor care of her troubled dad. With that thought also was the thought of how troubled he looked and a murmur of loving, hasty, very childish plans for helping him. They were all friendly, unquestioning thoughts, unchilled by any question or criticism. Never mind what he might be outside this house; here within, with his daughter Sara, he remained the great man, T. Wallace Wooly, Jr. He did the best he could by way of a smile, a tearful, grateful one.

"Glad to see me?" she asked, a little breathless.

Was he glad! Headache and all, he sat up, and she put his slippers on his feet. Then he looked at his breakfast. He had to refuse the chilled raspberries, the bacon and eggs staying warm in their little silver igloo, the hot biscuits. He tasted some coffee. She, seated on a bench on the other side of the low table she'd arranged, was ready to eat all he didn't. But seeing his misery, she asked, "Hang-over?"

The word, on her lips, shocked him. "What do you mean?"

"Bentley told me you'd have one."

"The rascal!"

"Oh, but I insisted I should know why you didn't eat breakfast these days. Seems so queer for you."

"Have I changed?"

"Not a bit, really," she said. "You're still my dad. Wait, I'll run down. Oh, *don't* ring, I'll be quicker— just be patient a moment. In the meantime there's aspirin."

She was back in a minute with ice and bottles of what he wanted. While she gobbled he sipped. It was a splendid breakfast for both of them. It improved steadily as it progressed.

In the midst of laughing at some old family gag she suddenly couldn't laugh any more. She asked: "You're in great trouble, Dad, but what is it? I can't find out! Bentley won't say a word; Cook won't. Nobody will. They all know something I don't. Of course it seemed crazy to have—ah—Jennifer die and be buried without me even being brought home and then to go straight to camp. And now this mystery. Tell me, Dad. Is it some crime? Have you been counterfeiting or something? Murder? If it is, I'll understand."

He considered telling her all. Was she old enough? It occurred to him that she was, indeed, young enough.

"Sara," he said, having made his decision, "Jennifer, your stepmother, was a witch." He waited for the exclamation of incredulity that did not come.

"And so?" said Sara calmly, coolly.

He told her enough: the climbing down the trumpet vine, and here the fascinated Sara went to the window and herself examined that unconventional stairway. He told her of the goat in moonlight. She was thrilled. Of the lame stranger Jennifer met at midnight at the bottom of the garden. She shuddered. He told her most of the story, explaining the curse Jennifer had placed upon him and how, more or less by accident, he had discovered the method of circumventing that curse, at least temporarily. Sara listened, understood, questioned no detail, condemned nothing. . . .

When the tale was done Sara said, pouring another glassful for her afflicted father:

"What have you done for poor Rummy?"

He did not understand her.

"But," she said, "why not try conciliation?"

This had never occurred to Mr Wooly.

"You see, Dad," Sara said, "it all makes complete, sensible sense. That is, up to the point where you just abandon the poor beast in the barn."

"She's been tethered in the field every afternoon," Mr Wooly objected.

"Yes, but she isn't an ordinary, dumb horse," Sara said. "She must be dying of lonesomeness—for lack of conversation with her equals. She can't talk to Goat or to Ass, not satisfactorily, do you think? So she stews. She's a haunted horse, and you've deserted her, poor thing. How much is she Jennifer and how much still stupid old Rummy? We simply don't know! The point is, Dad, don't you think, that if the life of the curse is related to that haunted horse you should, we should, turn all our attention to her. Maybe we could somehow placate her?"

"Placate her? How?"

Sara wondered too. At last she said: "She's female, you know."

Mr Wooly, taking another long pull at his brandy and champagne, asked: "What do you mean by that?"

"The worst thing you could have done," Sara said, "was to neglect the poor thing. Let's go down and try to make friends."

"In an army tank?" asked Mr Wooly.

"She's locked in her stall, and we can stay at a safe distance," said the practical Sara.

June had gone. Here it was July. The gardens to the south of the Wooly house were ablaze, the trees at their fullest and darkest. The fountain made a pleasant sound. While Swanson, glooming in a chair at the foot of the outside stairway of the garage, was obviously withholding deserved praise from this magnificent day, no other creature, winged, four- or two-footed, was with him. It was a round, golden day, as filled with a rich warmth as a ripe grape; it was a day that made walking seem like swimming in a gracious flood. The birds cried and called; from the hen runs, softened by distance, came the sudden egotistic chatter and brag of the unpersonable hens. Up in the air, halfway to the sun itself, it seemed, a sharp-shinned hawk metallically screamed. Mr Wooly and his slim daughter stepped out upon the south veranda and so to the circular graveled drive, passed the fountain to the barnyard, giving no eye to Swanson or to Bentley, who, happening upon the kitchen porch, could not help but stare. Inside the barn a dusty evening, for all this outer high noon, presided. Rummy turned her long head to gaze at her visitors.

"Darling!" said Sara.

The horse looked at her briefly and turned her head away.

"Rummy," began Mr Wooly, "we have come to talk things over. Now in the first place——" Sara interrupted, whispering, "Please, Dad, let me talk to her first, and if she won't listen to me then you try. . . ."

This was O.K. with Mr Wooly. He gave the stage to young Sara.

At first the animal sulked. She acted like a horse and a very stupid horse. This made both of them a little self-conscious; it is all right to argue with a horse if the horse gives some indication that it understands the argument, but when you present abstract ideas to a creature who merely stamps slowly and eats and even in midsentence, so to speak, does that which a horse but never a person is permitted to do wherever it happens to be, why then it is difficult to hold to the thread of your discourse. In

fact, Sara faltered and stopped. She looked appealingly at her father.

"'S no use," said a voice. "It is yust no use at all."

This was Swanson. He was in the doorway.

"If that horse was mine," Swanson said, "I would not stand and yaw with her; I would yust shoot her!"

Rummy's ears slightly moved; her tail swished languorously. She ate. She acted, in fact, as if either she hadn't heard or couldn't understand words.

"She is lonely," Sara said.

Here Rummy lifted her head around and gave the girl

a long and, as it were, beseeching look, as one woman to another.

"She understood that!" Sara said. "She wants *something*. Oats?" Rummy slowly shook her head.

"She is fat as a pig already," Swanson said and spat. Rummy's hoofs made a loud drumming noise as she tried in vain to back out far enough to kill Swanson with her hoofs.

"Go away, Swanson!" Mr Wooly said. When the chauffeur had gone Rummy calmed down somewhat, but she was still breathing hard.

"You see?" Sara said.

"No," Mr Wooly had to admit; he didn't see.

"Is it company you want?" Sara asked the horse.

No answer.

"Ask her if she wants a bottle of champagne," Mr Wooly suggested. She didn't. Any other sort of bottle? No.

"Shoes?"

She didn't.

Mr Wooly was getting restless. It didn't seem to him that Sara was getting anywhere. "Ask her," he suggested morosely, "if she would like a shave and a haircut."

Rummy glanced at him. It was a withering, contemptuous glance.

"Rummy," Sara went on, "I think you should listen to reason. It is true Father is in the trap you set for him, and he has no peace."

Here Rummy permitted herself a slow, gloating smile. She rolled her eyes toward Mr Wooly.

"It is true," Sara continued, "that he must go about

crocked as he is this minute or he cannot stand it. It is true that he has been given the gift to know himself as others think of him." Rummy opened her mouth in a silent guffaw. "His ego is in aching ruins," Sara conceded. "He tosses on his bed through the long nights, tortured by the despair of an endless future of alternate mental hullabaloo, drunkenness and hang-over. But"—she paused, and the horse sneered triumphantly—"but, Jennifer, you are in rather a spot yourself, aren't you? You're trapped there in a horse. Evidently you can't get out because if you could, it seems to me, you would. I," said the girl with conviction, "wouldn't like it. Stables smell all right —for part time. If I were where you are I'd feel uncomfortable, I am sure. And just a little foolish. You have maintained your spirit, of course, by considering the dreadful effects of your mischief, but aren't you cutting off your own nose to spite your face, more or less, darling? And what's the good of that? Why can't we effect some sort of compromise? If there's anything we can do to get you out of there we'll do it, but of course first you'll lift the curse off poor Dad. . . ."

From sneering defiance the horse had gone, it was plain to see, into a mood near to despair. She closed her eyes, hung her head. Evidently Sara's estimate of her situation was not far wrong.

"Do you trust me?" Sara asked.

The horse opened one utterly disillusioned eye, shook her head slowly, emphatically, as one who would ask at the same time: "Hell, no. Would you?"

"But we will prove we are trustworthy. We will do things for you, make your days less lonely, even pleasant."

Outside the day, framed by the wide doors. Warm dusk in here with dust motes slanting across the beamed sunlight, and a rich barn smell and quiet. The goat and ass were out tethered in the orchard. Swanson had gone back to his seat on the stairs of the garage. In the street a motor's horn sounded, far and small. Now the horse looked from girl to man. It was an unusual scene. The horse, resting her head on the edge of the stall, ears slanted attentively forward, listened in utter silence, her gray lips twitching from time to time. Sara, still pleading, exhorting, stepped from here to there and back and used gestures prettily, seeming to offer her argument to the animal as in a basket, with pansies.

"If you were a woman," Sara said, "it would be so much simpler. Stockings, I'd suggest then. You don't want silk stockings, do you?"

Sadly the long, melancholy head shook a no to that, and Sara saw a large tear gather in either brown eye and roll down a face that seemed all nose when you came to think of it as a face. "I'm sorry," Sara said quickly. "So sorry!"

"For what?" wondered Mr Wooly.

"Hurting her feelings," Sara whispered. "Of course she doesn't want silk stockings, not with legs like hers. It is very difficult." Sara sighed and, to help her think, drew out a compact (her very first) and put lipstick on her lips. Her father gazed at this with as much surprise as the horse plainly showed.

"Do you do that?" Mr Wooly asked.

Sara laughed and flushed prettily. "I forgot you didn't know I did, Dad. But I waited a year longer than most of the other girls. Oh, look at her. . . ." For the horse was reaching eagerly forward, her eyes burning. "Why, you don't think . . . ?"

"I hope not!" groaned Mr Wooly.

"But she does. Powder?" Sara asked the horse. "Want powder on your nose, darling? No, not powder. Oh, but . . ."

"Oh no," groaned Mr Wooly.

Sara, anxious not to hurt the poor thing's feelings again, hurried on: "A little lipstick?" she asked with a false but adequate smile, and the horse nodded joyfully.

"Be careful!" cried Mr Wooly. Sara was fearless, knowing a horse who had been longing for lipstick on her wide, gray, dry lips for all this time wasn't likely to bite her hand off, not at least until the lipsticking had been finished. "You can see for yourself," Sara said to her father, "that she couldn't possibly do it herself; how would she hold a little teeny lipstick with her front feet? Not even fingers. Poor dear!"

It took all of the lipstick, which was a new one, and the effect was remarkable, to say the least. Rummy raised her head and bared her square, old-ivory teeth, made to seem far yellower now by lips redder than fresh-cut beefsteak.

"Smile," whispered Sara to her father; "don't stand there looking horrified!"

Mr Wooly creased his face as best he could. But inwardly he shuddered. The effect was so downright feminine, after all. She looked like the kind of secretaries his father had always had about.

"There," said Sara, tossing the empty shell of the lipstick in a corner. "Is that all, dear?"

The horse shook her head and trod the boards of her stall anxiously, trying to get some other request over to the girl. What was it now? It took a little while, but eventually Sara guessed right again—a mirror.

As Sara went out to find one Mr Wooly stepped out with her. "Don't!" he warned. "She'll faint if she sees herself. She will never forgive you and, what's worse, she'll never forgive me! Remember, that's mostly Jennifer in Rummy now; whatever spirit Rummy ever had is so shoved into a corner, I suppose you could say she *was* Jennifer."

But Sara shook her head. "She'll love it," she said confidently. While she dashed upstairs Mr Wooly dashed into the now well-stocked sideboard of the big dining room and poured himself three, one right after another. He needed to keep his mind well guarded—in a word, tight—in such an emergency as this. But what a smart girl, his daughter! She understood psychology, that girl. And a bit later he watched Sara hold a hand mirror for Rummy and saw that foolish animal shake herself and stamp with conceited satisfaction! A revolting sight. Yet it had not reached its grotesque apogee, not yet. Sara had another inspiration. She found the old straw sun hat with two holes for ears, worn years before by some other and forgotten Wooly steed. To the crown of this she added a few feathers and a cluster of artificial grapes; she placed it carefully on the horse's head, again held the mirror.

The animal gazed, held its head this way and that, looking one-eyed at her reflection, smiling with her crimsoned mouth, trembling all over with the joy of vanity gratified. . . .

Everything was wonderful. Surely soon, with this good beginning, some deal, a sensible truce, could be effected and the curse lifted.

But suddenly the mare became angry. She thundered her anger, stamping, kicking, till it was hard to understand how her stall and her halter held.

They were dumfoundered, almost in despair, again.

"She wants to go shopping, I'm afraid," Sara said at last.

"Don't be silly!" her father objected. "They wouldn't let her into the stores. Even if she confined herself to window shopping, painted like that, hatted like that, I'm afraid a lot of people would notice her, and not with approbation! Even an ordinary unadorned, unpainted horse looking into millinery and underwear windows might cause comment, and as she is, that nightmare . . ."

Mr Wooly was saying this outside the barn, out of Jennifer's hearing.

"But she's all dressed up," Sara said, understanding everything. "She loves the hat I made. And it *is* becoming, if I do say it myself. Couldn't we just take her for a walk downtown so she could see people and be seen?"

"Good heavens!" said Mr Wooly. "If I looked like her I'd not want to be seen by *anybody*."

"You're not her," Sara said as emphatic as she was ungrammatical. "You don't understand. She'd like to parade herself. She would like . . ."

"Parade?" said Mr Wooly with the air of a man who has thought of something. "Next week's the Fourth of July. . . ." They gazed at each other.

"Bands!" said Sara. "Boy Scouts! Coast Guards!"

"American Legion," agreed Mr Wooly.

"D.A.R. float," Sara countered. "Police on motorcycles."

"Fire department." Mr Wooly went silent, thinking. "I mean—I'll have to be in that parade with the fire department. How about that old 1850 hook 'n' ladder—drawn by"—he used his thumb—"by her? Hat and all? Crowds, excitement, all eyes on her!!"

"But marvelous, Dad," cried Sara, kissing his cheek. "Oh, *wonderful!* She'll love it! She'll do anything for us then; we will work out some system of communication so she can help you figure out a formula for getting her out and away from that horse, with suitable guarantees, of course. . . . I don't know how we can do it, but, oh, Dad, I am beginning really to have hope. It won't be long now!"

Mr Wooly, comfortably soaking himself with brandy in his library that afternoon, permitted himself the most audacious hopes. He thought of phoning Betty but forbore to do that. "When I am free," he told himself, "I will go to her and tell her all, and then, after a suitable interval, we will be married. After that we will be strangers to anxieties, natural or unnatural. We will live confident always of tomorrow, companioned always by hope, and so strangers to unhappiness. When I awake at night," he thought, "I will awake to her presence, her dear and unsurprising presence by my side; she will not be crawling down the wall, singing on the roof with ill-bred cats. . . ." He thought other thoughts, that she was golden blonde, for instance. Both the other Mrs Woolys had been brunettes. He felt that he would like learning about a blonde.

By dinner he was so well fortified against the thoughts of others, not to mention his own anxieties, that Bentley had to guide him to the table, wagging his head toward Sara. Little did Mr Wooly notice of this; little would he have cared! And little, indeed, did he know what the Fourth held for him and for that horsy.

CHAPTER XXI

—And Now, in Conclusion

FOR SOME YEARS Warburton's Fourth of July parade had
been lead by the Warburton Women's Drum Corps, the
majorette of which could swing a very swift baton and
walk for miles, leaning back from her waist, her knees
shooting up to her chin. And love it. These drummers
wore white uniforms, white bootees and high white caps
with red pompoms. When Mr Wooly (Swanson beside
him) drove up to the starting point their success was immediate. They were cheered immoderately. The horse
smiled, bowed from right to left. Even the Women's Drum
Corps applauded. But after a brief wait the horse realized
by their movements that the Drum Corps females were
going on before. She reared up on her hind legs. She
wanted to be first instead of Lena Oglethorpe, the above-
mentioned drum majorette. She was outraged. She trotted
ahead. Mr Wooly, pulling back on the reins, said, "Now,
now, there's a good girl. Whoa, whoa, I say. Stop, Jennifer, please. We'll be off in a jiffy; don't be impatient.
Whoa, Rummy," and so on, for, indeed, he could not
know how much she was plain horse, how much Jennifer.
She wouldn't whoa. She hurried forward, cantering now.
She left it up to the people—men, women and innocent
children—whether or not they were to be tramped on.
They fled away from her hoofs. She was soon ahead of the

Drum Corps. This foremost position she plainly meant to keep.

The fire chief and Bat-Ears Reilly, who were marshals, came running up. Mr Wooly himself, in full fire regalia, explained that the horse insisted on leading. They scratched their heads, disliking this break with tradition. The horse looked around at them and smiled her best. This was their first sight of her make-up and her millinery. They scared Reilly, rather a superstitious man. But the fire chief, like most of those lining the curbs, was only amused. "Oh, hell," he said, "let her lead then." Reilly reluctantly agreed. They told Miss Oglethorpe, who was sore about their putting horse before art, but could only agree as gracefully as possible.

After the Drum Corps, a band, then the Coast Guard boys, then some official cars, the floats, the American Legion, and so on. A long and varied parade, involving so many of Warburton's good people that one wondered how there could be any left for audience. However, all the length of Brick Street there were watchers, papas and mammas and their children. The air was filled with sunshine, the popping of firecrackers, the hot braying of the band. The horse looked to right, to left; she bowed; she smiled. Sara, in one of the official cars next to Mrs Williams, wife of the chief, was delighted. Swanson, seated next to Mr Wooly, was dressed up as Uncle Sam. Mr Wooly begged him to cheer up. "Swanson," said Mr Wooly as he lightly flapped the late Mrs Wooly with the reins, "Swanson, you could be sent to Alcatraz for looking the way you look. Your impersonation of our uncle is downright subversive. You fill out so perfectly the specifications of his severest critic. You not only look hopeless and decadent; you look mean! You look as if you had spent the night trying to collect a war debt and were now out to raise everybody's income tax. Smile, can't you? This is a holiday."

Swanson smiled.

"As you were!" exclaimed Mr Wooly. "The smile is worse!"

As for Mr Wooly, he was tight. He felt fine.

Swanson sighed. He looked about him wearily. The parade was approaching that corner of Brick Street nearest to the Civic Center, the white stone and warm red brick of whose buildings shone handsomely through the shade of the tall trees there.

On a signal from a traffic policeman Mr Wooly pulled the horse to a halt, at the same time raising his right hand like a field marshal to the marchers behind him. Traffic cut across before them, a taxicab or two, some private cars and a rickety farmer's cart hauled by a discouraged white horse. Its head hung but its eye seems to have been roving, for now it caught sight of Rummy, with her make-up, her hat, and this picture scared the conservative old animal out of its daze. It fled, cart, startled farmer and all. "Which is she most?" Mr Wooly wondered. "Jennifer or old Rummy?" Here she turned her head to look at them. She grinned.

"Whoever she is," Swanson said gloomily, "she's too much!"

"What are you thinking about, Swanson?"

"My bones."

"Ache?"

"Not just exactly, Mr Wooly. They feel in them like something is making up its mind."

"To do what?"

"To happen."

"To whom, Swanson?"

"To us." He sighed. "I tank I go home, Mr Wooly."

"Wait till the parade is over. We need you."

Swanson sighed again, a long, tragic sigh.

Judge Gilead and Mrs Gilead sat in their car by the curb. Not far away from them, standing in the shade, Mr Wooly also saw Mr and Mrs Tiddle. The slight Tiddle had his handsome blonde wife securely by the arm. They looked like a youngish suburban couple out to enjoy a holiday, in spite of themselves. Mr Wooly bowed nicely to them. Mr Tiddle was delighted and felt honored. He tipped his derby, smiled broadly, remembering, no doubt, how Mr Wooly had got him pardoned after only a couple of those thirty days Judge Gilead had given him for speeding. He jiggled his wife's arm, said, "Look. Mr Wooly himself."

"I'm looking," she said ungraciously.

"Just like we were all friends," Tiddle exulted. "You ought to be more grateful, sweetie." (Sweetie was what *Tiddle* called her.) "After all, if it wasn't for Mr Wooly you wouldn't have me today. You ought to remember that."

"That's what I am remembering," she said.

Mr Wooly waved a debonair greeting to Judge Gilead. "Morning, Judge!"

"Don't speak to the lecherous little backslider," said

the dignified and intellectual Mrs Gilead, but Judge Gilead disobeyed. He spoke a grave, a very civil, good morning. He was no connoisseur of parades and could not just then think of any reason to love Warburton's leading citizen, sitting there under his fireman's helmet in that ridiculous old hook and ladder; on the other hand, he felt better than he had for some days, for hadn't it been his luck to see Honey Pot? And while he could not feast his eyes upon his estranged inamorata but only take quick little nibbles or sips, as it were, from the corner of his eye, lest his watchful wife observe him, still that little was far better than utter famine.

Now the last of the cross traffic had gone, or almost. Here came a bright little open car driven by the husband of one of Betty Jackson's friends. This obscure, innocent and wholly unsuspecting couple were in the front seat, while alone in the back sat Betty herself. Halted for a moment by the stalling of the car ahead, Betty had full opportunity to turn about and so from a distance of about twenty feet face Mr Wooly. Her lovely eyes darkened with loving admiration as she saw his confident posture, his red helmet, not to forget his leading position in the parade. She leaned forward to the driver of the car, suggesting that instead of crossing Brick Street they turn left into it and so somewhere farther along find a parking place and see the parade go by, especially Mr Wooly. Her friends were agreeable, and the turn was made.

Betty, all in white save for a filmy green fichu about her neck, looked back and threw Mr Wooly a number of loving kisses right between the ears, as it were, of the painted horse. As Betty threw the last of these she noticed the horse and was startled. Then she screamed, and that thin, silvery splinter of sound was heard blocks away, or so people declared when the whole series of dreadful events of which it was the first, the detonator, was later reconstructed and examined. Betty screamed because just as the car straightened out and slowly began to go on ahead of the parade she saw the horse jump, literally jump into the air and hurl herself forward, that terrible crimson mouth wide open.

Mr Wooly, utterly surprised, lost the reins.

"Yeesus," groaned Swanson. "I told you! She's all Yennifer now!"

The driver of Betty's car, startled by Betty's scream, had stepped on it, but he had to change gears, while Jennifer gained. Snap! And she had the green fichu in her teeth! Had it been tied securely, this would have been a tragic tale. Certainly then, noosed by the fichu, caught between the divergent pulls of car and horse, she would have been dragged to the pavement, done to death by strangulation, by being stamped upon by a madly jealous horse. But the fichu was not tied at all, merely pinned; the pin gave; the car gathered speed. Betty was saved by inches. Try as she would, the horse could not quite keep up. But how she tried! The car went faster, was half a block away. The horse kept at the vain chase. The light wagon behind her jounced and bounced from side to side, every moment threatening to go over. The horrified crowd on the curb saw Uncle Sam take the air, flung from his seat as the wagon lurched, saw him after a brief flight make a three-point landing, counting as one point each, his hands and his chin, the latter's contact with the macadam somewhat cushioned by the false beard, but not much.

On went Jennifer, the wagon, Mr Wooly! On and on! Now the conveyance of her hated rival was all of a block away, but still her four hoofs beat their maniac tattoo. Just beyond Elm Street one wheel of the wagon departed. It was unbroken and continued to roll by itself for some yards, but the wagon sagged at once; the axle reached the pavement at about the same time that Mr Wooly, thrown clear, encountered his office manager, the fat Mr Simpson, head on. Down went Simpson, and remained down. Beside him lay Mr Wooly.

In the distance Betty and her friends turned right on Macdonald Avenue because at the intersection a street-department excavation was carefully marked with red lanterns, W.P.A. signs and arrows with the word "Detour" printed large upon them. Betty and her friends turned right to safety. The maddened horse, still pursuing, did not turn but went on, hell-bent, blind, dragging the splintered remains of the antique hook and ladder at her tail, right through the signs, the thin wooden barricade, and so into a tangle of water mains, gas pipes and electric cables at the bottom of a ten-foot hole.

Mr Wooly was surrounded by people and the vast murmur and rush of their thoughts. "I'm sober," groaned Mr Wooly. "How are you?" Mr Simpson did not reply. He was unconscious. So it was Mr Simpson who was popped into the ambulance alongside of Swanson, who was already there, bruised but unbroken, groaning. Mr Wooly got up. He kissed his daughter Sara, who was gasping for breath, having run so hard and for joy too. Police officers came to help.

How did Mr Wooly feel now? Everybody wanted to know that, of course. But it was Dr Mannix who got the reply, accompanied by a slight laugh, at once nervous, incredulous, joyful. "I'm sober," said Mr Wooly. "Completely sober," and he touched his poor ears, his poor head. "But it's gone," he said, meaning that the invading thoughts were gone, that the unnatural faculty that had deviled him for so long had faded away! "It's gone," he repeated.

"So's your horse," Dr Mannix said.

Poor Jennifer. Poor Rummy. Yet she was not an ugly sight, lying down there in her last resting place, for in falling some of the earth had caved in after her, and very little of her showed. Her eyes were closed. She was dead. She had been killed instantly. There had been a crowbar standing up. It had gone through her heart as she fell upon it.

It was decided that very day to leave her there, ten feet under, securely staked, dead, at the intersection of the well-traveled Macdonald Avenue and Brick Street. She would not roam again. With her had died her curse. And with her poor Rummy had passed away, too. Good-by, Jennifer. Good-by, Rummy. We will not see you again!

"Betty, my love," said Mr Wooly to his wife something like six weeks later. (They were on board a steamer bound for Bermuda.) "Betty, my love, what are you thinking about? You looked at our young captain in such

a grave and thoughtful manner while we dined at his table tonight. And since then you have said very little. What are you thinking now? Do tell me. I won't mind in the least if it is that you noticed how tall and slim and dark-eyed the fellow is or that his voice is deep and pleasant, or whatever. What are you thinking about, darling? Tell me, for I love you so!"

"Oh, my dear," Betty replied gently, "I am only thinking about you and how happy we shall be. That is all."

"I wonder," wondered Mr Wooly. Ah, when he could have known every thought she thought he had avoided knowing. Now that he could not he wished, he longed, to know.

But who among us is satisfied?